Pride Publishing books by Aver Rigsly

Single Books
Starling's Again
The Beauty Beneath

I0598596

THE BEAUTY BENEATH

AVER RIGSLY

The Beauty Beneath
ISBN # 978-1-83943-914-8
©Copyright Aver Rigsly 2020
Cover Art by Louisa Maggio ©Copyright September 2020
Interior text design by Claire Siemaszkiewicz
Pride Publishing

Published in 2020 by Pride Publishing, United Kingdom.

Pride Publishing is an imprint of Totally Entwined Group Limited.

THE BEAUTY BENEATH

Dedication

Forever to my loved ones who always have been,
and continue to be, my greatest supports.

Chapter One

Justin Turner loitered on the dark street corner of Ninth Avenue and West Thirty-Seventh Street, shuffling his feet and wiping his sweaty hands off on his jeans. It was Sunday night, and already the people scurrying along the sidewalks were starting to dwindle. Across the street loomed a nondescript building, its bottom floor a Pakistani deli smooshed together with a chic, pricey liquor store. Both were still open, and the warm orange light inside spilled onto the sidewalk out front. Off to the right of both storefronts was a hidden black-glass door tucked into the stairwell on the side, and labeled in small, silver lettering *Eros Elite Services, Inc.*

A security camera blinked a red light up in the eaves of the stairwell and an intercom buzzer gleamed next to the door, but Justin couldn't find the courage to cross the street and push the button.

"Dammit, dammit, dammit," he cursed. It had been terrifying enough clicking on their website, nerve-racking downloading and submitting the application and answering the call from the secretary to make this appointment. All that and he still hadn't died from embarrassment, so, for the love of God, he could do this.

He waited for a pair of lumbering taxis to pass by and jogged across the street. His ratty sneakers splashed in the shallow puddles from the afternoon's drizzle and Justin crammed his hands into the pockets of his old red hoodie and tried to make himself as invisible as possible. He ran up the steps of the stairwell and glanced around.

Now or never.

He forced his hand not to shake and hit the buzzer.

"Eros Elite Services," a woman chimed out.

"Um, hi. It's Justin Turner. To meet with Mr. Morita."

"Hello, Mr. Turner. We're happy you've arrived. Please, come right inside." The door buzzed and Justin fumbled to grab the handle before it locked again.

Inside was a short hallway and at the end, past an elevator, stood a dark-red wooden door with a fogged glass window at eye-level. *Barney W. Gold, Attorney at Law* was stamped on the glass and underneath *Real Estate, Estate Planning, Probate.* The office space through the window was black, but at nine on a Sunday, Justin figured most of the offices had to be empty.

On the wall beside the elevator, a plaque listed nineteen different floors, starting with Barney W. Gold on the first, and at the very top, *Eros Elite Services, Inc.*

Justin hit the elevator's up-button and waited. Were all elevators in Manhattan this slow? On cue, as if to say, *'screw you, buddy,'* the elevator dinged, and the doors slid open. The interior was very posh, and he admired the mirrored ceiling and gold-plated handrails. Lit crystal-cut buttons lined the panel on the side, and he hit number nineteen with gusto.

The foyer to Eros Elite proved to be a surprising modern space that screamed money. There were mahogany-paneled accent walls, sparkling white floor tiles and gold on every fixture and dripping from the chandelier hanging in the center. The two hallways in front of him branched out behind the front desk and more ornate lighting fixtures dangled down both corridors from behind doorways covered by floor-length black curtains drawn back with golden ropes.

A beautiful, young, Irish-looking girl sat behind the sleek oak counter, her bright-red hair curled out from her ivory face in a big bushel fit for a supermodel. As Justin got closer, he saw a spray of freckles across the bridge of her nose.

"Good evening, sir. Mr. Turner, I presume?" she asked, her smile perfect, like the cover of a magazine.

"Yes. I'm uh, Mr. Turner. Justin Turner."

"Excellent. I've already let Mr. Morita know of your arrival. He should be out in just a moment. Please, make yourself comfortable." She gestured at a pair of leather chaises planted in the corner.

"Oh, thank you very much."

He shuffled over but didn't feel like sitting down, so he tried to waste time looking at the art hanging on the walls. A series of abstract oil paintings, thick with heavy strokes of red and orange and pink curves of paint, lined the section of the waiting room. They all looked warm and lazy and gave the small space a cozy feeling.

While Justin was trying to figure out the curly swirls and twists of paint, a strapping Japanese man with neat dark hair strolled out into the lobby from down the right hallway. He wore an expensive-cut black suit, highly polished black dress shoes, and gold cufflinks sparkled at his wrists.

"Mr. Turner?" he asked.

"Yes! That's me," Justin said, his voice cracking halfway through. He walked over and shook Morita's hand. He worried that his palms were sweaty and prayed Morita didn't notice.

"I'm so glad you could make it," Morita said. He turned and directed them back down the hallway that he had come from. Morita was fit and tall, and Justin had to keep looking up in little glances as they walked.

"I have to admit," Morita said, "I was very excited to have you come in for an interview. Your application intrigued me greatly."

"It did?"

"Oh, yes. You might be surprised, but almost all our employees tend to be female. We have a serious lack of good young men around here to serve our clientele."

"I see."

"Now, please, come on in." Morita opened the door at the end of the hall and Justin walked inside a long, glamorous office with a fish tank built right into the wall on the opposite side from the desk. A rainbow of tropical fish swam about while a line of teeny white bubbles danced up from the gravel bottom.

Morita strolled over to his desk and sat in the tall-backed office chair. Justin shuffled over and lowered himself down across from him. His foot started tapping on the carpet and he caught himself and stopped.

"So, Mr. Turner, welcome to Eros Elite Services. My name is Stephen Morita and I'm the owner and creator.

My little company has been in business for eight years now and we're thriving."

"Yes, I read that on your website. Very prestigious."

Morita beamed. "Well, thank you."

"And I saw a law firm on the first floor?"

"Oh yes, Mr. Barney Gold. Barney is a wonderful attorney. There are many different offices here, but I own the whole building. I picked the nineteenth floor for Eros Elite because I liked the view."

"It is a very nice view," Justin agreed, glancing around. "The whole place seems nice."

"And we're always looking for new talent. Speaking of, how about we take a look at your application?" He leaned forward and snagged a print-out of Justin's application from the top of a pile of papers. Justin readjusted himself in his seat.

"'Justin Stanley Turner, age twenty-one. Brown hair, brown eyes, five-foot-eight, one hundred and forty pounds. Born and raised here in Manhattan, I see."

"Yes, sir. Just me and my grandma, Julia Turner. But everyone always calls her Jewels."

"That's sweet. I was very close to my grandmother back in Japan. We used to call her Baasan. She made the best soba in the entire world, and I still haven't been able to find its equal anywhere in the city. I loved her dearly."

Despite the posh environment and pricey outfit, Morita still managed to come across as a normal guy. Maybe it was the easy way he held himself. It seemed more relaxed than what Justin expected from a C.E.O., but then again, he seemed so young to own such a prestigious company.

"You've indicated here that you are interested in men," Morita said.

"Uh, yeah."

"That's good. Like I said earlier, we could use more men on our team, regardless of sexual preference. They come in all shapes and sorts here, Mr. Turner. We don't judge."

"That's good," Justin laughed. It was a nervous breathy sound.

"And it looks like you were able to complete the Comfort-level Questionnaire as well. Did you have any questions about that section?"

The Comfort-level Questionnaire had been the most difficult two pages Justin had ever had to complete for a job interview — questions on a scale of one to five, from *'not comfortable at all'* to *'very comfortable'*, about toys, acts and body parts that had made him squirm and blush. Hell, he'd even had to Google some first, and that had been mortifying.

"I think I answered everything right. I mean, after some research."

"That's fine," Morita assured him. "'I know that part of the application is a bit overwhelming to consider at first, but you're allowed to change any of your answers at any point working here, and all of our customers are strictly instructed to never cross a comfort-level without asking beforehand. That's just how we operate here, and the breaking of any of the rules is disciplined immediately."

Morita's face was stern, and Justin got the impression that his employees' safety was not a flippant matter. This was the first time since meeting Morita that he'd been intimidated by him. He nodded to show he understood and Morita's face broke into a smile.

"How about, since this is your first time here, I give you the grand tour? We'll show you the ins and outs of our operations."

"Okay. Yeah. That sounds great."

"Perfect. Then why don't you follow me?"

Morita stood and led them out of the office back toward the foyer, stopping by the redhead at the front desk. "Cassidy, you aren't still here, are you?"

"Don't worry, Mr. Morita, I was just shutting everything down and heading home."

"Okay, good. Be safe out there—it's already late."

"I'll be fine, Mr. Morita. Goodnight."

Morita led them down the left hall, which was just as nicely decorated as the first one, with similar doors branching both left and right along the length.

"Over on this side are guest rooms for the clients." He gestured to his left. "They can place their clothes and belongings here, take a relaxing shower or use the private saunas. There are also similar accommodations for the employees on the other side. On this right side of the hall, though, are our 'Eros Elite Rooms'," Morita said. "These are where all the magic happens." He pushed open the first door on the right and motioned for Justin to walk inside.

The room was almost three times the size of his own tiny bedroom and looked nice enough to be a suite in any fancy hotel in Midtown. A huge plush bed stood centered against the wall across from them, adorned with a plethora of multi-sized throw pillows. Justin drifted in farther to glance around.

The walls were dark red in here as well. Maybe it was supposed to put customers and employees in a romantic mood, but the fire-engine shade was exotic and daunting, just like the rest of the place.

"You see, every room is monitored for safety by our discreet security team. There, and there," Morita explained. He pointed to the front and back corners of the room, where tucked up high on the ceiling were two cameras in dark little bubbles. One pointed toward the doorway and the other the bed. *Nowhere to hide in here.*

"All these rooms are essentially the same, just some minor alterations to the decor here and there. Basically, though, each one comes with the vanity sink, the fully stocked mini-fridge and a set of drawers with anything one might need during their experience. There's also a supply of fresh linens, Bluetooth speakers for music and Wi-Fi. We like comfort to be one of our main focuses here at Eros. Now let me show you the other side of the room."

Justin took one last look around. Could he even imagine being on the satin sheets of that bed, naked and vulnerable like he had never been in his whole life before he gave his body to some stranger? The thought alone was dizzying, and Justin twisted the sleeve of his sweatshirt with a sweaty palm.

They walked out to the foyer and this time, the main lights had been dimmed and Cassidy the secretary was nowhere to be seen.

"I hope you don't mind," Morita said, "but on Sundays we like to close up early. Most nights we're open until at least two in the morning if there are clients, but on Sundays, I like to give the staff a bit of a break. It's not much, but it makes for the perfect time to show someone new around. A lot less pressure." He smiled. Justin returned it with a sense of relief. He didn't need the anxiety of meeting a bunch of other *workers* here just yet.

"And this hallway on the right is where the employees enter the Elite rooms from. Employees are always sent to the rooms first so that they can get themselves settled before the client enters."

Morita pushed the first door on the left of the corridor open for Justin. He walked in, but this room was so small the two of them barely fit inside. Another section of bed, much smaller in this room, was pushed up against the wall. The wall itself was very strange. A rectangular section at bed-level reminded Justin of a dog door someone would install in their kitchen. There was a semicircle cut out of the bottom of the sliding rectangle, but instead of a clear flap, a black curtain of heavy-looking fabric draped down.

"There's a rack up here and a coat hook on the door for your things. The showers at the end of the hall are there for you to use anytime. We have a spacious dressing room and all the employees have their own stations to get ready at. And over here, is our dividing wall." Morita stepped past Justin to the far wall where the tiny bed was pressed against it.

The 'Dividing Wall', Eros' website had titled it. It had to be the most curious idea Justin had never considered before and it was fascinating to get to see it in person.

"The idea is that the employee lies here..." Morita demonstrated, sliding the square of wall with the cut-out section up on smooth, inlaid tracks so that it lifted out of the way and clicked into place. Justin could see the mound of throw pillows on the larger, nicer bed from the guest room side. There was just enough bed space on this side of the wall for him to rest his head and shoulders down, but the rest of him would be lying in the other room, splayed out on that extravagant bed.

"Then, when you are settled," Morita continued, "you lower this division back down, so it rests at about mid-ribcage. Your arms can stay on this side of the wall if you please. You at no point are ever required to place your arms through the division. That is completely up to you and your comfort levels."

Justin couldn't help but stare at the hole in the wall. He could imagine doing what Morita described with painful clarity. It would be like approaching the guillotine. He'd crawl up onto the bed, stick his feet and legs through the square hole and, lie on his back, blink up at the ceiling like a man on the chopping block and the sliding division would come down like the executioner's blade.

Okay, so the soft velvet fabric would be painless and there would be plenty of room to fit in the cut-out section, especially since he wasn't a very big guy, but it would still be like a beheading. His head would be separated from the rest of his body as it lay prone on the other side, helpless, like being dipped in murky, shark-infested waters.

Morita must have seen the nervous look on his face because he laughed and slapped a reassuring hand on Justin's shoulder.

"Don't worry, we have our security measures in this room as well. There's another camera on the ceiling, and see this button right here? If at any point you need to end the session, for whatever reason at all, you push that and our security team will immediately come to assist you and also see the client out of the room."

"Has anyone ever needed to use it?"

"Only once. But it was only because the employee came down with a sudden bout of stomach flu. You can imagine the mess that would have happened if she hadn't ended the session early."

Justin snorted. "Yeah, I can."

"Here, let's go back to my office," Morita offered. "We can discuss the rest of the details there."

"Okay, sounds good."

Justin needed to sit, that was for sure. His head was racing with a thousand thoughts a minute and yet at the same time, deep down inside he had already decided.

"So? What do you think?"

Back in his office, Morita tugged open a drawer in his desk and pulled out a wooden cigar box. He plucked one out and offered it to Justin. The powerful scent of tobacco drifted over and he could just make out the word *Churchill* printed on the side of the plastic wrapper.

"Oh, no thank you."

Morita shrugged and took it for himself. He placed the box back and glanced up at Justin, the still-wrapped cigar dangling from his fingers.

"But really, what do you think? I'm very curious to hear your thoughts."

"I think...I think I'd feel comfortable for one night. To try it."

"And that's fine. Some of our employees only work once or twice, and some of them love it! I have a team of regulars that have well-paying opportunities here every other week."

"Wow. I didn't realize it was so popular."

"Oh yes. We run a very tight ship here and we pride ourselves on the level of services we provide. Naturally, we want both our employees and clients to be happy, healthy and for them to find whatever it is they are looking for."

"And what exactly *are* people looking for here? Why do your clients come here instead of just going down to the red-light district? No offense, I mean!"

Morita chuckled and nodded. "None taken, I promise. That's a very fair question." He shifted in his seat, straightening his shirt collar. "I'll be very honest with you, Mr. Turner. A lot of our clients, the majority really, are the sort of people with too much money and little or no romantic relationships in their lives. The reasons vary, but most of them are looking for the sexual experience without having to worry about the social interactions. Our operation here offers anonymity *and* the possibility of physical affection in a comfortable environment."

"Oh, I see." It made sense. After all, besides the money, that was what he was here for too, wasn't it? For the sex with no panic-filled dating where he would only make a scared fool of himself?

"And I'm told by our employees that it can be very rewarding as well. Sort of a sense of helping others. It's not charity—I can assure you that you will be paid very well for your time with us. Even so, our employees often enjoy the same benefits that we offer our clients."

"Um, Mr. Morita? This all sounds great, but there's just one thing I didn't tell you. There wasn't really a place for it on the application form but uh, I still thought it was important to say."

"Yes?"

"Well, um…" Justin squirmed. It felt like a burning spotlight was on him in front of an audience of hundreds. "I've never actually *slept* with anyone before."

"You're a virgin?" Morita asked. His eyebrows rose and he leaned forward in his chair.

"Yes," he whispered. "Is that going to be a problem?"

"Hmmm, this is a first." Morita leaned back, his elbows on the armrests, and he fiddled with his cigar. He looked Justin over with a critical eye. "Well, you'll still have to comply with our mandatory health screening process but other than that, I don't see why it would be."

"Oh, yes. Absolutely. I'll do everything you need."

Morita grinned and Justin felt the first bit of relief since he'd walked into the place.

"Well then, I'd love to get you started as soon as possible. There's a health clinic that we work with on one-oh-eight. Head there tomorrow if you can and we'll need a blood, urine and semen sample. I know it might seem like we're asking for everything including the kitchen sink, but we test for numerous things. Mainly though for sexually transmitted diseases—we insist that all employees and clients are clean and safe and get checked regularly. House rules."

"Yes, sir."

"Good, good. The lab work usually takes a couple of days, but we should be able to schedule you for something next weekend."

"Wow, really? That would be great."'

"All we'll need is for you to sign this, and you'll be good to go."

He grabbed another sheet of paper off the corner of his desk and slid it in front of Justin. He leaned forward to scan over the page and Morita pulled a pen from inside his suit jacket and offered it to him.

"This is our employee contract," he explained. "It simply states you'll follow all of our procedures and rules that have been established, and that you agree to work on a per diem basis for as long as you wish with our company, unless violations have occurred. I'm sure you read everything on our website, but I can always give you hard copies of those documents if you need."

"Oh," Justin said. He sat blinking at the contract, hardly hearing a word Morita said. Was this how Faustus felt when he made a deal with the devil? If Justin squinted, Morita could possibly be an embodiment of Lucifer himself across the desk with his slick smile and pricey suit, but Justin wasn't signing away his soul, just his virginity. *Right?* He took the pen and shook his head. "No, I already read them all. I'll sign."

Morita smiled. "Then put your name right there on the bottom line next to the X."

The nib of the fountain pen touched the paper and he signed his full name, Justin Stanley Turner, in the neatest cursive he could manage. The date was already printed beside it, so he pushed it back to Morita without further ado.

"Thank you very much, Mr. Turner," Morita said. He snagged the contract, blew on the wet ink and slipped it away in his desk drawer. "It will be a pleasure having you working with us."

"Oh, thank you."

"You know…" Morita said. He seemed to be in the middle of a great thought and a smirk played at the corner of his lips. "Seeing how this will be your first time working with us, and another important first at that, I think I know the perfect client to give you."

"You do?" he squeaked. That was fast.

"Oh yes. He's a real great guy and a close friend of mine. You might be just the sort of person to get him to open up."

"You think?"

"Absolutely. Either way, I can vouch that he is very respectable with our employees, although," Morita chuckled, "he's a bit of a talker."

"Well, that's okay," Justin blushed. He had been a quiet guy his whole life. He was used to listening to people talk.

"Perfect, perfect. Just bring this paperwork to the lab tomorrow—the address is there at the bottom of the page—and I'll give you a call to set up your appointment in a couple of days."

"Thank you so much, Mr. Morita. I can't tell you how much this opportunity means for me."

"Times rough?" Morita had that look of recognition on his face that screamed that he was used to this by now.

"Yeah, you can say that. Just, um, thank you."

"And thank *you*, Mr. Turner. It'll be a pleasure having you here with us." Morita reached across the desk and shook Justin's hand in a tight, professional handshake. "Head to the lab, and you'll hear from me personally in a couple of days."

"Okay, will do. Thanks again."

"Take care of yourself, Justin."

Morita saw him out and closed the office door behind him. Justin stood in the soft-lit hall and, for a second, couldn't believe everything that had just happened. Part of him was relieved that things had gone so well. The other half of him, however, was even more frightened now that it was over, and Morita wanted him to start as soon as next weekend.

How in the hell was he supposed to not die from a panic attack in the meanwhile? There was no turning back now. If he did, he'd be letting down the most important person in the whole world to him. Not that she knew that he was here tonight, and she most definitely never *would* learn of any of this if he had his say.

He was going to carry this burden alone.

Chapter Two

"Look alive, motherfucker! We're back!"

The back-room door slammed open and two men burst in, causing a ruckus like a couple of buffoons. Adam Creed sat in the tattered recliner with his work boots propped up on the coffee table in front of him.

"I take it everything went well," he said dryly. His older brothers, Billy and Michael, settled in, tossing their backpacks down on the table and slapping Adam's legs to make him move.

"You bet your ass it did!" Billy said. He combed his hair back with his fingers, making the long greasy strands a tangled mess. His usual twitchy energy grated on Adam's nerves like nothing else.

"We did even better than last month," Michael agreed. He stood towering next to Adam slumped in the chair. As much as Adam hated the thought of being associated with the two of them, he had to admit they all shared the Creed men body build. His matching dirty blond hair and big frame made him fit right in with his brothers.

Michael and Billy made themselves at home in the back room of warehouse seventeen-C in the Bronx. Sitting near the bank of the East River, it was one of the many locations the Creeds owned around the city that housed the different 'wares' that their family sold. Of course, the cops knew of the place, but they were all either wise enough or paid enough to leave them alone. If Adam's brothers wanted to party and get a little rowdy, the 'clubhouse' in the back room of warehouse seventeen-C was where they made themselves comfortable.

"Yeah, Adam, we made a fucking butt-ton," Billy said. He sat across from Adam's recliner. "When old Mr. Cortez saw us, you should have seen the way he almost shit his pants. He opened that register faster than anything and gave *very* generously this time."

"Well, after that fractured eye socket you gave him last time, I'm not surprised," Adam said.

"The geezer deserved it! I mean, come on, he honestly tried to give us only four hundred. Can you believe that shit? After all our family does for him? Keeping that shit-hole restaurant safe for him like we do everyone else."

"The nerve of him."

"Hey," Michael said, slapping Adam in the back of the head. "None of that sarcastic bullshit. Not tonight. Billy and I raked in enough to earn a little reward for our hard work. What do you think, Billy?"

"Fuck yeah we did!"

"So how about you wipe that dumb frown off your face and join your brothers in celebrating a little, huh?" Michael walked to the mini-fridge and pulled out a six-pack of beer. He tugged one loose from the plastic ring and tossed it to Billy, who just managed not to drop it on the ancient rug, and he tossed another one to Adam. He cracked it open even though he knew he wouldn't end up drinking it. Still, he reminded himself to play nice.

"Yeah, sure. I'll stay for a bit."

"That's the spirit." Michael pulled out the thirty-eight special snub-nose revolver he kept tucked down the back of his jeans and put it on the side table gently, as though it were a cherished child. "Empty the bags for me, yeah?"

Adam put his beer down and tugged over the first backpack to unzip it and start laying out the contents. There had to be at least twenty-five grand in cash altogether. Michael and Billy had spent most of the day hitting up every spot in their territory. Every little restaurant, deli, laundromat and mom-and-pop shop in the South Bronx, Mott Haven and Port Morris fell into their radius, never mind the few other spots in Manhattan the Creeds had under their control. Between Michael, Billy and a couple of other guys like Jones and Miller who worked for the Creed family, they raked in a great deal of 'protection' money at the end of every month.

Billy eyed the pile and whistled. "Dad will be happy to hear how we did."

"Dad doesn't give a shit about this chump change," Adam scoffed.

"It's not about the money," Michael interrupted. "The money's a part of it, but it's *really* about making sure everyone around these parts knows who the streets belong to. Dad brings in the big money, but *we're* responsible for keeping the order. Get it?"

"Yeah, Mike," Billy said. Adam nodded.

Michael sat himself down on the couch next to Billy. He reached over to mess up Billy's hair even worse and tried not to spill his beer as Billy shoved him back.

"You know, Adam," Michael said, turning serious and giving him a stern look. "This is the third month in a row that you haven't gone with us for the monthly round-up."

"You're getting soft on us," Billy added.

"Why don't you just shut the fuck up and snort another line, cokehead?"

"Maybe I will! I've got enough cash here for a mountain of coke!" Billy walked over to the bureau across the room. He pulled out a small baggie from his back pocket and tapped out a line of white powder. Michael didn't pay any attention to Billy though.

"I'm serious, Adam. If Dad hears that you've been skipping out, he's gonna be pissed."

"I'll come along next month. Believe it or not, cruising around town with the freaking Bruise Squad isn't my idea of a good time."

"Like it or not, it's a big part of the family business, little bro, and us Creeds stick together. You're in this just as much as the rest of us."

"Like I don't already know that." Adam scowled, shifting in his seat. Michael only raised his voice.

"You can drink and smoke and hang out at that fucking whore house all you want, but at the end of the day, you're representing the Creed name just like Billy and me. I don't want you to tarnish the name and I *definitely* don't want to see what Dad would do to you if you did."

"I get it."

"All right, whatever. I'm just looking out for you, Adam."

"Yeah, I know, *Michael*."

Even with the sass, Michael seemed pleased. "I'm gonna call a few working gals and we can really get to celebrating — how does that sound?" he asked. Across the room, Billy snorted a quick line of coke and hissed. He coughed once and grinned over at them, pinching his nose.

"Make sure you get Chantel. She's my favorite," he said in a nasal voice.

"Yeah, yeah, I'll get your favorite whore. Any other requests, dear brother?"

"Go fuck yourself."

"I don't think so. Chantel can bring two of her friends and Adam and I will fight over the prettiest one."

"Sorry, but you can count me out, guys," Adam said. He got up from the recliner and grabbed his leather jacket off the arm of the couch to put it on over his navy button-up shirt.

"What? You don't want to stay, bro? Having trouble getting it up?" Michael teased, making Billy scoff out a laugh.

"Don't you 'member, Mike?" he asked. "Adam's into those twink faggots now."

Like a strike of lightning, Adam shoved him hard enough that he tumbled backward in the bureau holding the television up and almost sent the flat-screen tumbling over. Billy managed to catch himself on the bureau corner and keep his footing so he didn't end up on his ass.

"Don't you fucking say that," Adam growled. Michael stepped up and slapped a hand on his chest to keep him back.

"Easy, easy boys. I don't give a shit what Adam's dipping his wick into. Just let it go. He just better fucking make sure Dad doesn't hear any of this shit."

"Yeah, well, as long as you two assholes don't say anything, he never will."

"Don't be stupid," Billy sneered. He straightened himself out and shuffled back in place to start lining up another pile of coke. "You know that you can't keep anything from Dad. He hears everything in this freaking city."

"Come on." Michael tugged Adam back toward the coffee table and away from Billy. "You know how he gets once he's flying. Just leave him be."

"I don't give a shit what he's on. He's getting on my last nerve."

Billy laughed like an asshole. He didn't bother looking up from his new line of coke he was working on, otherwise he might have seen the daggers Adam was shooting his way.

"Well, I don't fucking care," Michael said. It seemed like his full-time job wasn't working for their father, but rather keeping Billy and Adam on short leashes. "Sit your ass down and drink your fucking beer."

Adam fell back in the recliner and Michael sat on the couch, shifting to one side so he could tug his cell out of his back pocket. Adam picked up his abandoned beer off the table and sat quietly while Michael dialed. Billy hissed as he snorted the second line, shaking his head like a wet dog.

"Hey, Jimmy, how's it going?" Michael said. There was a burble of Jimmy Vincenzo's voice. "Yeah, man. Exactly. I was thinking our usual weekend request. You know Billy wants Chantel. Yeah, he's a man of simple tastes, what can I say?"

"Oh, you're one to fucking talk." Billy laughed.

"Yeah, but make sure you send two other lovely ladies with Chantel, okay? I want it to be a fucking party over here. The real deal."

"Fuck yeah," Billy said, bouncing over to the mini-fridge and grabbed a flask-sized bottle of vodka out of the freezer drawer at the top. He unscrewed the cap and tipped the bottle back for a good swig.

"That sounds perfect, Jimmy. And would you put a rush on that? We've had a long day and are looking forward to some well-deserved R&R, *capiche*? That's my man! You're a fucking lifesaver. Yeah, see you later, guy."

Michael hung up the phone and tossed it onto the coffee table with their loot.

"There. Now don't say I never do shit for you two."

"Yeah," Billy said. "Sometimes you're not a complete dick."

"Ha-ha, you're a fucking riot. Get me another beer." Michael grabbed a stack of bills off the coffee table and started straightening them out, counting them.

"Where are Jones and Miller?" Adam asked.

"Those two fucks? They went to Hooters in Times Square."

"Yeah," Billy said, walking over a new beer. "And not for the booty-shorts and tits. Miller's been trying to fuck that chick that works the bar. You know the one, with the nose ring and wrist tats?"

"Yeah," Michael agreed. He cracked open the can and started gulping it down. Adam had no clue who Billy was talking about but didn't say as much.

"Well, I guess he's been going every night for the past two weeks. Pathetic, right? I mean, honestly? What pussy's worth all that trouble?"

"Amen, Bill." Michael lifted his beer and clunked it with Billy's vodka. "I'd rather pay for it than be a slave to it, any day."

"Hey," Billy said, rubbing his dripping nose on the sleeve of his denim jacket. "Do you guys wanna smoke? I can roll us something."

"Why not? Adam?" Michael asked. He glanced over at Adam and the hard glint in his eyes felt like a dare, like he was saying *come on, just try me tonight.*

"Fine, whatever."

"All right, cool," Billy said. He went back to the bureau, his own personal drug station, and pulled out a plastic box from the top drawer. He lined up all his tools, like an artist preparing to craft the finest blunt this side of the Mississippi. Adam couldn't hold his tongue though.

"I'll stick around for a while, Michael, but honestly, I'm gonna head out soon," he said. Michael shook his head and finished counting the first stack of cash. Only after he placed it neatly back on the table did he answer him.

"What? You got somewhere important to be tonight?"

"I've just got plans to meet Steve. It's our usual night to get drinks."

"How is that asshole anyway? Is running a prostitution ring still as glamorous as they say?"

"He's doing good."

"I bet, charging what he does over there. *I'd* be doing fucking good too."

Adam didn't like talking about Steve's business, not with his brothers, so he cleared his throat and tried to move on. "Well, anyways, I'll tell him you said hi."

"Yeah, but first you're going to stay and say hello to the nice women I have on their way," Michael said in a tone that made it clear he wasn't talking just to talk. Michael wasn't stupid like that, and neither was Adam, so he got the message and shut his mouth.

Billy hopped over, holding an ashtray and a massive blunt that reeked from all the way across the table. The stench of freshly ground marijuana and the vanilla-flavored cigar wrapper he'd sealed it in was strong without even being lit yet. Billy sat down next to Michael on the couch. He dropped the grimy plastic ashtray down and saddled up to flick his lighter and hold it steady, so the wavering flame hit the end of the blunt evenly.

They passed it around, Billy then Michael then Adam last, who took a quick hit for show then passed it along. He liked to smoke from time to time, but he wasn't in the mood tonight and the pot did little to settle that itchy desire to leave.

Michael's cell phone buzzed harshly as it vibrated on the wooden table. He grabbed it and checked the text on the screen. Billy leaned in just a bit, snooping over Michael's shoulder to see what it said, but Michael just nodded and dropped the phone back down.

"Billy, the girls are here. Go get them," he ordered. He reached for the last pile of cash and ignored the long sigh that Billy huffed out. When the passive-aggressive sass didn't work, Billy didn't argue. He took another gulp of his vodka to polish off the bottle and strolled out of the room.

Adam waited for the door to click shut and glanced over at Michael.

"Don't you think Billy's overdoing it a bit, huh?"

"What are you talking about?"

"I just mean with the booze and drugs. I'm not preaching that he should stop. I'm just saying, don't you think he's going a little hard tonight?"

"Give him a break — he's had a busy day. He worked his ass off, which is more than you can say."

He didn't bother bringing up that he had his own job that he worked at all week, Wednesdays through Mondays. The door swung open and Billy walked in with three ladies of the night behind him, Chantel one of them.

Michael got up from the couch and strolled over to smile at another. "Jade, it's been a while. And you are…?" Michael trailed off, turning to the other girl.

The blonde smiled, flashing her bleached teeth, and held her hand out for Michael to shake. "My name is Barbie."

"It's nice to meet you, Barbie," he said. "I'm Michael. How are you doing this lovely Sunday?"

"I'm doing wonderful," she said.

"Then come 'ere, girlies. Come lend us some company, huh?"

"Sure, Mikey," Barbie said. She was bubbly and effervescent, and she sauntered behind Michael to slide herself onto Adam's lap. Adam let her settle in, but he avoided touching her.

"Hey," she said. Her lipstick was hot-pink and matched the shimmery pink eyeshadow she had plastered on. A huge pair of faux lashes fluttered to her rosy cheeks each time she blinked at him. She certainly looked like a doll, if that was what she was going for.

"Hey."

"What's your name, handsome?" Her voice was sweet and high, yet she spoke slowly and deliberately like a phone-sex operator.

"Adam."

"Well, it's very nice to meet you, Adam." She shifted herself in his lap, rubbing the black leather of her miniskirt against the dark wash of his jeans.

"You Jimmy's new girl, Barbie?" Michael asked.

"Yeah. It's my first week."

"Congratulations. Jimmy's a great guy, and I'm sure you'll be seeing a lot more of us Creed boys."

"Good. I hope so," she said, turning back to Adam to give him a wink.

"You think you can keep up with us?" Michael chuckled. Jade was slowly inching her hand up Michael's thigh toward his crotch. She kissed the side of his neck, along the curly font of his *Bronx* tattoo. "We like to move fast around here."

"I've been known to be as quick as I need to be," she said. She placed a hand on Adam's shoulder and played with the collar of his shirt.

"Well, I like the sound of that. What do you think, Billy?"

Billy had his ass pressed up against the bureau, his hands clutching the edge while a lit cigarette dangled from his fingers. Adam could just see the top of Chantel's head bobbing over the back of the couch where she was currently on her knees in front of Billy, working hard already. "She should fit right in then." Billy tangled his fingers in Chantel's hair and the wet sound of her coughing came as Billy fucked her face, still puffing on his cigarette between thrusts of his hips.

Barbie traced her fingers along Adam's neck, running them up and down with lazy passes. She spoke to him this time as she found the top button of his shirt at his throat.

"Why don't I just prove it to you?" she asked.

Before she could get the button undone, he reached up for her dainty hand, gripping it easily so she couldn't keep going.

"Don't."

She looked surprised but caught herself and slipped her hand from Adam's, who let her pull back without a struggle.

"Oh, don't be shy," she said. It was a light, easy sound as she played him off. "I promise you're going to enjoy yourself." She reached again for Adam's shirt and this time he grabbed both her hands in his, standing up and forcing her off his lap in one swift motion.

"Hey, sweetheart," Michael interrupted with a soft chuckle, as though he was amused by the outburst. "Don't fuck with the shirt. He's a little sensitive about it."

"I don't need you to fucking talk for me," Adam growled at him. "You know how much I goddamn hate it."

He pushed past Barbie, around the other side of the couch to avoid Billy, but Chantel had already stopped at the shouting. Billy spat out a curse and tucked his wet dick back in his jeans.

"Where the fuck do you think you're going?" he shouted.

"You need to stay out of my business."

"And you need to stop acting all high and mighty!" Billy tossed an empty beer can from the bureau top at his boots, but Adam just tugged open the door.

"Just let him go, Billy," Michael shouted. "Adam wants to be a stick in the mud, then let him!" The door slammed shut behind Adam before he had to listen to anything else.

* * * *

Adam sat in the back of Ginny's Bar in the middle of the Lower East Side. He liked Ginny's. The place was nothing more than a narrow hole in the wall sandwiched between an apartment building and a laundromat, but roomy enough for a couple of tables, booths and even a pool table for anyone looking to kill some time. He sat at one of the booths in the corner, underneath a stuffed bear's head on the wall, and nursed a mug of beer.

Stephen Morita slipped in through the front door. He nodded to the bartender who, without asking, opened and handed him a bottle of Corona. Steve shuffled past the gaggle of people chumming at the bar and into the booth across from Adam with a huff like a deflating airbag.

Steve was not only the owner of Eros Elite Services, Inc., but also Adam's oldest friend. If he was intimidated at all by the Creeds, that intimidation didn't spread down to their youngest, and Adam appreciated it. They didn't have enough time to see each other often, but made sure to keep their Sunday nights at Ginny's a regular thing if they could. So, he knew Steve well enough to see that he'd had a rough week.

"Sounds like you might need a little something stronger than that Mexican piss-water."

"Meh." He shrugged. "It was a long day but overall, I'd say pretty productive. What about you? It's the end of the month again. You must have been busy."

"Nah, I let Tweedle Dee and Tweedle Dum handle it."

"Again? Don't you think they're gonna get pissed you flaked again?"

"Jesus, you too? I thought you were on my side, Steve."

"I am! I'm just saying, *I* wouldn't want to get on Michael's bad side. Everyone around here still remembers what he did to Johnny Scott. You can still find the poor asshole down at the Liquor Depot on East One-Thirty-Seventh in his wheelchair behind the register."

"That was a long time ago and, besides, I'm not afraid of Michael."

"I guess if anyone could take him it would probably be you. But still…"

"Still what?" Adam lifted his mug and chugged down the rest of his beer.

Steve looked around but no one was near. The group of friends at the front had left for the night and now they were alone except for the bartender and one Haitian man sitting at the counter.

"*Still*, your old man is someone to keep in mind. People that cross him end up in the Hudson, in a burlap sack."

"I'm just sick of it," Adam said. He rubbed his face in his hands. "I'm sick of the way people look at me — the way they walk across the street when they see me coming. And more importantly, I'm sick of being trapped under the names Shawn and Michael Creed. For Christ's sake, I'm fucking thirty-one years old."

Steve leaned back in the booth with a sigh and tugged on his tie to loosen it.

"Look, I get it. It sucks being judged before someone gets to know you. That's why I keep telling you that you're not like them. I know that, you know that and if you actually tried to open up and find someone special like I've said, you might finally start believing it."

"Not this again."

"What?! What's so wrong with going on a couple of dates? What about, uh, Sandy?"

"Susan?"

"Yeah! I thought things were going well with her."

He laughed. "We went on one date and afterwards, I found her in the clubhouse with Michael, sucking his dick."

"Ah, shit. I'm sorry."

"Don't be. The second she heard my name, I saw it on her face. It was a lost cause. Just another one of those danger junkies who loves the idea of rolling with the Creeds. Besides, I could already imagine the look she'd give me when she got an eyeful of the shit show under my shirt."

"Hey, it's not a shit show."

"Yeah, just a mangled mess of scars that cover sixty percent of my torso."

"Jesus, Adam. I think you'd be surprised by people in this world. Sure, maybe not every bimbo chick off the street would be dropping their panties after seeing that—"

"Oh, thanks."

"But that doesn't mean that someone out there honestly wouldn't mind."

"I wouldn't hold my breath but thank you, oh great and wise love doctor."

"Hey, it's my job," Steve said, taking a sip of his beer. "Oh! And speaking of my luminous career and love, I've got someone new at Eros."

Adam shook his head. "I appreciate it, Steve, I really do. I'm just not feeling it."

"Adam, man. Aren't I always looking out for you? Don't I know your type?"

He raised an eyebrow at him and Steve laughed.

"Maybe."

"Then trust me when I say I have something special here and you are not going to want to miss out."

"Okay, fine. I'll bite."

"It's a young guy."

Adam leveled him in a look that might have scared off anyone else if it wasn't Steve, who knew better.

"Hear me out," Steve bargained. "It's a young guy. Twenty-one. Born and raised in Manhattan. A little skinny and quiet, but listen to this… He's a virgin."

"You're shitting me."

"No, sir. He seems a little skittish, I have to admit, but maybe if someone eased him into it, then I could have a great new employee in the making."

"Someone like me?" Adam asked. He had to admit he was curious now.

"Why not? I can trust you not to be an animal, right?" Steve smiled and Adam chucked a coaster at him. "Just show the kid a good time, show him the ropes and you'll be doing me a solid."

"You still gonna charge me?" Adam teased.

"Of course, jerk. But for you, the family discount."

"Fine," he agreed, caving like he always did when Steve tried to butt into his love-life. "Just tell me when."

"Will do. You're a lifesaver. I was gonna worry about that kid all week. Now order us another round."

"What am I, your maid? You know, you're lucky I like you. That, and the fact that you run the best whorehouse in New York," he said, standing up from the booth.

"We're an elite service!" Steve yelled as he walked away.

Chapter Three

It wasn't until Thursday that Justin got a call back from Stephen Morita. He was stretched out on his bed, propped up in his mess of pillows and blankets and reading a horror novel while listening to the cop-drama show his grandma loved to watch every night in her recliner before she went to bed. The television down the hall was loud enough that he could hear every police siren and shoot-out in the show, but it didn't bother him. He was so used to it that the sounds faded into the ambient background noise.

Jewels was a stouter woman who immediately gave off the impression of being someone's grandmother, probably because of her cheery smile and warm eyes that wrinkled around the edges. Now though, just after her seventy-sixth birthday, she had begun to change.

Jewels had been a nurse for almost fifty years and was used to moving all day at a busy clip, but now got tired more easily, winded after only a couple of minutes. She needed a little extra hand with everything, which Justin didn't mind, of course, but watching her get short of breath at any bit of strain nagged at the back of his mind. It had worried him something terrible, and it had only gotten worse the more she tried to reassure him that it was nothing.

He had managed to break her down and make her agree to go to the doctor's, but she must have known what the doc was going to say because she put up one hell of a fight. Jewels, a smoker for over thirty-five years of her life, had two stents in her heart already and when she'd seen Doctor Morris, he'd confirmed the worse. She needed a third.

The looming surgery was enough to keep Justin up at night all, but that was only the first part. He knew that the surgery, the hospital stay and the medication would all cost money. Money they barely had. He already worked almost fifty hours a week at the bookstore downtown, and between his measly pay and her social security checks, they just managed to make rent each month and pay for groceries.

However, he also knew that he would do anything for Jewels. She had taken him in when there was no one else left in his world. Now there was no one else to help *her* besides him.

His cell phone buzzed in his jeans pocket and he bolted upright in bed as though it had electrocuted him. He read the name *Eros*.

"H-Hello?"

"Hi, Justin?"

It was Morita, and Justin's throat went dry.

"Yes. It's me."

"Great, this is Stephen Morita from Eros Elite."

"Yeah. I mean — it's great to hear from you again."

"Same here. I hope I didn't call too late."

"Oh, no! I'm sort of a night owl."

"Good, good. Look, I called to see if you'd be available for an appointment Saturday night. I understand if it's a bit short notice, but I'd love to get you in this weekend."

Justin's heart thumped in his chest so hard he could hear the blood rushing in his ears. "It's okay. I-I'm free Saturday."

"Around ten o'clock?"

"Yeah, absolutely."

"Amazing!" Morita sounded genuinely happy to hear that. Justin, on the other hand, was a delirious combination of excited and terrified. "Um, Mr. Morita?"

"Yes?"

"Do I need to bring anything or wear something in particular? I mean, like, is there a dress code or something?"

"Oh, no. You don't have to worry about anything like that. We provide any clothing if there are requests by the clients, but typically employees come in their own clothes. Why don't you come by around nine and you can get ready in our dressing room? I'm sure some of the girls would be happy to show you around and get you settled."

"Okay, yeah. That sounds good." He fisted his fingers into the jeans on his knee and squeezed the bunched-up denim in nervous pulses.

"And, Justin?" Morita said. "Try not to stress out too much. Everyone is nervous for their first appointment, but I think you'll be pleasantly surprised."

"Okay, thank you." Justin's face had to be as red as a tomato by now if the heat he felt radiating off his cheeks and neck was anything to go by.

"Goodnight, I'll see you at nine on Saturday."

"Yeah, have a good night too, Mr. Morita. See you Saturday."

He hung up and blinked in disbelief, trying to absorb the past few minutes. It was really going to happen. He was going to give up his body to a complete stranger. This Saturday.

He jumped to his feet and padded in his socks over to his door. He pressed his ear near the door frame and held his breath.

The racket of the television had dimmed at some point during his call. The soft cheery voice of a saleswoman on one of the shopping networks echoed down the hall. At ten every night like clockwork, Jewels would click off the lamp next to her, flip to one of the home shopping channels, turn the volume down and fall asleep right there in her recliner. Justin backed away and turned to stand at the foot of his bed.

How in the hell am I going to go through with this? He didn't know. The idea was that he was supposed to lie back on the bed and just let it happen. *I'm going to be naked in front of a random stranger.*

And that was just supposed to be the first step.

He turned toward the full-length mirror on the back of his closet door and his throat bobbed as he swallowed. His brown hair was messy from absent-mindedly running his hand through it. He tried to smooth it back down, parted neat and perfect on the left side. He looked over the features of his face with a critical gaze.

His nose wasn't too small or too large, but it did have a little bump at the bridge from being broken when he was fourteen. He disliked the way his ears stuck out a little too much, but they could be worse, and he considered himself lucky. Even more lucky he noticed was how clear his skin was. He just prayed he didn't end up breaking out like he sometimes did under stress.

With shaky hands, he reached down to the hem of his green T-shirt and yanked it up and off. He kept his head down, unbuttoned his jeans and shoved them off his legs to the floor. He ripped both socks off and pulled in a deep breath before he tugged down his boxers as well and dared to look back up at his reflection.

The blush that had started on his cheekbones had blossomed to his ears and down the slope of his neck where it just barely hit his collarbone.

His immediate thought was the one that always came first looking at himself—he was scrawny. He didn't have time to go to the gym and work out. He didn't have time for anything really, but the one thing he wished now was that he had made time for dating. He didn't know how to flirt, and he had no idea how to ask someone out without looking like an idiot, but boy was he horny.

Sex crept up into his thoughts constantly. On the subway downtown to Union Square to work at the bookstore, re-shelving put-back books in the aisles packed with towering shelves, watching television at home—it didn't matter. He'd imagine the feeling of his lips brushing against someone else's, the slick glide of tongues as they kissed, and more often than not, the way it would feel as a pair of hands stroked down his back and stomach and lower to where he dreamed to be touched.

He glanced down his flat stomach to the trail of hair leading from his belly button to his crotch. He usually kept his pubic hair trimmed as short as possible. Should he shave it before Saturday? Would that be better, or would it just be weird? Watching porn, he noticed a lot of guys were completely shaven, and that *really* seemed to be the norm for skinny guys like him.

He finally looked at his penis hanging between his legs. It wasn't really anything special but, to be fair, he was more of a grower than a show-er. He was uncircumcised and he gave himself a tug as he grew heavy.

Somebody else is going to be touching me.

Justin shivered. His heart rate was picking up and he continued to lazily touch himself.

A man is going to reach between my legs and touch my cock, my balls, and is going to slide his fingers inside me.

He panted out a sharp breath and gripped the base of his shaft. His length throbbed in his fingers and he was good and hard now, the light pink tip of his cock peeking out from the hood of skin. He used his other hand to roll his testicles and went back to slowly pumping his fist.

He tried to imagine how the guy's hands were going to feel on his skin. Would they be soft and gentle, or maybe rougher and more demanding? God, he hoped they would burn trails down his body. He was starving and dying for a touch like that.

He's going to stretch me out on his fingers and, whenever he wants, he'll push his cock inside me.

The thought was both terrifying and thrilling. He wanted with a desperate urgency to know what it would feel like to have someone inside him. Even feeling *any* sort of sexual intimacy would be a blessing at this point.

He'll start to pump his hips as he takes me, burying himself inside me again and again. Maybe he'll even jerk me off while he does.

He increased the speed of his hand and slid his other back up his torso. His nipples were small and pebbled on his chest and they were very sensitive. He pinched the little bud and while it felt nice, it was so much better imagining it was the hand of his mystery man, and that sent a jolt of pleasure down his spine.

Maybe he'll use me until I can't take it anymore. Maybe he'll come inside me as he pounds his cock in.

He was suddenly right at the edge of his orgasm, his breath locking in his chest as it crested, and he pumped his hand harder to chase it down. He came fast and his body spasmed and tried to curl in on itself through the waves of pleasure. His cum dripped over his fingers, falling to the floor, and he shivered when he pulled his cock slowly, inching his way back down from his orgasm.

"*Shit*," he hissed, looking down at the mess on the floor. As nice as the quick jerk-off had been, the rush of adrenaline and endorphins were gone as quickly as they'd come. He sighed and walked over to grab his box of tissues off his bookshelf next to his bed.

He cleaned himself up and took care of the floor. At least he had managed to miss all his clothes and he was a tiny bit grateful for that.

More than anything else, though, he really wanted to know what it would feel like to have another person touch him. He was dying to know what it'd be like.

Justin sighed and felt the little twinge of fear in his heart again. He'd get to find out sure enough, and maybe sooner than he was mentally prepared for, but either way…

Saturday was the day.

Chapter Four

Friday nights after work, Adam liked to stroll over to Famous Greco's Pizza. The place was a stone's throw away from Eros Elite, which *was* a bit out of his way, but he enjoyed the walk and was a firm believer that they had the best over-the-counter New York-style pizza in the whole goddamn city. This Friday was no different, except there, on the sidewalk, three buildings down, stood Billy. It must have not been Adam's day, because the second he noticed Billy, his brother looked up through the people shuffling by and spied him. He pulled the cigarette from his mouth.

"Hey, Adam!" he called out. "Come 'ere!"

Just fucking perfect. Adam cursed his luck and stuffed his hands into his jeans pockets and headed over. Billy was wearing his favorite denim jacket again, making him look like a trucker from the Midwest, especially when wearing the matching blue jeans to complete the look.

"Get your ass over here," Billy said.

"Yeah, yeah. What are you doing?"

"Just waiting for Michael. You wanna smoke?" Billy held out his pack of cigarettes, but Adam shook his head. At least Billy didn't seem to be harboring any hard feelings from the other night. Billy had a wonderful ability to get under his skin, but things always blew over after a day or two. Although, there was always a new argument brewing on the horizon.

Billy shrugged and put the pack away. "Eh, whatever. Oh nice, there's Mike." He nodded over Adam's shoulder.

The stream of people walking by parted around Michael like the Red Sea. People tended to just naturally move out of Michael's way and Adam couldn't blame them.

"Hey, man, what perfect timing," Michael said.

"What were you doing?" Adam asked.

"Me? Just running some errands here with Bill. And *you* are just in time to help us with the last one."

"I'm sure you guys can handle it without me," Adam tried, but he wasn't getting out of it that easily.

"No, no, no, we could definitely use your help." Michael slapped a hand on Adam's shoulder, heavy and squeezing with a powerful grip through the leather of his jacket. He got the not-so-subtle order and tried to keep the scowl off his face.

"All right."

"Great, then let's go."

Michael used his hold on Adam's shoulder to spin him around and off they went. Billy followed behind the two of them, finishing up his butt. Michael finally dropped his hand and Adam's skin crawled from the touch through his clothes.

"Where are we going?" he asked.

"Just right up the street here." Michael stared up ahead. He led them around the corner but then stopped. They stood in front of a tiny storefront with a hanging plastic banner over the door reading *Vapetown Suppliers*.

"Here?"

"Yeah. After you..." He held his arm out for him to go. He glanced back at Billy, who tossed his cigarette onto the sidewalk and stepped on it before he shoved past him. He opened the door, and Adam sighed and walked in after him, Michael last.

The inside of the smoke shop was tiny. It was more like a long hallway but the walls were packed with goods and a narrow counter against the left side displayed rows and rows of glass pipes, grinders and varieties of vape pens and cartridges. The store was empty except for one man behind the counter, who looked up from his cell phone at the chime of the bell over the door.

The guy was maybe a bit younger than Adam. He put his cell phone down next to a half-eaten tuna sandwich and stood up.

"Hey," he said, his voice rough like he needed to clear his throat. He wiped his hands on the bottom of his too-long gray T-shirt.

"Hey, man." Billy walked right up to the counter. "Maybe you can help me."

"Yeah, sure."

"I'm looking for some bowl screens, but not those shitty, fake-steel pieces of crap that fucking burn. You know what I'm talking about?"

"Of course, man. I've got some gold-plated ones here that will last you at least twice as long. Hold on..." The clerk spun around and bent down to the shelf by his knees to pluck a tiny paper envelope out of a box. He turned around and slid it across the glass counter. "Ten in a sleeve. Two-fifty for one pack or five for ten."

"Uh-huh," Billy said, nodding. "Why don't you get me ten packs? Why not?"

"Sure." He turned around to count out nine more and Michael took a step forward, right up to the glass counter.

"Hey, you look pretty familiar," he said.

The clerk twisted his neck, eyeing Michael up and down.

"Do I? I'm not sure we've met."

"Yeah, you do. Actually..." Michael snapped his fingers. "You're not the new guy my friend mentioned at Jack's Club up in South Bronx, are you? Sammy, is it?"

"Scotty," the clerk said. He stood slowly back up. "And yeah, I've been around Jack's a couple nights the past few weeks."

"That's it," said Michael. His voice was dripping in sarcastic surprise, and Adam got the feeling he was playing dumb. It felt like a cat toying with a mouse. He shifted his weight from one foot to another and tucked his hands into his jacket pockets.

"Who did you say your friend was again?" Scotty asked.

"I didn't."

Confusion flashed across Scotty's face, but it was quickly wiped off when Michael's fist went sailing over and connected with the side of his head, smashing his ear hard enough that it was going to swell up later.

Scotty almost collapsed down to the floor, but Michael grabbed a fistful of his red hair and yanked it up, forcing him to stand. Scotty let out a yelp like a beaten dog and scrambled to hold himself up on the counter.

"Adam, lock the door," Michael said, tightening his fist in the guy's hair, making his face twist in pain.

"Michael, don't you think —"

"Get the fucking door, Adam," he growled, shooting a look over to him. There was a burning look in his eyes, reminding Adam of a shark that smelled blood in the water.

He nodded and turned around. There was a round lock near the handle of the door and he twisted the little metal tab to the left, sliding the bolt into place.

"Please, please," Scotty begged, his voice cracking. "If you want the money, just take it. Everything's in the register."

"I don't want your fucking money," Michael said. "What *I* want is to know where you get the fucking balls to be selling blow down at Jack's?"

"I don't know what you're talking about," Scotty cried.

"Goddamn fucking *LIAR!*"

Michael used his hold to slam Scotty's head down to the glass counter. The *thunk* of his forehead hitting and his nose breaking against the glass was sickening. It was a miracle that his whole head didn't go through the counter in a spray of glass shards and come out like ribbons on the other side. Michael yanked his head back up and Scotty looked like he was two seconds from passing out, his eyes rolling back in his head. Blood was already pouring from one nostril and down over his lips.

"I fucking know you've been pushing, so stop trying to play cute," Michael warned. He brought his face right up to Scotty's. "And I also know that you picked the wrong neighborhood to be setting up shop."

"What do you m-mean?"

"I *mean* that Jack's and all of South Bronx is Creed territory. And if I ever fucking catch you poaching our customers again, I'm gonna rearrange your face so that your momma would get fucking sick just looking at you. You understand me, Scotty?"

"Yeah, okay, yeah," he gasped, blood spitting from his lips. "I get you, I get you."

"You better goddamn get me, because I won't be so kind as to explain it to you again."

Michael shoved him away, letting go of his hair, and this time Scotty finally fell. He went tumbling backward and the back of his knees hit the shelving. He went down, falling hard on his ass. The shelves broke easily under his weight and boxes of rolling papers and cheap cigars went scattering across the ground.

"Let's get out of here," Michael said. He ran his hand over the buzzed hair on the top of his head and stepped away from the counter. The skin on two of his knuckles had split from his right hook but Adam doubted that he even felt it.

"And don't forget your screens, Bill," he said.

"Yeah, good thinking." Billy snagged the packets of little round screens off the counter and shoved them into his pocket. He didn't leave any cash.

The two of them brushed past Adam and he stood there while Michael unlocked the door and left. Scotty groaned from the ground and his feet shuffled on the floor without finding purchase, but he didn't do any more than that.

Adam felt like complete shit inside, but he turned around and followed his brothers out of the door.

Chapter Five

That dreaded intercom buzzer sparkled in the neon and headlights of the Saturday nightlife. It was amazing how much fear the sight of a single metal button could bestow on a person, but Justin felt as if it were glaring at him, *daring* him to come press it. He shook the feeling as best he could and bit the bullet.

"Eros Elite Services."

"Hi, Cassidy. It's Justin again."

"Oh, good. Please, come right inside."

"Thank you," he said and tugged the door open as the lock clicked.

The new hall off this service entrance was quiet and devoid of anything besides the gleaming metal elevator at the end. The bustle and cacophony of the New York street dropped to a distant murmur. He could just see the outlines of cars and people through the tinted black glass and it was strange to think how many people walked by this spot every day and never found out what was only nineteen floors above their heads.

The elevator took him up, faster than he could wrap his head around the fact that this was really happening. Upstairs, he was going to have sex with a stranger, and when it was all done, he was going to walk out with a check big enough to keep both him and Jewels set for a while.

Hopefully.

The elevator came to a stop and Stephen Morita stood there in the small hallway. He was scrolling through something on his phone but whipped his head up as the doors opened. He smiled at Justin and tucked the phone away inside his suit jacket.

"Mr. Turner, great to see you again." He reached out and Justin shook his hand.

"Yeah, same to you, sir."

"As explained, this is our employee entrance. It's a bit more discreet. The front of the house can have some heavy foot traffic on Saturday. But even better is the fact that this door leads directly to our employee dressing room." He started walking toward the end of the hall and Justin had to tell his heavy feet to follow him. "This door locks when closed, but if you push this button here, the bell will sound, and someone inside can let you in."

Morita didn't press the button, though. He reached into his back pocket and took out a key card that he swiped through the door lock. He pulled the door open and held it for Justin to step through.

Inside was a circus. The dressing room was a long stretch of space but bustling with women as they chattered and laughed to each other across the room. The walls on both sides were lined with heavy wooden vanities. Each had their own bench, set of drawers and glowing light bulbs around the mirror.

There were about a dozen and a half women milling about in every stage of dress. Most were wearing sets of lingerie that he had only seen in pornos and Victoria's Secret catalogs. Two dark-haired ladies wearing matching black sets of lingerie walked right past them toward the hallway of bedrooms, and he had to blink twice before he realized they were identical twins.

"Hello, Mr. Morita," the first one said.

"Hey, Steve," said the other.

"Hello, Lillian. Hello, Jillian."

Jillian tossed a wink back to Morita and both girls sauntered out. A blonde girl with huge curls and sleepy-looking eyes came dashing in, tiptoeing in her heels as she pushed past the twins and ran off without a word.

"Here," Morita said to Justin, "how about we find you a spot to put your things?"

He shut his gaping mouth and followed inside behind Morita. Some people tossed a look at him, but most only gave a passing glance before going back to dressing.

"So, you'll be in room eight with Adam tonight. Age thirty-one," Morita said. "Unfortunately, that's all I can say, but that's the policy here. Your first name and age are public knowledge and anything else is solely up to your disclosure. Most people like to remain as anonymous as possible"

"Oh, okay. That's good to know."

Adam. His name is Adam and he's THIRTY-ONE.

"Over here looks perfect," Morita said, pointing to an empty vanity beside a large African-American woman doing her makeup at her station. As Justin got closer, he realized it was really a muscular man wearing an ivory nightgown. The racy silk garment clung to his strong chest and thighs, and it looked perfectly matched with his big blonde wig.

"Missy, I'd like to introduce you to our newest member of the team, Justin. Justin, this is one of our veterans, Missy."

Missy put down her foundation powder and held her hand out for Justin to shake.

"Why, hello, Mr. Justin. Aren't you just a little scrap of a thing, sweetie? My stage name is Miss Rude when I'm performing down in Brooklyn at some of the older drag clubs, but everyone usually just calls me Missy."

"It's nice to meet you, Missy," he replied. He had never actually met a drag queen before, but his coworker Andrew Carlson said he saw them all the time taking the F-line to Coney Island.

"Missy, will you please help make sure Justin gets settled in before his appointment?"

"Oh please," she said, tossing her hand. "Of course, I'll make sure this child is ready. Don't you worry about it, Mr. Morita." Missy's voice was deep yet sultry. It did little to hide her masculine side, never mind her body-builder physique.

"Much thanks, Missy," Morita sighed. He clapped his hands and rubbed them together. "Is there anything else I can do for you before I go, Mr. Turner?"

"Uh, no. I think I'm all set." It felt a bit like being dropped on a stage and told to perform even though he didn't know the routine.

"Perfect, and I apologize, but I have a meeting I must get to. Missy will take good care of you," he assured Justin.

Justin nodded and Morita straightened his suit jacket and rushed out.

"So, first night here. How exciting," Missy said, drawing his attention back to her. Justin slipped his bag off his shoulder and sat down at the other vanity next to her.

"Yeah, it's still kinda unbelievable."

"What's unbelievable is that it's been six years now since my first night here. I'm telling you, Justin, time goes fast. And speaking of, sweetie, it's already twenty-past. Now, if you want to wash up, the showers are down past that wall over there. Yes, right down there. Towels and toiletries are on the shelves to the left and there are changing benches in the stalls if you'd rather get undone in there," she said with a knowing look.

He gave a meek smile in embarrassment but thanked her before he grabbed his bag and headed down. The showers at the back of the dressing room were spacious enough for ten roomy stalls and full of shampoos, lotions, hair nets, soaps and piles of puffy towels.

He grabbed a towel and a bar of soap, slipped into the very back stall and started the hot water. As the steam began to grow, he undressed and folded his clothes on the dry bench. From his bag, he pulled out a red pair of boxer-briefs. They were the best-fitting pair he owned — *and the red has to be kinda sexy, right?* Morita had just said to wear his own clothes after all.

He got into the shower and, for a moment, it was like the calm before the storm. The hot water pounded down on him and the heat soaked deep into his skin, muscles and his very bones. The water was hotter here than his ancient apartment building and it was luxurious in a way he'd never really thought a shower could be. Maybe he'd take an even longer one after it was all said and done, just because he could.

He didn't have any time to waste now though. He grabbed the bar of soap and started at his hair and worked his way down. He scrubbed meticulously, and after his usual routine, reached behind himself and braced a hand on the wall to slide a slippery finger inside himself.

He tried to be as quiet as possible as he stretched and washed himself. He had to bite his lip when a second finger joined in with the first, but he worked in a quick and efficient manner. Time was shorter than he'd like.

He stopped the water and it was as though his little safety bubble broke. He wasn't at home. He couldn't just walk down the hall, listening to detectives interrogate suspects on the television, and push his bedroom door open to fall into his tangle of sheets on his bed.

He was going to lie in a bed all right, but it wasn't going to be his. His whole body shivered.

He stepped out and got himself dry, jumping into his underwear, jeans and T-shirt with haste. He rubbed the towel through his hair hard enough to start a fire, but he was nervous, and he didn't want to think about how close ten o'clock was getting.

Back out in the dressing area, all the girls were happy and casual while they talked with each other. He wished he could feel even half as relaxed as they seemed. He sat himself back next to Missy and tried to comb his hair down neat again with his fingers. Missy was still doing her makeup. He didn't see what the point was, not when the client was never going to see her face, but maybe she felt more comfortable done all the way up.

"Missy?" he dared to ask.

"Yes, sweetie?"

"Do you, um, have any advice for someone who's never done this before?" Justin squirmed in his seat. Missy smiled and put down her compact.

"Nervous, are we?"

"Yeah." He laughed a soft, anxious chuckle and Missy leaned over to pat his knee. She reached up and flipped a lock of his hair, trying to straighten the part and he blushed and ducked his head.

"We were all nervous our first time, so don't you worry about that. Just relax and don't fret about every little thing. No one is perfect. Momma used to say that and bless her soul, it's painfully true. But, most importantly, remember that it's all about feeling *good*. So, if it feels good, then don't worry. I imagine Stephen gave you his whole speech already, about the sorts of people that come here."

"Yeah, when I came in for my interview."

"Well then, let me tell you that he was right. They aren't a bunch of sicko perverts out there. Trust me, I've seen plenty in my day. That's the God's honest truth. But the people that come here, Justin, are a lonely sort of folk. And we've all known what it's like to feel lonely, right?"

"Yes," he whispered.

"Then you have nothing to fear from them. Just open your heart and your legs, honey, and I'm sure the two of you will have a good time," Missy chuckled, picking her powder back up. She had a deep baritone laugh but it was full of warmth and Justin *did* feel a little better now thanks to her. "Plus, I bet Steve lobbed a softball at you for your first go. He's a big softie like that. I'm sure he didn't give you one of the kinkier ones like Martin or Geoff, you'll be just fine."

"He said I'd be in room eight with Adam tonight."

Missy stopped mid powderpuff to her nose and looked at Justin's face in her mirror.

"Adam, you say?"

"Yeah...why? Do you know him?" Justin's heart picked up and his palms were starting to get sweaty again.

"Oooh," Missy drawled. "Every gal here has had Adam once or twice. He's one of the jumpers, we like to call it. You know the kind? Most clients like to pick a favorite or two after a while, but not guys like Adam. It's never the same person twice in a row. But, to be fair, he'll definitely give you a run for your money in bed."

Justin cleared his throat. Missy caught the flush on his cheeks and chuckled while she reached for a glue stick and started pasting down her eyebrows, although he couldn't think of why someone would put glue on their face like that.

"Could you be a doll, honey, and tell me the time?" she asked.

"Oh, sure." He pulled his phone out and peeked at the screen. "It's nine-forty-five."

She hummed like that was an appropriate answer. She glanced over to Justin and did a double take as she gave him the up and down.

"Are you wearing that?"

"Um, yeah, I mean...Mr. Morita said to just bring my normal clothes. Although I did change into my nicest pair of boxer-briefs."

"Mmhmm, well, it could use some improvement. I'd say lose the shirt and jeans, and head to that closet over there next to Zelda's station. Get one of those pairs of black joggers and make sure they fit right. You want to be able to show off the goods a little before your clothes end up across the room on the floor."

"Okay," he agreed, his face burning up. The closet contained stacks of clothing. The bottom two shelves were lined with pantyhose and garters in almost every color imaginable. The middle two shelves had silk bathrobes, see-through nightgowns and lacy bras stacked in neat piles. The very top two shelves appeared to be men's clothing, and he reached up on his toes to tug down what had to be sweatpants.

Justin held them up and they looked like they might fit, but he'd have to try them on. He glanced around. No one was paying him a lick of attention. He made up his mind and stripped off his shirt and jeans without any further hesitation. He tugged the black pants up and the ends clung to his ankles and the elastic band was just right around his hips. The top of his briefs peeked out just a bit and he had to admit that Missy had been right. He looked a little more fit for the part now.

As he walked back to his station and took a seat, the blonde woman who'd run in earlier came rushing over to Missy, all upset.

"Oh, Missy, you haven't seen my other pink thigh-high, have you? You know it's my lucky pair and I've got Eric next. He'll be so sad if I can't find it." She started digging around in the top drawer of Missy's vanity and Missy shooed her back.

"Honey, you know I could never pull off that Barbie-ass pink. Did you check that drawer of yours where you always keep them?"

"Yes, of course," the blonde woman cried. She walked around Justin to her vanity and tugged open the third drawer. "I looked there first and it wasn't—oh."

"You need to get your head on straight, Zelda," Missy said with a shake of *her* head. "You're on in five minutes, girl."

Zelda jumped her way into her other stocking and settled it with a relieved sigh on her thigh. "Oh, I didn't even notice your friend, Missy."

"This is Justin. Justin, this is Zelda. Tonight is Justin's first night here," Missy said with a smirk.

"Oh! How thrilling! I remember my first night here. It was months ago with Timmy —"

"Jimmy," Missy interrupted.

"That's right! I remember now!"

"How about you walk Justin to his room, Zelda? Number eight, right? I think he'd appreciate the company." She gave him a soft smile and he sheepishly returned it.

"Thanks, that'd be great."

"Of course!" Zelda exclaimed. "Let's go, dear!" She grabbed his hand and started tugging him to the door. He managed to grab his sweatshirt to put on over his exposed chest, and Missy gave a little wave of her fingers goodbye and went back to her mirror.

Zelda led Justin down the employees only hall and his heart began to race like he was a dead man walking. He could barely focus on the small chit-chat she was trying to make, but it was still kind of nice to have the noise. Zelda talked in a sweet manner, as though she were constantly surprised by the world around her, but it was endearing at the same time. If only he could hear past the blood rushing in his ears. His stomach rolled uneasy in his guts. What if he got sick and had to push the button too like that other girl?

Before he was mentally ready, Zelda stopped at one of the doors and pointed to the one next to it down the hall.

"That's yours, Justin."

He crept toward the door and glanced back to Zelda. She must have seen the blind panic on his face because she gave a warm, reassuring smile.

"Remember, have fun!"

"Thanks," he managed to croak out of his tight chest. She opened her door and went inside, and he was left all alone in the hall. The round crystal-cut doorknob sparkled, and he curled his fingers around it. It was chilling in his sweaty palm.

It was now or never.

Chapter Six

Adam slipped inside Eros Elite Services and brushed the hood of his black sweatshirt off. As the elevator ascended, his cell phone buzzed a text from Michael.

Where are you tonight? You're not home.

Adam rolled his eyes and put his phone back in his pocket. Michael didn't need to watch over his every waking move despite how much he seemed to love doing so. *Fuck him.* He could wait a couple of hours.

The elevator reached the nineteenth floor and Steve Morita was waiting for him in the lobby. He gave Adam an easy smile.

"Hey, man," Steve said. He was dressed in another one of his impeccable suits. Adam didn't even want to guess at how much that guy's wardrobe had to be worth.

"Hey. So, what did you need me to come in early for?"

"Here, follow me. Let's go to my office."

Adam tossed a nod to Cassidy as they walked by. She smiled back, watching them go with a curious look, but she didn't stop them. Steve led them to his office and when Adam walked inside, he gave a whistle of appreciation.

"You know, I always forget how swanky it is in here."

"I worked very hard making this place *swanky*," Steve teased. "You want anything to drink?"

"Yeah. How about a shot of that whiskey I know you keep in the bottom drawer?"

"All right, I'll join you."

They sat down and Steve pulled out a half-empty bottle and two shot glasses. He poured himself one and pushed the bottle across the desk for Adam. He didn't wait for him to finish pouring his before he got right into it.

"Michael came by yesterday wanting to talk."

"He did? When?"

"Late. Around nine maybe."

Nine o'clock? That had to be right before he ran into the both of them on the street.

"What did he want to talk about?"

"He said he's worried about you."

Adam snorted. "Yeah, that's a lot of bullshit."

"Maybe, but even still. He wants to know if you've been working other shit on the side. Like shit besides that crappy day job at the grocery, I mean. He said that you've been flaking out on them the past few months."

"Jesus, Steve. I'm not pulling some side-shit, okay? And I hope you told him that!"

"I did, I did! It's just that Michael doesn't take too kindly to being fucked around with."

"Yeah, I know," he mumbled. "I got that job unloading trucks at Maria's because I liked the quiet and having my own fucking money that Dad didn't have anything to do with. If Michael's getting paranoid, then I'll talk to him, all right? I don't want him to come around here any more than you do."

"Okay, okay. But I'm trusting you on this one, Adam. The Creed gang haunting around this place is bad publicity. Don't look so insulted — you know I don't mind *you* being here. Why else would I let you pout around here all the freaking time?"

He broke and laughed. "Because I'm such wonderful company?"

"Ha, that's a bit of a stretch." Steve turned solemn again. "But for real, Adam? Why are you being so pissy and giving those two jerks a reason to stir shit up?"

Adam was quiet at first. He fiddled with the armrest and shifted in his seat like a man in a slowly boiling pot.

"I guess…I guess I *do* want to flake out on them," he admitted. "I don't want to be what *they* want me to be. I don't want to be a Creed anymore. I want my own life, my own job and my own place. And maybe, just maybe, I'd be able to find someone who wouldn't get dragged down into this life like I was. I wouldn't do that shit to anyone."

"Have you tried talking to your father?"

"He'll barely even look at me. I swear, he hates me more than Michael and Billy combined."

"He's your father. He can't hate you."

Adam raised an eyebrow at Steve and leaned forward to pour himself another shot.

"You've clearly never heard the way he talks to me. And besides, I have a plan."

"Oh really? A plan."

"Yeah. I've been saving up."

"For *what*?"

"My own place, far away from here. Anywhere I can fucking get where my name doesn't mean shit."

Steve scoffed. "So, you're just gonna leave? And you expect them to be okay with that, given everything you know?"

"I'm not going to tell them."

"Are you insane? They'd find you."

"Not if I do it right," he declared.

Steve shook his head. "Sounds risky at best."

"It'll work. If I play my cards right and wait for the right time, I know I'll be able to slip away."

"And when is this *right time* supposed to be?"

Adam glanced over to the picture window where the glowing and vibrant city was thrumming outside. "I'll know it when it comes."

"Well, hopefully when it does, you won't tell me where you're going. I don't want to have to lie when they come looking for you." Steve took the bottle back and poured himself another small one, then tucked the whiskey away. Adam tossed his shot back and put down his glass.

"I would never put you in a position like that, Steve. You're the one guy in this shit-hole city that doesn't care what my last name is."

"Oh, I care," Steve retorted. "I'm just not scared of your false tough-guy exterior. You can try all you want, but you can't fool me. I can smell bullshit a mile away. Now Michael? *He* scares me shitless."

Adam rolled his eyes. "Like I said, I'll talk to him. He won't touch a hair on your professionally styled head."

"Good. I pay a lot of money to look this nice."

"Why, I'll never know."

Steve was a good guy in Adam's book, and he trusted him more than his brothers or his father. Steve could keep a secret. After all, he was the owner of an elite escort service. The man dealt in nothing but other people's most private secrets.

Steve sighed. "It's been a while."

"It's kinda lost most of its appeal. No offense to everything you've built here, Stevie-boy."

"None taken. It just proves what I've been saying for a while. You want something more. A *real* relationship with someone. Not just anonymous sex."

"You might be right, but anonymous is the only real option I have though. At least in this town."

"Maybe." Steve didn't seem to want to argue and Adam let it go, but Steve didn't get what it was like. Anytime he tried looking for a real relationship, he couldn't escape the shadow of his family. Never mind the fact that he was damaged goods, at best.

"But tonight," Steve said, shaking him from the rut of depressing thoughts that were too commonplace nowadays, "you're going to have some fun. And afterwards, you can worry about your life choices.

"Go get settled. It's almost ten. Room eight tonight."

"What was the kid's name again?"

"Justin. Go easy on him, all right?"

"Aye, aye, sir," Adam teased. He stood and strolled over to the door. "I'll see you at Ginny's tomorrow night, right?"

"Of course. I wouldn't miss our one night a week to get fucked up and play pool for anything."

"Okay, good. See ya."

"Have fun!" Steve called out, but Adam was already gone.

Chapter Seven

Justin crept into room eight and the door clicked shut with a clean snap. He blinked at the teeny bit of bed on his side of the wall then shut his eyes, scrunching them tight.

Time to man up and do what you have to.

That's right. The money. Jewels needed him now and this was a sure, safe way that would pay enough. The little butterfly of silly hope and romantic love in his chest had to be crushed down. There was no Prince Charming. There was no Fairy Godmother who was going to swoop in and fix Jewels' heart good as new.

He couldn't afford to save his virginity for the childish dream of true love.

He couldn't lie to himself either though and say that part of him wasn't eager and curious to find out what sex was like. How often had he spent the night, trying to bring himself off under his sheets in the quiet dark of his room, but only ended up more wistful when it was all over? The brief moments of pleasure didn't wash away the loneliness soaked deep in his heart. He wanted to know what it was like with *someone else*. So hopefully tonight, he'd be able to get the money and satiate that curiosity all in one swoop.

Justin stripped off his sweatshirt and hooked it on the back of the door. He reached over to the wall and hoisted the diving section of wall, teasing it up. The square of padded leather wall slid on smooth tracks, nice and oiled, and he let it fall back down again to the sheets. He fingered the downy velvet curtain of black fabric hanging down from the half-circle cut out of the sliding wall.

It was two minutes to ten.

He crawled up onto the bed, shimmied under the black curtain and slipped his legs through the wall to get settled. He wiggled down as far as possible and let the divider fall back down to the smooth mattress. The velvet brushed over the line of his nipples and he tucked his arms behind his head to keep them out of the way.

Even though the mattress was comfy, the sheets under him expensive and silky, it was still like lying down on the surgeon's operating table and waiting for the first incision. Or maybe he was one of those magician's assistants, waiting for the saw to cut him in two.

The second hand on the clock ticked by. How long before this guy showed up? If Justin had to wait until even ten-ten, his heart was going to pound straight out of his chest and explode in a spray of viscera.

Suddenly, there was a knock on the door from the other side of the wall. His voice stalled out in his throat for a second before he got it working again.

"Come in!"

The door clicked open and a man's voice spoke out.

"Hey, I hope I didn't keep you waiting too long," he said, closing the door behind him.

"N-No, it's okay."

"Good," the man said. He was closer to the bed now. "It's nice to meet you. My name is Adam." Adam's voice was masculine and light, friendly and rough, like he had smoked a cigarette outside before he came in. It surprised Justin how much he immediately enjoyed it.

"Hi, Adam," he gasped. It was hard to catch his breath. "My name is Justin."

"Hey, Justin. Would you mind if I put some music on?"

"No that's fine." Adam synced his phone to the Bluetooth speakers and an R&B song with a bass-y beat came on just loud enough to hear from his side.

Adam sat down on the bed and his weight shifted the mattress on Justin's right side. He could smell Adam's cologne from this close. It was warm and spicy and reminded him of fall. He squeezed his hands into fists behind his head and waited, waited for the touch from Adam he knew was coming, just not when. There was something to say about the thrill of anticipation, even with his nerves.

"So, you're the new guy here," Adam said.

Justin opened his mouth to answer but Adam didn't give him any time.

"Steve also told me that you're a virgin," he said, addressing the elephant in the room without hesitation. His voice had an amused tone like he didn't believe it was true. Justin let out a chuckle, but only because he was incredibly nervous, and it slipped out.

"Yeah. I guess my plan of pretending like I know what I'm doing is out the window now."

Adam laughed, a rich, lovely sound, and it made Justin shiver. "Yeah, the cat's already out of the bag. No need to sweat it now."

"Okay."

"And besides, if you're nervous, this doesn't have to seem like some crazy, kinky thing. If you want, we can just pretend that we're on a date."

Justin gulped. Embarrassment was going to be the death of him for sure at this rate. "I've...I've never actually been on a date before either."

"For real?"

"Yeah."

Adam hummed, mulling over this new information. "Well, if you could go out anywhere, to do anything just for fun, where would you go?"

"Ummm, the movies, I guess. I love going but it's hard to find someone else to go with me."

"The movies are a great choice. Do you know that little place on Second Ave on the East Side? The Village East Cinema?"

"Yeah," he said. He had been there twice before. Both times he had gone alone after work.

"Then how about we pretend like we're on a date at the movies? What are we seeing?"

Justin shifted and tried not to wiggle too much on the bed. "I don't know. Something scary?"

"Ah. You're one of those horror nuts?"

"I guess you can say that."

"All right, then maybe you can settle this for me. Do you actually think Jason Voorhees would win in a fight against Freddy Krueger, or was the ending to that movie complete bullshit like I thought?"

Justin couldn't help but smile. He fiddled with the hair on the back of his head, running his fingers through the short strands there.

"I thought Freddy should have won too."

"Good, then it wasn't just me," Adam chuckled. "I can get down with a scary movie. What if we sat all the way in the back? Just the two of us in the dark with no one around to see us? If I whispered in your ear and asked real nice, would you let me put my hand on your knee?"

Justin placed a hand over his thumping heartbeat at the base of his throat.

"Yes," he whispered.

"Good. Then, I'd wait for the suspense to start to build and reach over when I thought you looked tense."

His hand came up and touched Justin's knee, almost making him jump out of his skin. Adam's hand was huge and warm, even through the cotton of his pants. His thumb rubbed the knob of bone and Justin let out a shaky breath.

"Don't worry, sweetheart. I promise I'd be a gentleman. I'd make sure to move nice and slow to make sure you didn't want me to stop." His hand crept up Justin's thigh, but only an inch before he paused.

"No," Justin said. "I-It's nice. Don't stop."

"All right, I won't," he purred. "I swear that no one would see us. I could lean in nice and close and feel you up without anyone knowing. Just look at these gorgeous legs. I love the way they feel under my hand."

"Really?"

Adam's hand crept up even farther and his fingertips massaged into the tender flesh of his upper thigh. Adam was so close to his crotch now and Justin's cock twitched in his pants. He felt a wave of embarrassment at the thought that Adam must have been able to see it through the thin fabric but, thankfully, if he did, he didn't mention it.

"Fuck yeah. So nice and slender, but I can tell you've got some muscles. I bet you've got an *amazing* ass. Do you think," he started, scooting up a little closer on the bed, "that if I was gentle enough in the back of the theater, you'd let me feel you up under your shirt?"

Oh, that was a tantalizing thought. He could imagine sitting in the back row, pressed close to the bulk of Adam beside him. What would Adam look like if he leaned in and whispered that sexy question in his ear? Would his pupils be blown with lust and desire, asking Justin to let him touch him in their little bubble of darkness? Would he say yes to him if they were there?

Absolutely.

"Yes. Yes, please."

"Good, because you look like a dream. How have you been keeping the guys off you?"

"It's easy when you work all the time," Justin confessed. "No one really ever looks twice at you when you work all day and go home to watch T.V. with your grandmother and read in your room."

"Let me guess, you like horror books too? Oh, have you read those kids books, uh...*Scary Stories to Tell in the Dark*?"

"Um, I don't think so, but I love reading just about anything new."

"Wait, so you're smart too? Damn, now you really are out of my league."

"Oh, I don't know about that."

"You are definitely a catch—just look at you." Adam's other hand landed on Justin's left thigh and both dragged upward, creeping over the jut of his hip bones and the delicate skin on his flat stomach. The callused pads of Adam's thumbs traced the bottom of his ribcage and made his skin tingle and goosebump. Adam found the pebbled nubs of his nipples at the curtain's barrier and gave them a teasing rub. Justin sucked in a breath at the wonderful sensation. It was so sharp and powerful, and he felt the shock of it all the way down to his dick.

Adam must have enjoyed the reaction that he got, because he lingered at Justin's chest and brushed his nipples with little flicks.

"*And* you're so friggin' sensitive. I could spend all night just playing with these little tits, baby boy."

Holy shit. Morita hadn't been lying when he said that Adam was a talker. Justin had *never* had anyone talk like this to him before, but it rolled out of Adam on a silver tongue. Just the sound of his voice was like gravel and dripping honey, and it was so hard not to melt a little at the shameless way he spoke.

Justin was still afraid, but it was too easy to push that scared little voice to the back of his head when Adam was saying downright sinful things.

"So," Adam said, dragging his hands up and down Justin's sides, "you better believe I'm a lucky guy for managing to get you all to myself in the back of this theater."

Justin chuckled. He was enjoying their made-up date, even if it was goofy given the circumstances, but he played along.

"Well, a guy that takes me to a reboot of *Alien* and splurges on the extra-large popcorn deserves a thank you, in my opinion."

"Justin, baby, I'd even let you put on *all* the butter you wanted."

He let out another laugh, but it got caught in his throat when Adam's thumbs dipped over his hips and rubbed under the waistband of his briefs where he was sensitive and ticklish. Adam was so close to where Justin really wanted him to touch, but he didn't dare ask for it.

"Can I take these pants off you, Justin? Would that be all right?" he purred. His hands were holding Justin's hips, fingers digging just a little into the sides of his butt and thumbs rubbing tiny circles on his hip bones like he was trying to short-circuit Justin's brain.

"Okay, yeah. That'd be fine," he said. He hoped it came out sounding confident but he doubted it. Adam slipped his fingers under the waistband of his pants and had no trouble tugging them down the length of his legs. When Justin's bare legs touched the satiny silk of the sheets, it was beyond luxurious. The material was so soft, but it tried to cling to the heated skin on his back and thighs.

"Oh, Justin," Adam said. He adjusted himself on the bed, shifting by Justin's legs. "Just look at these sexy briefs you have on. You know, my favorite color is red."

"Really?"

"Mmhmm. And these are skintight and doing all the right things. Trust me." Adam's hands felt huge and hot on the delicate skin of Justin's ankles.

"Okay. I'm glad you like them."

"Oh, I do," he reassured Justin. This time, when his hands moved upward there was nothing between Adam's strong hands and Justin's sensitive skin. He got to Justin's knees and used a guiding nudge to spread his thighs, wiggling even closer. He kept his hold on Justin's knees and massaged the joints.

"But what I really want to know is, if you'd let me sneak down in the back of the theater to my knees. Could I get down between your legs and taste you nice and slow? Take you into my mouth as the movie plays?"

Chapter Eight

Holy fuck.

"Would you really want to do that? For real?" Justin asked.

Adam chuckled, deep and baritone. He leaned down and Justin tried not to jump at the press of Adam's lips against the inside of his left thigh.

"I would love to, if you're okay with it. You don't have to say yes, but I'm hoping you will," he said with another kiss, just a little higher on his leg.

"Okay, wow. Yes, I mean, of course," he said, making Adam laugh again.

"Then just let me know if anything doesn't feel good, all right?" he asked with such tenderness that Justin wondered if he was being extra careful with him. If he was, Justin was a little grateful for it.

"I will," he whispered.

Adam blazed a trail of open-mouthed kisses up his thigh. His lips and tongue were so hot and there was stubble on his face that seared Justin's skin even more. He reached the line where the leg of Justin's boxer-briefs hugged his thigh and kept moving up, over the warm cotton, until he mouthed at the hard line of his erection through the material.

Justin let a small whimper escape his lips at the hot breath and the hard press of Adam's lips against his cock. It throbbed under the attention, begging for more even though he couldn't find the words for it.

"Fuck. Gotta get a taste of you," Adam groaned. His hands snaked up Justin's legs and before Justin knew it, he found his underwear slipped off, rendering him one-hundred-percent naked in front of a total stranger.

His cock landed on the plane of his stomach and he held his breath as Adam settled back in.

"Damn, you're working with more than I expected," Adam admired. "And just look at these itty-bitty hips. I bet I could nearly wrap my hands around your waist, baby boy."

Adam's little pet names were something Justin never thought he'd be into but *oh man*, each one seared up his spine like knots of wood popping under the intense heat of a fire.

Adam went back to kissing his way across Justin's stomach. This time, he started at the thin skin right under his belly button. It was hard to keep the muscles from fluttering under the attention, and Adam's hot breath made the rest of Justin feel so cold in comparison.

The side of his cheek brushed against the hard line of Justin's cock, but he surpassed it towards the sensitive junction of his hip and thigh. It was way too ticklish there and Justin's hands flew up to the wall to try not to squirm right out of Adam's hold.

Adam must have heard his palms hitting the wall because he gave a tiny laugh that Justin felt more than heard.

"Sorry," he said. "I'm sorry. No tickling, I swear."

He licked up the underside of Justin's cock without a single word of warning. The press of his soft tongue was so fast Justin barely had time to process the amazing feeling. Adam licked again and lingered a little more at the underside of his glans with the pointed tip of his tongue.

"*Oh God*, Adam," he moaned. His hips bucked upward without his permission but Adam's hands on his hips kept him still.

Adam wrapped his lips around the tip of Justin's cock, tight and with a hint of suction, and he sank down on his length with wiggles of his tongue to help him inch down.

Justin bit his lip hard, picking his head up and dropping it back down on the bed with a harsh exhale. Sliding into the slick warmth of someone's mouth was so much better than his own fist. Adam took him all the way down to the root, letting the head of his cock nudge into the back of his throat before he pulled off with a lazy drag.

Adam didn't take him back into his mouth again. Rather, he lapped along Justin's length and drifted a hand down to his balls. He rolled them in the palm of his hand, tugging them just a bit away from his body, and it was too wonderful and made Justin shake from the pleasure.

"Hey." Adam pulled back and put a hand on the inside of Justin's thigh and made him spread his legs wide apart again. "Just relax, sweetheart. You trying to crush my head with your thighs or something?"

"Oh, oh my God, I'm sorry," Justin squeaked out. He hadn't realized he was clenching his legs together.

"Don't worry a second about it," Adam soothed. "I'll just take it as a compliment to boost my ego."

Justin huffed out a shaky giggle. "You should. It feels really good."

"Does it? I'm glad. Just relax for me, Justin."

"Okay," he whispered. He tried to do as Adam said—he *wanted* to be good for him—but everything felt too new and incredible to make his body comply.

It must have been enough, though, because Adam kissed his way across the slope of his hipbone and took Justin's length back into his mouth. He re-adjusted his weight, scooting up a bit more, and used the bulk of his hard, solid body to keep Justin's thighs spread.

Adam bobbed his head with slow, glorious drags of his mouth and his easy pace let Justin feel every pleasurable nuance of his mouth that much more. The tight ring of his lips around his shaft, the velvety softness of his tongue as it licked around the head, the slick, impossibly smooth insides of his cheeks... It was all better than Justin had ever imagined it to be. It was so much to take in, never mind how his brain was still trying to process the fact that his dick was actually in someone else's mouth right now.

"Oh, *fuck*," he cursed.

Adam hummed a little noise almost in response, and the sensation of it bolted straight up Justin's spine, making him gasp.

"Adam," he panted. "I'm getting really close."

Adam pulled off all the way and let Justin's cock fall back onto his stomach. He used the second to catch his breath. Adam's mouth had been so very hot and now that it was gone, it made his wet skin chilly in the air.

"I want you to try to hold it back for as long as you can, Justin. Can you do that for me?"

He gulped and nodded his head before he remembered that Adam couldn't see it. "I'll try my best," he said. He had no idea how he'd be able to control it, especially if Adam kept it up like that.

"That's the spirit," Adam encouraged. He placed a little kiss on the glans under the slit of Justin's cock and laid kiss after kiss, working down the shaft. Justin shook out a breath and tucked his hands behind his head again to brace himself.

Adam reached down to Justin's balls and took a couple of minutes just to mouth at him there, taking first one into his mouth before moving on to the other. Adam's lips and tongue massaging where Justin was so sensitive made his cock twitch off his stomach.

Adam set up a slow, torturous pace. He finally slid down on Justin's cock again, sucking just enough, and the feeling punched the air out of Justin's chest. Adam's hands were hot brands on Justin's hips and his mouth was a scorching, wet suction intent on bringing him apart at the seams with every bob of his head.

"Adam? I'm getting close again," he rushed out. Adam pulled off for just a second to speak.

"Hold it, baby boy," he purred. "Damn, sweetheart. You taste so fucking good. And you're leaking— look at that." He flicked the point of his tongue over Justin's slit.

His mouth sank back down, just as wonderful as before, but he moved even slower, sucking just a bit harder. Justin squeezed his eyes shut, clenching his hands on the back of his neck, and tried to take measured, even breaths. His cock throbbed in the tight heat of Adam's mouth, but Adam was moving so sinfully slow. Every bob of his head made the nerves in Justin's blood-swollen flesh zing with spikes of pleasure and he couldn't hold back for much longer.

"No, no, no, Adam. Please. I'm still so close," he warned. He didn't want to come. He wanted to do what Adam told him, but he didn't have any way to stop the intense bolts of pleasure as they came.

He thought that Adam would pull back, but he didn't. He crept at an even slower pace, barely moving at all anymore, but his tongue wiggled and massaged right below the head of Justin's cock.

"Oh God, I can't." Justin shook his head to himself. "I can't, Adam. I can't hold it anymore."

Adam ducked his head and took him all the way in and down into the back of his throat. He started his quick tempo again, but it only took him a couple of pulls along Justin's cock to shove him clear over the edge of his orgasm.

Justin whimpered in shock at the rush of pleasure. The first pulses of his cum flooded into Adam's mouth and he couldn't believe that Adam kept him deep and sucked him through the duration of his orgasm. His whole body tried to curl inward, spasming from the intense bliss, and a long moan pulled from his lungs.

"Oh fuck, oh fuck, oh fuck," he panted. Adam's throat squeezed, swallowing down everything Justin gave him before he pulled back.

"Damn, baby boy," Adam said. His voice was raspy from deepthroating and Justin found out that Adam's sexy voice *could* sound even better. "You make the most perfectly hot noises when you come."

Justin laughed. Endorphins were soaked in his veins. That had to be the hardest he had ever come in his whole life.

"I'm serious!" Adam defended. "Was that good for you?"

"Are you kidding? I think you've turned every bone in my body into Jell-O."

Adam shifted, sitting himself up on his knees between Justin's shivery legs. Justin felt a little shy again now that he had come, but Adam stroked his sides with languid touches. He adjusted Justin's legs so that his thighs were draped over his own, right in his lap, the denim of Adam's pants under Justin's ass and legs. The distinct sound of his zipper being tugged down set goosebumps on Justin's skin.

"I've gotta come while I've got your gorgeous body here in front of me," Adam groaned. Justin heard shuffling and a noise he worked out was Adam spitting before the slight jostle of Adam's arm came against the inside of his leg, brushing his bent knee. Adam was jerking himself off. "Will you let me come on you, Justin? Mark you up?"

"Yes, absolutely," he replied. After that mind-blowing orgasm Adam had just given him, that was the least he could do. In fact, he thought that he should try to do at least *something* to return the favor.

"Could I touch you?" he asked.

Adam's arm stilled and he sat in silence for a moment, making Justin bite his lip and wait with bated breath.

"Where?" he asked.

"You know, just to help you get off? I could g-give you a hand job..." Adam didn't answer, and Justin continued, "Jerking off is actually the one field where I have some prior experience."

Adam let out a laugh. It was light and breathy, and Justin thought he sounded tense beneath it.

"Okay, just…just nowhere else besides my dick," he said.

That was a little curious, but Morita had said that people here came in all sorts, and everyone had their own reasons for needing the unique sense of anonymity this place provided. Adam clearly had a thing about being touched and he could respect that.

"No problem. I promise."

Justin placed his right hand on his own chest and slid it down underneath the black curtain, out to the veiled *other side* of the wall. He reached out and Adam's hand intercepted it in the air. He held it in his own larger one and Justin's eyelids fluttered for a second when Adam pressed a kiss to the palm of his hand.

He moved Justin's hand down and wrapped his fingers over Justin's as he gripped the hard warmth of Adam's erection. He felt bigger than Justin, but it was familiar enough for him to feel confident, even if the angle of his wrist was a bit awkward. Adam gave his fingers one last squeeze before he let go and let him do his own thing. A deep groan rumbled out of Adam's chest and it only reassured Justin more.

"Oh, damn. That's nice," Adam hissed. Justin rubbed his thumb along the underside of Adam's cock. He never got the angle to touch himself like this and he felt the delicate texture of Adam's veins with the pad of his thumb and the way his cock flexed in his tight fist from his meticulous pace. He made sure to do everything he knew felt good for himself, and it sounded like it was doing the trick, because small moans rumbled out of Adam from time to time and he panted.

Adam's cock was rock-hard in Justin's hand and when he squeezed the shaft tight, he could feel Adam's heartbeat. The tip of his cock was slick with pre-cum and Justin made sure to rub his thumb through it to spread it around. The tacky slide of it only helped him rub the head of Adam's cock against the smooth webbing of his thumb and palm every time he reached the tip and gave a little twist of his wrist.

Adam groaned again and his hips twitched forward, trying to chase the sensation. If Justin's own cock hadn't been completely spent and tingling still from his orgasm, it would have grown heavy and stiff from just touching Adam like this, from just listening to him enjoy it.

"Unngh, oh yes. Keep going, baby boy. You're gonna make me come."

A swell of pride bubbled up in Justin at knowing that he could make someone else feel good too. Adam moaned and sucked a breath in through his teeth, and Justin doubled his efforts to get him there. Adam's breath panted out in soft huffs and his swollen cock twitched with need in Justin's hand. He held his breath as Adam finally lost himself.

Adam's cock throbbed once more in Justin's fist and this time he felt the hot spray of Adam's cum when it hit across his stomach. Warm rivulets dribbled over his fingers and the back of his hand, and Adam's hips bucked through Justin's fist. He milked every last bit out of him, making him groan deep and satiated before finally stopping.

"Shit, that was good," Adam sighed. Justin pulled his hand back and wiped it on his stomach. He was a mess, but it was a good thing the showers here were so nice. Adam pressed his forehead to Justin's right knee and groaned.

"Damn, our time is up."

"I'm sorry," Justin peeped out.

"For what?"

"I f-feel like you didn't really get your money's worth. I mean, it was just a lousy hand job."

Adam chuckled and kissed the inside of Justin's knee.

"It was anything but lousy, sweetheart. And um, I was hoping that maybe, you'd like to do this again next Saturday?"

Justin's heart fluttered. Again? Next weekend? But Missy had said Adam was a jumper. Maybe he felt unsatisfied after what just happened, and he wanted to get more for his buck.

"I mean," Adam said, breaking the long silence as Justin's mind raced, "*I* had a really good time and I hope you did at least a little bit too." He smiled against the skin of Justin's thigh then placed an open-mouthed kiss right there and Justin melted into the feeling.

"So, is that a yes?" Adam finally asked.

"Y-Yes. I would really like that."

"Awesome." Adam snaked his hands up and down the outside of Justin's legs and shifted back. "*God*, this cute, little body. I'm going to be thinking about you all goddamn week."

"Yeah, I'll be thinking about you too," he admitted. Even after all that had happened, his face was still burning hot.

"Mmm, perfect. Just give me a second to help clean you up a bit, sweetheart, and you can go."

"Oh, okay," he whispered.

Adam jumped off the bed and after a second, the sink ran nearby. The bed dipped as Adam returned and the warm press of the damp hand towel against Justin's chilly skin was surprising but pleasant. Adam swiped gently to clean up the mess so Justin wasn't walking down the hall dripping in cum, and Justin was grateful for the help.

"Here, I'll leave your clothes next to you." Adam was gone from the bed again, and Justin heard him zip up his jeans and shuffle farther away.

"Thanks," he told Adam before he left.

"Thank you, Justin. I hope you have a good night."

"Yeah, you too."

"See you next week," Adam said softly, and out the door he went.

He was all alone again. He lay there in awe for a moment, still dazed by everything that had happened. Eventually he made himself get up, wiggling out from the bed, and he slipped his briefs and pants on to head back to the dressing room.

He lingered extra-long in the showers just like he had planned, savoring the scalding heat. He let the warmth wash away the last traces of cold nerves. He had managed to live through tonight. Maybe he hadn't gotten to lose his v-card in the first go like he'd wanted, but there was still hope that it'd happen soon.

Adam hadn't been what he had expected, but maybe Morita had been right in picking him. He had felt strangely safe with Adam, and he noted that maybe *that* was something to think about.

He shuffled his street clothes on, headed back out to the dressing room, and there was Morita waiting for him at his station.

"Hello, Mr. Turner. How was your evening?"

"It was nice," he said, cramming his hands into the pockets of his hoodie. He prayed he wasn't blushing.

"Good, good, I'm glad. I've been told that Adam has requested you again for next weekend. Did you accept?"

"Yes," he whispered.

"Perfect. I'll let Cassidy know and we'll pencil it in. Oh, and, Mr. Turner, before you leave. This is for you," he said, reaching into his suit jacket and pulling out an envelope which he handed over. It was blank and letter-sized, and Justin looked at it for a second before he tucked it into his jeans pocket.

"Thank you, Mr. Morita."

"And thank *you*, Justin. Cassidy will give you another call to confirm a time and, in the meanwhile, if you need anything, just give me a call."

"Thanks, will do. Have a good night." He made for the back door and Morita raised a hand to wave.

"You too, Justin."

* * * *

It wasn't until Justin crept back into his apartment, tiptoed around Jewels who was snoring up a storm in her recliner and flopped down on his own bed that he remembered the envelope in his pocket. He rushed to pull it out and held his breath.

The check inside was printed on beautiful ivory paper with silver embellishments bordering the edges. The name *Eros Elite Services, Inc.* was written in fancy script and there, underneath that, was his name. Beside it was the amount of four thousand, five hundred dollars. He blinked his eyes and looked again, but it was still the same numbers and the same number of zeros at the end.

"Holy crap," he gasped. This was more money than he had ever seen on one check. This amount alone was going to cover at least half of Jewels' surgery.

And Adam wants to see me again. Next weekend.

He swallowed. How could he turn down that much money knowing how badly they needed it? And Adam? Well, the fact that it was going to be with Adam again might have been the real reason he had agreed in the first place. He still needed the money, but at least now, having Adam a second time at Eros, he had some idea of what he was in for.

Or, he hoped so at least.

Chapter Nine

Eight-thirty Sunday night rolled around at a lazy clip and Adam sat in the back room of Maria's Grocery, a mom-and-pop market in the East Village on Avenue B right across from Tompkins Square Park. On Saturday afternoons, most of the delivery trucks made their stops, and the smaller-sized, family-run store got a couple of pallets worth of stock each week. So, on Sundays, Adam spent his shift in the back of the store, breaking down the pallets and unloading the freight into easy piles of stock. It was laborious and almost mindless work, but he got to spend his shift in the back, which was what he really wanted.

Nobody saw him besides the Ramirez family, who owned the place, and the delivery drivers. He could hide away from the world and just work an honest shift. Sometimes Maria Ramirez herself, all five-four, one hundred and ten pounds of sweet Latino great-grandmother, would send him home with containers of homemade dishes and leftover foods that didn't sell. It only made the job more appealing because he sure-as-shit could only boil water. Home-cooked food was something he'd never turn down.

When eight-thirty finally came, all the pallets for the weekend were broken down and as soon as the last of the trash bags were in the dumpster, he washed, hung up his apron and slipped out of the back door on the loading dock and into the night. He pulled the hood of his sweatshirt up and crammed his hands into the pockets, making his way down the store's side-alley and out onto the sidewalk.

The walk to his shit-hole apartment was quiet and no one bothered or stopped him. He only had to go three blocks north to his place. It wasn't anything grand, just a space big enough for a bedroom, a tiny bathroom and a room that worked as a kitchen, dining room and living room all at once.

He climbed the three stories to his apartment and unlocked his door, dropped his keys on the rickety side table and locked the door behind him. He didn't bother to turn on the lights. He could see enough from the glow of pink neon coming from the window over his couch. A huge sign for a low-key bar next door, *The Velvet Chair*, was bright through his open shades and he made a beeline for his shower.

His phone buzzed and he tugged it out of his jeans while kicking his boots off. It was from Steve.

Gonna be able to wrap up early. See you at Ginny's in a bit, get me a drink!

He smiled and rolled his eyes.

All right, but you're getting the second AND third rounds.

He put his phone down on the sink counter and pushed aside the clear plastic shower curtain to turn on the hot water. He had just enough time to take his shower and head down to Ginny's, which was thankfully only four blocks below the grocery store. He planned on getting good and tipsy, maybe playing a round or two of pool, and probably watching Steve make a fool of himself and hit on every single lady in the bar.

He shrugged off his hoodie and reached behind his head to tug his T-shirt off. He didn't want to, but he glanced over to the mirror above the sink.

His blue eyes stared back at him and maybe he looked a little tired today, but that wasn't what he cared about. At the top of his left collarbone began the mangled patchwork of burned scar tissue. The mess of skin extended downward, over his left pec, and spread out over the plane of his abs and stomach. If he turned, he'd see the collage of pink and red scars continue over his ribs and toward the muscles of his back. It was gruesome to look at and he could only stand it for a couple of seconds at a time.

He ducked his gaze and finished getting undressed. His jeans were unbuttoned and shoved down his hips along with his boxers. Finally, he took off the thin gold chain around his neck. Dangling on it was a delicate twenty-four-carat-gold cross. It had been his mother's, Kathleen Corcoran before she had become Kathleen Creed, and he only took it off to shower. He placed it down with care on the counter and made a point to not look back at the mirror again.

The water in the shower was hot but not steaming. He eased himself in and winced as the change in temperature made his scars ache and prickle. They were very sensitive, especially to heat and cold, and he worked with speed to get himself soaped up and washed off. By the time he was almost done, the water had cooled off just enough and his scars quieted down.

He knew that Steve was going to ask him about his time last night. Truth be told, he had spent all day pushing thoughts of Justin from his mind. Damn Steve for being right, but he hadn't been wrong. He did know his type.

Justin's body had been a sight to see. He was slender, trimmed in smooth muscle and looked so cute under Adam's palms. He had been a sight, that was true, but Adam had been surprised by the kind of person Justin seemed to be.

What kind of kid walked into a whorehouse like Eros and offered up his virginity to a stranger? It was a ballsy move, and even though Justin had seemed nervous to be in that bed, he had still gone through with it.

Adam respected that bravery. He reached down between his legs and took a moment to massage his cock. He had been half-hard all day and he sighed in relief at finally indulging.

Justin's voice and his sweet, breathy chuckle at Adam's goofy comments were amazing, and Adam had adored the sounds. His cock twitched in his slippery grip as he remembered the way Justin had moaned out his name when he swallowed his cock down.

Adam groaned and rubbed at his swollen tip, just a second, before fisting his shaft again and pumping harder.

He remembered pinching and rubbing the little nubs of Justin's nipples and the way his whole body quivered. He could imagine the way he would shake apart if Adam sank his fingers inside him and stroked his prostate.

"*Fuck*," he grunted. He gripped himself tighter and worked his fist faster to get himself off. It felt good and satisfying but not as good as how Justin's hand had felt on him. Those long, dainty fingers with his bony knuckles had squeezed just right and made the heat in his gut flare up like a rampant flame.

Would Justin let out another of those teeny whimpers if Adam nudged his cock inside him, or would it be more like that shocked gasp he had made when Adam had pushed him over the edge of his orgasm? Would he cry out Adam's name again if Adam was balls-deep and made him come on his cock?

He slapped a hand to the tiles in front of him and came hard.

His hips bucked and his body shook from the bolts of pleasure. His cock throbbed and his cum hit the tiles in front of him and ran over his fingers with the water. He tipped his head down, the shower spray running over his head and down his spine. He shook his head and let go of his spent cock.

"*Shit*," he sighed. The water was getting cold now. He shivered and cleaned up to get out and get dressed.

He tried to push thoughts of Justin away again, but it was difficult. He couldn't believe how easily Justin had accepted it when Adam had told him not to touch him. He hadn't even asked why. It was scary to let himself imagine that maybe Justin would accept the scars if he knew about them, maybe if he even *saw* them. Adam knew better than to let his mind wander down that road, though. He couldn't risk letting anyone that close, no matter how sexually intrigued he was by the mysterious new kid. He knew he had to keep to his own rules. Justin was just more anonymous sex and that was it.

Chapter Ten

If Adam had thought that he was going to have a relaxing night out at Ginny's with Steve, he was a fool for thinking he could escape Michael for that long. Apparently, blowing off Michael for more than twenty-four hours put Adam at the top of Michael's shit-list. He had hardly gotten halfway through his beer before his phone in his pocket started buzzing a string of rapid texts.

Where the fuck are you? You never answered me last night.

You have five minutes to text me back or else.

I'm not joking. You better get your ass over here to the clubhouse. I've GOT to talk to you tonight.

He knew how much worse it would be for him if he didn't respond, so he gulped down the rest of his bottle and typed out a reply, trying to keep his anger in check.

Fine. On my way.

Steve hadn't given him any shit for bouncing early, thankfully, so Adam had slipped out and made the long subway journey up to the Bronx. The whole ride, however, he sat in the nearly empty train car and thought about what Steve had asked the second he sat across from Adam at their usual booth.

'Wait, wait, wait,' Steve had said. He'd lowered his glass of beer and wiped at his mouth with the back of his hand. *'You didn't fuck him?'*

'No. But, Jesus, Steve. The kid was shaking like a leaf. I wasn't about to throw myself on him.'

'So what? You just talked?'

'Do you know me? Hell no. We did a little talking, but I got an amazing orgasm in the end.'

Steve had snorted. *'Yeah, you always do. And, may I also point out how one-hundred-percent correct I was. My jaw almost hit the floor when Cassidy said you requested a second appointment with him.'*

'Yeah, well, I'll give you this one. I don't know, he was...interesting. And besides, I told you I'd help you out.'

'You gonna fuck him next time?'

'Yeah,' Adam had said, brushing him off.

He didn't want Steve to worry about it, but really, *he* was worried about pushing Justin, worried about moving too quickly and hurting him. The kid deserved to have a nice first time, even if it was at Eros. If it took some time, fuck it. It wasn't like he had to worry about the money. This curious situation was too fascinating to pass up.

* * * *

Rock music was bumping behind the door to the back room of the warehouse. Adam heard a couple of guys talking over each other and the distinct wheeze of Billy's laugh. He pushed the door open and saw his brothers and a couple of their friends sitting around the plastic card table. Peter Jones and Eliot Miller were there, playing poker with Michael and Billy, and they both tossed a nod to Adam.

Jones and Miller were Billy's friends from school, the two guys who helped the Creeds out more than any other of their 'acquaintances' from the streets. Almost every night of the week they'd turn up for one reason or another, to drink and smoke usually, so Adam saw plenty of them.

Michael glanced over his cards and threw Adam a glare before he lifted his glass of whiskey and took a sip.

"Look who decided to show up."

"Yeah, yeah, I'm here," he said, shuffling forward. Smoked filled the room and both cigarette butts and marijuana roaches were smooshed in the ashtray. Billy was sniffling like he always did after snorting lines, and all of them looked well on their way to fucked. Except Michael. He looked like a man waiting to pick a fight.

"It's about time."

"Believe it or not, I was in the middle of something. What did you want?"

Michael lowered his glass and put his hand of cards on the table.

"Let's go somewhere to talk. Guys? Hang tight for a couple of minutes, yeah?"

"Fine, but hurry up," Billy said. "We're gonna order some pizzas soon."

"Sure thing, Bill." Michael got up from the metal folding chair and slapped a friendly pat to Billy's shoulder. Adam followed Michael through the door and down the hall out onto the warehouse floor.

It was dark in the main space. The swinging doors to the back were propped open and the light from the bulbs in the hall cast a bubble of light across the floor. Michael led him to the outskirts of it and leaned against one of the many wooden crates. He tilted his head and gave him a curious look, his face half covered in shadows, before he spoke.

"Why didn't you answer me last night?"

"I was out and forgot to do it later."

"When I need to talk to you, I want you to answer me. I don't have time to worry about where your dumb ass could be."

"I'm here now, so why don't you just tell me what you want?"

Michael sighed. "We've got an important date coming up."

"For what?"

"Dad wants us to move a big order of blow. He's got a buyer down in Newark and *you're* going to help us get it there."

Adam ducked his head. This was the exact shit that he was trying to break away from. A cocaine deal? A *big* one? He knew how important a sale like that one was.

"I don't want to hear a single fucking peep from you," Michael warned, his patience thread-thin. "These are orders straight from Dad. You've got a problem with it, then you're gonna have to take it up with him."

"I get it, I get it."

"Then good. The end of the month, the last Tuesday. That's the date. It should be a calm night. You, me and Billy in one car, and Jones and Miller in the other. We're gonna get the order down there, safe and sound, and once it's over, we'll be swimming in cash."

"Yeah, all right."

"There you go," Michael said. "We'll work out all the details and make sure we're ready over the next two weeks. I don't want those fucking Perez-gang assholes getting any funny ideas and trying to fuck with us. That's the last thing we need — to get caught with our goddamn pants down. Oh, and when I tell you we're meeting, I want you to be there."

Adam looked him right in the eyes and made himself nod. "I'll be there."

Michael stared at him, reading his face, and nodded as well. "Good. After all, you're a part of this gang. A part of this family." He paused but Adam just stared back at him. "And you hiding down in the East Village doesn't look good."

"I just want my own place, Michael. Not that apartment you and Billy live in with Dad. And I want my own job with a real, legit paycheck. I'm not doing any other shit than that."

"I know," Michael said, surprising him. "And I'll also know if you ever do."

Adam's hackles rose. He hated when Michael did this shit, acted like this. The heir to the throne, the golden boy — he was determined to keep the Creed gang at the top and he wasn't shy about bossing everyone else around him.

A thought popped into Adam's head. A big deal at the end of the month meant a lot of planning, a lot of distractions and, more importantly, a stretch of time where afterward everyone would be trying to lie low. Chances were, he'd be able to get a week or two of quiet before Michael called for him again. Even one week would be enough time for him to put a lot of miles between him and the city before anyone even noticed he was gone. He tried to keep his face neutral and looked at Michael.

"Like I said, I'll be there. You can trust me."

"Okay, I'm glad." Michael put a hand on Adam's shoulder and led them down the hall to the back room again. Inside, Jones was crooning along to a song and Billy was laughing like a buffoon.

"So," he said, glancing at Adam, "you wanna stick around for a while? Get fucked up?"

"I'm kinda tired after work, if that's all right with you. I think I'll just head home for the night."

Michael shrugged. "Fine by me. I'll text you to set something up next week. And friggin' answer me next time."

"Yeah, I will."

Michael opened the door and left him in the hall without a goodbye or another word. The racket died back down when the door closed in his face and Adam scrubbed at his eyes. He had a lot of thinking to do.

Chapter Eleven

The next Saturday, Justin's afternoon shift at Roger's Bookstore, the narrow, four-story place tucked between other retail stores facing lively Union Square Park, was painfully slow.

Roger's Bookstore was a family-run business that thrived in the extremely busy neighborhood. On a good day, there were two floor managers, three cashiers and at least ten floor staff clocked in to take care of the dozens, if not hundreds, of customers that came through the doors.

The store had four levels: the first for magazines and new releases by the cash registers. The second was for non-fiction subjects like health and fitness or self-help. The third floor was more of the same really. Things like cooking and arts, business and everything else from bibles to bibliographies. The fourth floor was solely for fiction, however, and books from romance to science-fiction were tucked all the way up there.

They were a busy place, but that helped the time go by. Justin thought the whole week would have dragged on, but it had been quite the opposite. Now though, at seven-fifty, he wanted to get home, get his stuff ready and head over to Eros. His second date with Adam was scheduled for tonight and hardly a few hours away.

Appointment, he reminded himself. These weren't dates. They were booked appointments and nothing more. It had been sweet the way Adam had pretended for him though. He hadn't needed to go through all that, but it had been nice, even if it hadn't been real.

Regardless of the formalities, he was still excited to go. The nerves weren't as strong as last time and they only served to ramp up the anticipation. He was hoping Adam and he could go further tonight. All this build-up to lose his virginity was daunting, but he trusted Adam enough now to have faith to get them there. Either way, whatever happened, it was bound to be something.

He had a surprise for Adam tonight waiting at home. An email had come in on his phone during his lunch break with Andrew, and Justin had tried to keep calm reading that his package had been delivered. It was a little something that he had picked out from a discreet website and dared to order without letting himself over-think it.

He finished checking the last aisle in the mystery and crime section he was cleaning and headed down to the first floor to where the employee break room was tucked away in the very back of the building. He pushed the metal swinging door open and stepped off the floor.

The employees' room was a mess of a place in the back of their stock room. Towering metal shelves filled the space and rows and rows of boxes were stacked full of stock. The shelves gave the whole room a cloistering feeling, but the staff made do.

Andrew was the only person back there, sitting in a folding chair with his feet propped up on a pile of cardboard boxes nearby. He was the closest person Justin considered to a friend after the past handful of years he'd spent at the bookstore. Andrew had a pair of earbuds plugged into his phone and Justin could hear the music blaring from the one not in his ear.

Andrew glanced up through his messy fringe of black hair and heavy black-rimmed glasses and smiled at Justin.

"Hey, getting ready to head out?" he asked.

"Yeah, just about to clock out. What are you doing back here? Aren't you on till ten?"

"Technically, but I needed to get away from Alec at the registers. He won't shut up about that video game he's been playing. So, I told him I needed to take a shit and to cover me."

Justin scoffed, shaking his head and taking his red sweatshirt out of his locker.

"What?" Andrew defended. "It's friggin' dead out there! I'll go back in a couple of minutes."

"Okay, okay. If anyone asks, I haven't seen you."

"Thanks, man. Got any plans for tonight?"

"Uh, no. I mean, not really. Just gonna stay in with Jewels, I think." He couldn't risk trying to explain what he did have planned. No one else could know about Eros Elite, not even Andrew.

"Eh." Andrew scrolled through his phone. "A night of relaxation is always good too."

"Yeah, that's the plan. Relaxation."

"Well, I'll see you Monday. I've got tomorrow off."

"Playing a show?" he asked hopefully. Andrew was trying to get his indie-electronic band, Winter's Edge, up and performing at some of the smaller joints around the city. He played the synth, and he and the band had been slowly gaining recognition over the past two years. They were even talking about renting some studio time and recording an album. The second they did, Justin was going to buy one. Andrew shook his head though.

"Naw, I wish. Just needed a day, you know?"

"Yeah, I hear you." Justin shrugged his sweatshirt on and clocked out using the pad mounted on the wall by the lockers. It was *finally* time to leave and he rejoiced inside. "Have a good weekend, Andrew."

"Yeah, you too, man."

He pushed through the swinging doors of the break room and tried to be as invisible as possible past the registers. Alec was there, ringing out a customer and talking his ear off. Justin kept on moving. He was in a hurry and didn't need anyone stopping him now.

* * * *

"Hey, Jewels. I'm home!" he shouted, unlocking the apartment and taking his shoes off at the door. He heard the muted sounds of a car chase from Jewel's cop-drama.

"Hi, Justin. Come here, honey."

He padded into the living room and Jewels put down the book of Sudoku puzzles she was working on. She had a tall glass of ginger ale and a Hostess cupcake on the side table next to her.

The living room was a small den off the main hall without a single window. Tucked back past the kitchenette, it was a small, dark room that Jewels had painted a shade of yellow that reminded him of lemon meringue pie. Yellow was her favorite color, and almost everything in the apartment was a cheery sunshine hue.

There wasn't a lot of furniture in the living room, but they did have a boxy television set on the right, a worn-thin loveseat on the left and Jewel's dearly loved recliner in the back corner by her reading lamp. The television set was tilted at a perfect angle so she could have the best view. The hanging pictures on the walls were all framed family photos, including a set of Justin from every first day of school from first to twelfth grade. They made him cringe every time he looked too closely at them.

Jewels gave him a soft smile. "How was work today?"

"It was all right."

"Good, I'm glad. I ordered us dinner. It's Chinese from Jade. I know how much you like their house Lo Mein, so I got you a large. Everything is in the microwave, so please help yourself."

"Thanks, Jewels." He loved how the first thing Jewels did every day when he got home was ask him about his day and proceed to go through all the food in the house like he hadn't eaten all at and was about to faint.

"Oh," she added, "and a package for you came this afternoon. I put it on the counter."

"Oh, yeah, thanks."

"Did you want to make a plate and come join me for a while? A new episode just started a couple minutes ago."

"I would love to, but, uh...I was just about to head back out."

"Oh?" she asked, clearly curious. "Where are you going?"

"Um, I'm just going to meet a friend and go see a movie. Nothing too exciting. I'll just be a couple of hours."

"Okay, no problem, honey. Oh, and do you mind putting away the rest of the food for me, please? I'm just so tired today."

"Of course, you just take it easy." Her surgery was coming up fast, already the Tuesday after next. With it being less than two weeks away, he kept reminding himself how lucky he had been getting these appointments at Eros. Jewels just waved a hand at him for acting like a mother hen.

"You know I will," she said. "I've got a hot date with Detective Marshall at nine o'clock on the dot, and I'm not moving an inch from this chair."

"Yeah, yeah, I bet." He smiled and shuffled his way to the kitchenette. He didn't think he could eat, not with the knots in his stomach, but he had to grab the package. Right there in the center of the island counter was a small, innocent-looking cardboard box. He glanced at it as though it were a ticking bomb, plucking the take-out containers from the microwave and putting them in the fridge before he finally picked it up gingerly. The tape was sealed and he thanked his lucky heavens that Jewels hadn't opened it.

He passed the living room and peeked at Jewels, but she was already entranced in her show again. He got to his room unnoticed and slipped inside.

He came to a stop at the foot of his bed and turned the package over in his hands. The shipping label was discreet and gave no inclination as to its contents. He found an edge of tape and tore it off. Inside was packed with a layer of bubble wrap and underneath that was a sealed thin plastic bag. He dropped the box down onto his comforter and ripped open the bag, unfolding the piece of fabric and holding it up in front of him.

A lacy red pair of underwear stretched between his fingers. They were from an exclusively men's web store and made to fit and hug his male anatomy just right.

His face was burning at the thought of putting them on, but he had bought them with tonight specifically in mind. With *Adam* specifically in mind. He hadn't forgotten that Adam's favorite color was red and how he had sounded pleased at the plain, boring pair he had worn last time. He just prayed that Adam liked these at least a bit. He wanted to hear more of those praises purr out of him. It was so nice to have some directed toward him for once.

He took the racy pair of panties and picked up his backpack from the floor to shove them to the bottom. He made sure he had his deodorant, a comb for his hair after his shower, the washed pair of sweatpants he had gotten at Eros and he double-checked around his room to be safe. There was nothing else he could think to bring and chances were, Eros would have anything he would ever need anyways. He strapped on his bag and headed out down the hall.

"Have fun! Make sure you stay safe," Jewels called out. He took a step back to see her.

"Will do, Jewels. Love you."

"Love you too, honey."

He felt terrible about lying to her, even more so than lying to Andrew, but he knew it was for the best.

Chapter Twelve

Justin felt like a pro now, sneaking in the secret entrance and taking the elevator up. That gut-wrenching nervousness he'd felt last time was gone, replaced with thrumming excitement. What would Adam say once he saw his new purchase? Would he make that happily surprised moan that had come out of him last time? God, Justin hoped so.

He shuffled backward just in time as the security door flung open and Zelda's head of bushy blonde curls popped out.

"Justin! It's you! Come on in," she said. "Missy and I were just talking about you."

"You were?"

"Yeah! We were hoping you'd be back. There aren't a whole lot of us that stick around here and it's always great when someone comes back for another night."

"Oh, well, it's nice to be welcomed back."

"Of course! Come on, come put your stuff down."

She led him over to the station between hers and Missy's again. Missy was in her seat, lowering a blonde wig onto her head and nestling it into place. Once it was properly settled, she glanced up in the mirror and smiled at Justin.

"Why hello. It's good to see you again."

"Yeah, same to you," he said. He sat down on his bench and shrugged his bag and hoodie off.

"How was your week, child?"

"It wasn't so bad. How about yours?"

"It was a whirlwind, let me tell you. I've got a set every Monday, Wednesday and Friday down at the Xtasy Lounge in Greenwood Heights and now, I've got a gig Thursdays and Saturdays at the King Arthur Club near Park Slope. I'm a certified stage girl, that's for sure."

"That's great."

"You ever been to the Xtasy Lounge?"

"Oh, no," he admitted. He had never been in a regular club, never mind one of the gay drag clubs in Brooklyn.

"They're a riot. You'll have to come see the show sometime," she said, adjusting the spaghetti-straps of her lavender-colored nightgown.

"Okay." It felt a bit crazy sitting there, chit-chatting with Missy and Zelda like a couple of friends. He hadn't expected everyone to be so friendly here.

"I think I'm gonna head to the showers," he said, picking his bag up.

He passed by the twins, Lillian and Jillian, as they traded high heels with each other. It was busy here again this week, and a couple of showers were already running. He grabbed a bar of soap and towel and went all the way back to the last stall again.

Despite how lovely the steaming water felt cascading over him, he couldn't ignore the bubbling excitement in his gut. He made sure to wash himself spotless with minimal loitering around his cock. He had been half-hard all day and he didn't want to get distracted. It was tough though, especially when he got his fingers soapy and propped a hand on the wall to reach back and finger himself. It was fast and perfunctory, and he willed his interested cock to behave. To be safe, after washing the soap off, he turned the water to cold.

The water was cool enough to make him shiver but it worked. He made himself stay under the spray until he counted to fifty. Finally, he snapped the water off and reached for the towel, sighing when the soft material ran over his goosebumpy skin.

He dried himself off, eyeing his backpack with wary eyes the whole time until he was done. At last, he reached in and pulled out the panties, his face turning hot again. He couldn't help it—they were just more scandalous every time he saw them. God, they were almost see-through. Why on earth had he picked this pair again?

Steeling himself, he slipped his legs in one at a time and tugged up the lingerie slowly. The silk material was smooth and wonderful on his thighs, and it was surreal when it settled on his hips and tucked his junk in so everything fit perfectly. The lace was so thin he could feel every sensation of his warm hands through the fabric. They were also surprisingly comfortable, tight but not pinching. It was a pleasant feeling, but he was glad there was no mirror in the stall. He would get cold feet for sure if he saw what he looked like in them.

He hopped into his sweatpants and made sure they were pulled up enough to cover the red underwear completely. There was no way he was just going to walk around in them for everyone to see. He would die of embarrassment.

Back at his station, Missy and Zelda were in the middle of a bout of laughter.

"Girl, he didn't," Missy said. "Without a little warning or anything?"

"No, none! He just stuck my toes right in his mouth and sucked!"

He tried to keep the shocked look off his face and rubbed at his damp hair with his towel. Missy was belly-laughing, deep and hard.

"Well, I've got that beat. You ever have Charlie?"

"Charlie? I don't think so..."

"The one with the stutter?"

"Oh, yeah!"

"Well, three weeks ago, we were right in the midst of it. You know, those jack-rabbit hips of his?"

Zelda laughed. "Oh, yes. That's the perfect way to describe them."

"Yeah, but out of the blue, he starts talking dirty about my armpits."

"No!"

"Yes! Like, vividly. I'm not kidding!" she defended as Zelda broke into a fit of giggles. "I swear. He would have licked them if I had let him."

"Okay, okay, you win."

Missy glanced over and she caught the aghast look on Justin's face while he combed his hair down neat.

"Oh, jeez. Don't listen to us, Justin. Just two hens clucking. Everyone's got a kink or two—ain't nothing wrong with that. I'm sure you won't have to worry about anything too crazy for your second time. Who do you have tonight, sweetie?" she asked.

"Actually, it's Adam again."

"Hold up, for real?"

"Adam, as in, Adam Creed?" Zelda gasped. She leant forward and propped an arm on his vanity.

"Shut it, girl," Missy hissed.

"But I don't believe it."

"Wait," he said, whipping his head to Zelda. "How do you know his last name?"

"Oh, Justin, who in this city doesn't know who the Creeds are?" she asked. He just gave her a puzzled look. The name didn't sound familiar to him.

"That's enough out of you," Missy whispered. "None of that shit out there matters in here. No point gossiping. Now leave it be."

Something was still nagging at Justin, though.

"Missy? I thought you said Adam was one of the jumpers. Why...why did he ask to see me again?"

"Don't you worry nothing about that," she said, patting him on the arm. "Maybe he just enjoyed your company a little extra. Did you at least have a good time last week?"

"Yeah, I did. Although, I feel like I didn't do enough."

"Oh please, like I said, don't worry. Most of these folks are just happy to have somebody willing in their bed. You clearly made him happy, otherwise he wouldn't have asked again. Life's too short, sweetie."

"Yeah, I guess you're right."

Zelda looked like she had something to say but her lips were pressed together in a tight line as she turned back to her mirror and fiddled with her hair.

Adam Creed. The name echoed in his head, but he couldn't make it mean anything. A feeling of guilt washed over him. He knew Adam's whole name. The whole point of this place was privacy, right? And yet every employee here seemed to know who Adam was, except him. So? What if Adam was Adam Creed, or Adam Smith or Adam Joe-Schmo? He was still a stranger to him. He decided to not bring it up. It was as good as forgotten. After all, that was Adam's privacy, and he could respect that.

Chapter Thirteen

Adam stepped out into the hall and closed the door behind him. Directly across the way was room eight, and he knocked on the door. He was going to see Justin again. Truth be told, he was glad he had asked the kid for another night. His curiosity about him was piqued, that was for sure, and he found himself wanting to know more about him. At the very least, wanted to learn all the things in bed that drove him wild.

"Come in," Justin called from inside.

He turned the knob and let himself in. The warm lighting in the scarlet room gave the space an intimate, sensual vibe. The white silk sheets on the bed glowed pink in the light, but his eyes were drawn to the gorgeous sight of Justin's half-nude body stretched out on top, his chest bare while he wore those black sweats from last time. He took a moment to admire his cute body again, walking slowly around the bed.

"Hey, Justin. How're you doing?"

"Hi," he said, shifting a little on the bed. "I'm doing all right. What about you?"

"I'm much better now." He got a tiny laugh out of Justin and it made him smile. "How was work?"

"It was work. Really boring."

"What do you do?" he asked, putting some easy music on the speakers. Just some chill electronic music with gentle rhythms. Nothing too fast or too slow. Justin squirmed on the bed again, his scantily clad hips wiggling, and Adam wanted to run his hands over them.

"I…work in retail."

"God bless your soul. You're a saint."

Justin laughed. His stomach heaved with the motion and Adam saw the hard planes of muscles underneath the soft skin when they flexed.

"It has its days."

"I couldn't imagine working with the public like that," he said, sitting down on the bed next to Justin.

"I don't know, I bet you'd be good at it. It's all about making the customer feel comfortable, and you're really good at that."

Adam was speechless. He was thrown off guard by the compliment. Most people felt anything but comfortable when he was around.

"Hmm, maybe," he finally said. "But thankfully I work in the back of a grocery. It's just me, stacks of cardboard boxes and eight hours of quiet."

"Does it ever get lonely? I mean, not having someone to talk to for so long?"

Adam blinked, opening his mouth and closing it again. It took a second to gather his thoughts.

"Sometimes, but it has its benefits. And I'm not lonely now."

"Neither am I," Justin whispered.

He ducked his head. "Can I touch you, Justin?"

"Yes. Of course."

He watched Justin's breath pick up, his chest hitching, and he put a soothing hand on his knee. Justin's leg went lax under his touch and that willingness caused a heady sense of pleasure to bubble inside Adam.

He kicked off his work boots and shifted up on the bed. He knelt back on his heels and draped Justin's legs over his thighs. He heard him shift his arms on the other side of the curtain and blow out a shaky breath.

Adam leaned down, wanting to taste Justin's skin, but held himself back, making himself burn with the desire to. He brushed his nose against the smooth, heated skin on Justin's chest with little swipes, and he smelled the fancy soap that Steve stocked the place with.

"*Adam*," Justin sighed. The sound was like a spark flicking up his spine. He finally let himself taste, placing languid open-mouthed kisses to the center of Justin's chest and dragging himself in any direction that struck him. He moved along the slope of rib cage, the dip of his stomach and over the fluttering muscles under his belly button.

Justin's ivory skin was dotted with rogue freckles here and there. Adam kissed each one he found and enjoyed the soft pants of Justin's breathing, letting him know that Justin was enjoying the attention Adam lavished on him.

The sweatpants on Justin needed to go, like, yesterday. Adam slipped his fingers under the waistband of Justin's sweats so he'd be warned the second before Adam lifted his hips and tugged them down. With the article finally gone, Adam stared in disbelief at the sight before him.

His mind melted and his cock throbbed in the tight confines of his jeans at the stunning red lace pulled tight over Justin's hips and groin. He groaned and snaked his hands up Justin's thighs, running his thumb under the hemline of panties across Justin's stomach. It was possible he enjoyed the way he quivered at the touch a little too much.

"Damn, Justin."

"Are they okay?"

"Are they *okay*? These are wet-dream worthy. Where did you get them?"

"I ordered them online."

"Just for tonight?"

"Yes."

"Just for me?"

"Yes."

Damn, this kid was something else. He looked stunning in the provocative pair of panties. Bikini-small and stretched over the swell of his hardening cock, he looked good enough to eat. And they were *red*. Jesus, it was like Christmas.

He bent down and mouthed at Justin's cock through the thin lace, making him gasp. His cock twitched under the hot press of Adam's mouth, trying to seek out the source of heat, but it was trapped in the material. He took his time licking and kissing along the length, getting the thin fabric soaking wet, and he made sure to spend extra time and attention near the head.

After a couple of minutes, Justin was hard as a rock and beginning to drip pre-cum from the tip that tried to peek out of his waistband. Adam tasted it through the lace, giving the head a little extra attention. Teeny whimpers snuck out of Justin every time Adam's tongue did something nice, but Adam's mission was to have him howling by the end.

"I want you to flip over for me, sweetheart. Lie right on your stomach."

"Oh, okay," Justin said. He wiggled himself over and got settled, and Adam gripped around his waist and massaged up the plane of his back. He swung a leg over Justin's and sat on his heels above him.

He had been right—Justin *did* have a wonderful ass. The gorgeous red lace hugged his perfect tight cheeks and made quite a sight to see. Adam ran his hands over them and savored the feeling of the sleek fabric. As much as he really loved the panties, he didn't want to rip such a nice pair, and so they had to go.

He peeled down the material all the way off Justin's legs. He readjusted him into position, spreading Justin's knees around where he knelt between them.

"Yeah, I knew this ass would be perfect," he said, digging his fingertips into the muscles and pulling the cheeks apart. There was his hole, a tiny ring of pink muscles.

"*Fuck*," Justin whispered.

"This still okay?"

"Yes."

"I promise I'll be gentle, baby boy. Just stay nice and relaxed for me."

He started with tame little touches to Justin's hole, just stroking it softly with the tip of his finger without pushing in, and he watched the way it made Justin shiver. He was just so tight and pink and smooth, and Adam wanted it bad.

Figuring that it was now or never, Adam thumbed Justin's cheeks apart and held his hips tight in place. He leaned down and licked a long stripe from Justin's balls, over his taint, right across his hole and up all the way to his tailbone. Justin made a cute shocked sound and his whole body tensed up.

"Are you all right, Justin?"

He panted and gulped loud enough for him to hear from his side of the curtain.

"Y-Yes, I just…just wasn't expecting that."

"Can I keep going?"

Justin sighed out a moan. "Yes. Yes, please."

Cute and polite, what a catch.

He dipped his head and licked along the same path again, this time going slower and focusing on teasing the rim of muscles with the pointed tip of his tongue.

A real deep moan vibrated out of Justin's chest, and when Adam latched his mouth right to his hole like a kiss, Justin cursed under his breath. It was music to Adam's ears and he went to work in earnest.

He scraped his teeth just so, nibbling at the rim, and sucked hard. Thank God Justin sounded like he was enjoying it, because now that Adam had started, he could spend all night here. He tightened his hold even more on the soft cheeks of Justin's ass and pushed his tongue in as far as possible.

"Oh, *fuck*, Adam," Justin keened.

Adam smirked, pulling back for a second to let him get his bearings again. "Still doing all right?"

"Hell yes," Justin replied, not hesitating a moment to answer.

Adam leaned across the bed and over to the set of drawers next to them. Eros provided brand-new versions of every accessory a person could need during sex, and he picked out a small bottle of lube. The label claimed it was green apple flavored and he shrugged, popped the cap open and tipped the bottle to pour a glob onto his fingers.

"I'm gonna keep going," he said, closing the bottle and rubbing his wet fingers together to get them slick. "If you need me to slow down or ease back at any point, I want you to let me know."

"O-Okay."

"Promise me?"

"I promise."

"All right, then hold on, baby boy."

He rubbed his lubricated index finger over the ring of muscles, and this time it was loose and pliant to the touch. His tongue had eased Justin open enough that his finger rocked inside with easy, incremental pushes. He could have moved faster if he wanted, but it was too sexy watching the way the tight circle stretched bit by bit around his finger.

His cock twitched again in his jeans, desperate and jealous of his hand. He wanted more and dared to pull back to nudge two of his fingertips together, pushing them against the resistance. At first, they slipped inside without any trouble, but as the main girth of his knuckles breached inside, Justin sucked in a shaky breath.

Adam ducked in to lick around his stretched rim. He knew it would help ease any burn from the stretch, and he wanted Justin as lax as possible. The prominent taste of green apple flooded his palate, but underneath were the soapy, musky hints of his skin.

Justin's body eased open from the licking, and Adam pushed his fingers in the rest of the way. Justin whined and shifted his legs on the bed, spreading them a little farther as if he was presenting himself for him. He was being so good for him, and Adam started rocking his fingers and curling his fingers downward to stroke his smooth inner walls. He knew he'd found Justin's prostate when Justin choked in a gasp and gave a full-body shiver.

"Oh God," he groaned. His body bucked again when Adam repeated the motion.

"Does that feel good?"

"*Yes*," he hissed.

Adam started pumping his fingers with more determination, trying his damndest to aim for his prostate. The wet sound of his fingers sinking in was loud enough to be heard over Justin's harsh panting.

He tilted his head to the side and saw the flushed tip of Justin's cock as it peeked out between the sheets and the crease of his hip. Just the rosy head was visible and glistening at the tip as Justin rocked his ass backward on Adam's fingers with little bucks of his hips.

Adam used his free hand to pull Justin's cheeks apart so he could dip down and lick around his fingers again. Justin whimpered louder and Adam spread his fingers so he could wiggle his tongue in between them.

"Unnngh. Fuck, fuck, fuck."

God, he sounded desperate and it made Adam's resolve melt away. It was too easy to imagine what it would feel like if he replaced his fingers with his cock and the thought was driving him mad. He stopped taking his time and focused solely on bringing Justin to the edge. He rocked his fingers again and again, just a bit harder, to stimulate that sensitive spot inside Justin.

He must have caught Justin off guard because he sucked in a gasp, holding his breath, as his body locked up. His inner muscles clenched down on Adam's fingers. They squeezed ridiculously tight as Adam pushed hard against his G-spot, over and over while his orgasm hit.

Adam stared as the first pulse of cum from Justin's trapped cock hit the sheets and dribbled from his red-purple tip. He kept the rhythmic pressure inside him and with each press of his fingers, more cum pulsed out and his legs trembled on the sheets.

Justin found his voice again and cried out a keening sound, his knees trying to draw together around Adam's legs. He shook from overstimulation and his hole fluttered around Adam's fingers in lingering pulses.

Adam pulled his fingers out with an easy glide. His cock ached at the sight of Justin's hole twitching closed again, giving him one last peek at the soft, red insides where he wanted to be buried deep. He reached for the bottle of lube and opened it again to pour more slick between Justin's cheeks, shushing him reassuringly as the cool liquid hit his skin and dripped down into his twitching hole.

Desperately turned on by the sight, Adam unzipped his pants with messy fingers and tugged his painfully hard cock out. He squeezed the swollen flesh with his slick fingers and even a few pumps of his fist made waves of tingling bliss pool in his stomach. He was dying to come and had to do something. He mounted himself up so he could rut the hard line of his cock right between Justin's cheeks. A sweet moan croaked out of Justin and he took the positive sound as a go-ahead.

He started moving his hips, fucking the warm, slick skin along Justin's crease. His eyes were glued to the way the head of his weeping cock slid over his hole with every thrust of his hips, rubbing but not pushing past the loosened muscles. Justin held still for him, letting him grip his ass with both hands to massage and squeeze it around his cock.

Justin kept making the hottest little moans as Adam moved, and he groaned right back, losing himself in the fantastic sensation. It was too easy to imagine sinking his cock inside. Now, without Adam's fingers stretching him open, Justin's hole looked so tiny again compared to his cock every time he slid over it. Fuck, he would be so warm and slick and *tight* inside.

Adam's orgasm crashed over him and his cock flexed, swelling as the pleasure hit. The first shot of cum hit Justin's lower back, striping him while Adam kept moving his hips. He slowed down to rub the head of his cock directly over Justin's hole, smearing his come over it and marking it. He couldn't get enough of rutting against his skin, even as his cock twitched and slid through the sticky mess.

"Fuck," Justin gasped. His voice sounded wrecked and blissed out. His breathing was still heavy, and the stretch of muscles over his back rippled with every breath.

"Fuck, shit *and* holy damn," he groaned. Justin laughed and let out a slow, deep breath. His body went lax again under his weight, all soft and worn out, and Adam couldn't help but be a jerk and lean down to swipe his tongue over Justin's hole to lick off his own cum.

He gasped, but it melted into a weak moan when Adam flicked his tongue inside him a couple more times, just for good measure. He finally decided to take pity and left his sensitive rim to blaze a trail of nips and kisses along his ass cheek, up to his back, and he licked up any rogue spot of cum he found along the way.

"*That* was incredible," Justin whispered.

"I'm glad you enjoyed it."

He found the knobs of his spine and kissed his way up, stopping at each one to taste the skin there.

"Adam? Um, can I ask you something?"

"Sure."

"I know our time's just about up, but do you think we could maybe meet again next week?"

"You wanna?"

"Yeah, I want…"

Adam paused his kisses. "What do you want?" he whispered.

"I want us to go all the way next time. It's just, I don't think it'd be as scary if it was with you."

"You're scared?" Adam asked, leaning on his forearms and staying draped close over Justin's back.

"A little."

"Well, don't be. If that's what you want, then we can do that next time. I promise." He hadn't intended on seeing Justin again, but now? After the tender and shy way he had asked? There was no way he could say no to that. He tried to ignore the bud of protectiveness taking root in his chest and placed another kiss to Justin's skin.

"Okay," Justin said with relief. "Thank you."

"No problem, sweetheart. Hold tight for a second, all right?"

"Yeah, okay."

Adam got up and tugged his jeans back in place, tucking his spent cock inside and zipping up.

"Just a second and I'll have you cleaned up. Enough, anyway."

"Okay," Justin chuckled.

He was diligent yet careful, swiping up the mess of cum and lube with a hand towel, especially between

Justin's ass cheeks and over his hole. He watched the way it twitched from the soft terry-cloth, and he knew he'd end up jerking off thinking about the sight sooner than he cared to admit to himself. Finally done, he placed one last kiss to the center of Justin's back and stood.

"Thanks for the great night, Justin." He grabbed his sweatpants off the floor and placed them next to him.

"Thank you, Adam. I had a really good time."

He smiled. "Good. See you next week."

"Yeah, see you next week."

He let himself be greedy and raked his eyes over Justin's body one last time, then slipped out.

Chapter Fourteen

Justin's Tuesday shifts at the bookstore were by far the slowest and most tedious. The head manager, Chris Rogers, had Saturdays, Sundays and Mondays off. So, every Tuesday, Chris came in and he brought a laundry list of tasks he spent all weekend thinking up.

This Tuesday was no different, but that gave Justin a lot of think about last Saturday night. More specifically, about Adam.

Adam had promised him that next Saturday, they would go all the way. At the end of the week, it would happen. He'd no longer be a virgin. He couldn't even tell himself anymore that it was about the money — he had to have more than enough to cover Jewels' surgery by now. It was the desire to have Adam take his virginity that had driven him to ask, terrifying as it had been.

Getting a second time with Adam had been lucky, but asking for a third? He had been almost certain that Adam would say no. And if he had to start over with someone new? Someone else? That had been even more scary to think of.

Adam had said yes, though, and it made him shiver to think about it.

Besides having plenty to worry about this upcoming weekend, he kept replaying last Saturday over and over again. He had never come before without touching his penis, but Adam had pulled that orgasm right from him with expert skill. Even the memory of the hot line of Adam's huge cock rutting against Justin's crack was enough to make him half-hard in his jeans.

"Hey, I've got a couple of 'G's and an 'L' over here," Andrew said, shaking him from his thoughts. Andrew peeked around the corner of the tall aisles and passed three books over, sliding them on the carpet over to where Justin sat.

"Oh yeah, thanks."

He turned the books over to their spines and tried to find their alphabetical places. At the last second, he heard shoes on the carpet behind him before a man spoke out.

"Hey, excuse me, but do you work here?"

He whipped his head around and looked up. A man, older than him, stood there waiting. He seemed like a blue-collar guy in black work boots, jeans, T-shirt and heavy leather jacket. His jaw was covered in stubble and he had a tough air about him, although his blue eyes were warm looking, like the big brewing clouds that blew in during summer storms.

"Yeah," he finally said.

"Do you know where the horror section is?"

Justin blinked at him for a second before his brain caught up. Had he seen this guy here at the store before? He seemed familiar in a way, but when a person lived in a city with millions of other people, maybe they all just started to blend together after a while.

"Uh, yeah. It's just over there. Um, the far corner down that way," he pointed.

"Thanks," the man said. He spun around and headed toward the section. Justin caught the pleasing scent of his cologne, warm and spicy, like an open fire on a cold night. The man rounded the corner and the second he was gone, Andrew came flying around the aisle, clearly excited.

"Oh man, I thought you were about to get mugged or shanked or something," he gasped.

"Why?" Justin asked, furrowing his eyebrows at Andrew.

"Don't you know who that was? That was Adam Creed!"

Adam Creed.

The name made him jump in his skin. Everything in the world tilted slightly before clicking into place. Was that *his* Adam Creed?

"Are you sure?"

"Absolutely! Come on, let's peek," Andrew said, tugging Justin's sleeve and making him stand. Andrew scurried down the aisle and poked his head out as if he were checking if the coast was clear through a crossfire. Justin leaned behind him, holding his breath.

The guy stood at the horror section browsing, hands stuffed into his jacket pockets. He had blond hair that was buzzed short along the sides and just a bit longer on the top of his head. His chiseled jaw was shaded with stubble and between that and his bulky, muscular frame, he looked a bit intimidating.

Intimidating, and particularly handsome.

Justin tried to take in every detail he could. Adam stood with a casual air, taking his time looking and shifting his weight to one side every now and then. His outfit was almost entirely black, except for a fading blue band T-shirt he wore under his black leather jacket.

Andrew nudged him in the side. "Dude," he whispered. "I've heard that his family runs almost *half* of all the drug trades in the city. Never mind all the other illegal shit they do on the side."

"Really?"

"Hell yeah! You know the old guy that technically owns this place? Chris's dad? I heard that he has to pay the Creeds once a month because of a gambling addiction. Trust me, the last thing you want to do is to end up owing money to the mafia."

Wow, the mafia. No wonder Zelda had looked spooked saying Adam's name the other night.

"I can't believe it," he whispered.

"I know right?" Andrew asked, excited. "Thank God it's not the oldest Creed son, Michael. I've heard nothing but horror stories about him. And his father, Shawn Creed. You might have actually been shanked if it had been one of them."

Was that really the same Adam who had made him melt into a puddle on the bed? The same Adam who'd pulled him apart with his mouth and hands, exuding sexual prowess? The same Adam who had kissed his spine and whispered a promise to take Justin's virginity?

Holy fuck, it probably is.

Adam picked a book off the shelf, turning it over, but Justin couldn't make out the title. It must have been what he was looking for, because he turned around and headed back to the escalators. Justin watched him go the whole way until he disappeared from view, and he finally remembered to breathe again once he was gone.

Had he really asked a drug lord to sleep with him? It was surreal.

"Well, that was exciting," Andrew said. His face fell into a frown. "Now back to *alphabetizing*. Whoopty-doo."

"Yeah." Justin blinked, frozen in place as Andrew walked away to head back to work.

Exciting.

* * * *

"Hey… Hey, dude… Justin!"

Justin snapped his head up and looked at Andrew, who was sitting at the break table next to him and picking at his leftover spaghetti.

"Huh?"

"You okay, man? You've been staring at that turkey sandwich like it owes you money and trash-talked your grandma."

He blinked at his barely nibbled-at sandwich in his hands and saw he had smooshed the white bread around the edges from gripping it too hard. He put it down on its bag with a sigh.

"Oh. Yeah, I'm fine."

"Really? You've been super quiet all morning actually." Andrew was giving him a quirked eyebrow like he had the word *liar* stamped across his forehead.

"Sorry," he said, leaning an elbow on the table and rubbing his temple. "I've just been in my head all morning."

"Let me guess, you've found someone on Tinder."

Justin laughed. Dating apps? They seemed tame now compared to the truth. "Something like that."

"I could tell. You've got that pale, scared-shitless look on your face that screams 'new love'."

"Well, I don't know about that."

"Okay, okay, maybe not the 'L' word. But you can't stop thinking about them, right?"

"Yeah," he admitted.

"That's normal, dude," Andrew said. He scooped up a forkful of spaghetti and slurped it up.

"Have you ever had, you know, a girlfriend?" Justin asked.

"Eh, a couple."

"Sounds like you weren't too attached."

"Some of them were great but, you know, you can tell when it's not gonna work."

"Oh?"

"But seriously, if you're having a good time with this chick, don't worry about it. I'm a cynical asshole anyway."

"Thanks," Justin said, laughing away seriousness. Andrew joined in with him.

"No problem, man, and I'm here if you ever want to talk. Although you should honestly never take love advice from me."

"Duly noted."

He picked up his sandwich and took a bite. Everyone kept telling him not to worry, to relax, but at the same time, *everyone* seemed scared of Adam Creed. He wasn't scared though, not when all he knew of Adam was that strangely sweet man from Eros on the other side of the wall.

He was going to keep telling himself not to worry, and he was going to look forward to Saturday night. Now, if only he could stop picturing that insanely handsome man from this morning every time he closed his eyes…

He doubted he'd be able to, though.

Chapter Fifteen

Adam rolled into his apartment after work on Friday night around nine o'clock. He dropped a plastic bag of enchiladas that Maria had insisted he take home with him onto the rickety kitchen table, threw his jacket on the kitchen counter and reached into the cupboard for a paper plate.

He leaned back against the counter, rubbing his neck to get the crick out, and waited. The buzz of the microwave was lulling, and he stood with his eyes closed until the bell dinged and he took the steaming plate to sit at the table in the one chair he owned.

It was a mindless chore, blowing on it first so the melted cheese wasn't scorching hot. The walls of his apartment were old and solid, blocking out almost all the sounds of the other apartments around him. Outside behind the building some kids were shooting hoops in the lit-up courtyard, and he could just make out the garbled sounds of their shouting from the window over his couch.

Other than that, it was just the hum of the fluorescent lights and the too-loud sound of his blinking to keep him company as he shoveled through his plate. Justin's voice echoed in his head, making him frown.

'Does it ever get lonely? I mean, not having someone to talk to for so long?'

The truth? Yes. More so than he cared to admit, and not just at work.

'I'm not lonely now,' he had said.

'Neither am I.'

Wouldn't that be nice, not being lonely? Could he even remember what it was like, truly not feeling alone? His heart ached, like a sore tooth that hurt every time he poked it with his tongue.

Did Justin feel lonely too? Could that be why he had ended up at Eros? Adam wasn't dumb, though—he knew how well Steve paid his employees. Chances were, Justin wasn't so much lonely as he was broke. Times were at a shitty low in the city. He saw the fucking worst of it every time he went out. Every time the gang made their rounds.

He glanced at the digital clock on the microwave. It was time to go. Michael and the gang were gonna be waiting for him if he didn't get going.

He stood up, tossing his fork in the sink and paper plate in the trash. The rest of the leftovers went into the fridge so he would have something to eat tomorrow. He grabbed his jacket and flicked the lights off on his way out.

* * * *

The few working streetlamps on Elm Hill Ave that lined the row of warehouse fronts cast little bubbles of light that Adam passed under on his way to warehouse seventeen-C. The brakes on a truck screeched off in the distance but there were no other cars around that he could see. The gravel sidewalk crunched under his boots and he took one last deep breath of night air before jogging up the cement stairs beside the loading dock. He tried the front door, but it was locked. Shaking his head, he rang the buzzer and waited for someone to let him in.

Footsteps inside paused at the door, most likely checking the small screen for the surveillance camera. The intercom buzzed and a voice spoke out.

"Hey, Adam. It's just you, right?"

It sounded like Jones, and Adam hit the buzzer to answer.

"Yeah, man. Just me."

The metal door swung open and Jones gave him a nod hello and stood back to let him inside.

"Am I the last one here?"

"Nope, we're still waiting on Billy. Come on in, get a beer."

He followed a couple of paces behind Jones onto the warehouse floor. The lights dangling from the ceiling were glowing, and tendrils of cigarette smoke floated around them and up through the steel beams that held the sheet metal roof up. On the left were rows of ceiling-high shelves stocked to the brim, but the main space was dominated by rows of stacked wooden crates on the floor, all different sizes. They contained anything from rifle scopes to kilos of cocaine. In the center was a cleared-open space where Michael and Miller sat in folding chairs. The card table from the back room had been dragged out and on it was a road map, two six-packs of beer and an ashtray where Michael's cigarette sat parked and forgotten.

Michael looked up from the map he was inspecting and tossed a nod in their direction as they walked over.

"How's it going, Adam?"

"It's fine."

"Just fine?" Jones teased. "You sound miserable. What? Having trouble getting laid?"

"Sounds like a dry spell," Miller chimed in. Michael huffed out a laugh.

"Yeah, your friend Steve running low on good ass over there at Eros?"

"Eros Elite?" Miller asked, turning to Adam. "You've been? I was thinking about checking it out. My brother-in-law says that place is worth the money."

"Oh yeah, he's a frequent flyer," Michael joked.

"Yeah, well," Adam said, brushing him off, "it's better than those hookers you get from that pimp, Jimmy Whatshisname."

"Hey, Jimmy Vincenzo has some of the finest ladies in town."

"Sure," he said, sitting down in one of the chairs. "I'll be sure to have them chisel that on your headstone."

Miller popped the top off a bottle and held it out for him. Adam took it with a nod of thanks and gulped one swig before he put it down on the ground beside his chair. Miller handed a fresh one to Jones and they all got settled around the table in a loose circle.

"So, where's Billy?" Adam asked.

"He's on his way," Michael said. "We'll wait till he gets here and we can officially start."

"Start with what?"

"With making sure you rubes know exactly what the plan for next Tuesday is. I want to make sure we have every detail clear, so I don't have to worry about any of you fucking it up."

"Ye of little faith."

"I'll have faith as long as Billy's not doped out of his mind by the time he gets here. I told him to stay straight 'til we're done."

"You gonna nag *him* about being late this time?"

"That's enough out of you, smartass."

The buzzer rang from the front and Jones stood up. "Gotta be Billy, lemme get him."

"Thanks," Michael said. He picked up his cigarette and pulled a lighter from his jeans to spark it up. He took a long drag and squinted an eye as the smoke drifted into it.

They sat and listened as Jones' footsteps drifted to the front and the door clanked open. Billy and Jones chatted as they walked in, and Billy's boisterous laugh echoed through the warehouse. He had a lit cigarette dangling between two fingers at his side and he was wearing his ratty denim jacket with a matching pair of blue jeans torn at the knee. He smirked at Adam when he saw him.

"Oh wow, Adam actually beat me here."

"Very funny," Michael deadpanned. "Now get over here and sit down so we can start already."

Billy scoffed. He flicked the ash off the end of his cigarette at Adam as he walked past and plopped down into a chair. He reached over the table and plucked a beer for himself, popping the cap off using the edge of the plastic table with a bang.

"All right, listen up," Michael started. "Do you guys remember three months ago? That night when we met

David De Luca in Paramus to pick that shipment of blow?"

Everyone nodded and mumbled in affirmation.

"Good, cuz we're gonna do something similar next week. Our guy, a dude by the name of Moretti, is going to have his crew waiting for us in Newark for the delivery."

"How much are we moving?" Adam asked.

"Forty kilos of China White."

"Jesus, that's a lot," Miller whispered.

"Yeah, it's a good amount," he agreed, "but it's not the most we've ever done. And besides, the amount isn't what's important. If we do this right, it's gonna mean a lot more opportunities to work with Mr. Moretti. *That's* the reason Dad wants this to go without a hiccup."

"Is there any reason for it not to?" Adam asked. Michael took a second to have another pull on his cigarette, finishing it off.

"The Perez gang."

"Oh, fuck the Perez gang," Billy groaned. "Those assholes can't even come close to touching us."

"Maybe, but if they catch any wind about any of this, then they might be tempted to try."

Billy rolled his eyes and sipped his beer. Michael continued.

"So, we're gonna take some extra precautions. First off, we're gonna travel in two cars. I want half of the order in each—it'll be safer than risking all our eggs in one basket."

"Good thinking," Miller added.

"I know. That's what I'm here for. Now, I want me, Billy and Adam in the first car. Adam, you're gonna drive. Jones and Miller, you take the second car behind us, and Jones? How about you drive?"

"Yes, sir," Jones replied. Adam nodded.

"Okay. Now second, I want you on time. We'll meet here Tuesday at nine o'clock on the *fucking dot*, and we'll get locked and loaded."

"You don't mean we'll all be armed?" Adam asked. Billy barked out a laugh.

"Are you fucking kidding me? What, you're too scared to point a goddamn gun?"

"I'm just saying," he growled. "It might make the situation a little harder if someone gets an itchy trigger finger."

"And what the fuck is that supposed to mean?"

"Hey, both of you," Michael interrupted. "Shut it. I'm the one here deciding what we do and don't need, and I say everyone should be prepared. At least one per vehicle. I don't want us getting caught with our pants down. End of it. Now, fucking scoot closer. Let's look at the map."

Billy tossed Adam one last pissy look, but joined them to gather around to get a better view. The map covered all of Manhattan and the neighboring boroughs. Michael placed his finger on the dot across the river that read *Newark, New Jersey*.

"This is where we're headed."

"And what the fuck is in Newark?" Billy asked.

"Not much," Michael joked. "But we're going to meet Moretti's crew in the parking garage of the Best Western hotel across from Newark Penn Station. I want us to take the Holland tunnel on our way over."

"And on the way back, too?" Jones asked. He lit his own cigarette and Billy snagged the pack out of his hand to bum one off him. Billy always chain-smoked if he couldn't get high.

"No. No tunnel coming back. I don't want to take the same way. If anyone stakes out our route on the way there, they can't set up a hit point to catch us returning. We're gonna take the George Washington Bridge back."

"Isn't that the long way, though?" Adam asked.

"Yes, so they won't be expecting it. Okay, now just try to stay focused for a little bit longer. We're gonna go over the exact route starting from right here at the warehouse…"

* * * *

Michael had his work cut out for him, but he managed to keep them all, mainly Billy, in check long enough to get through his whole plan. By the time he was wrapping up, Billy was already tapping out a line of coke on the card table, right on the road map. Adam couldn't wait until he could get the hell out of there. His patience for this shit was wearing very thin.

"All right, okay, I'm done. Jesus, Billy, you're a fucking animal," Michael growled.

"What? I waited!"

"Hardly."

"Oh, fuck off," he said, leaning down to snort his line. Michael snagged the map off the table after he'd finished and shoved the cardboard boxes of empty beer bottles at him. "Go toss these in the dumpster," he ordered, "and wait for me. I'll be right out."

Billy did as told. Once he got high, he seemed to have no problem shoveling shit for Michael. Adam couldn't decide if he liked docile, high Billy or asshole, sober Billy better. It was a tough choice.

Billy stood up, and Jones and Miller started moving the folding chairs back against the wall. Michael turned to Adam.

"Do you mind helping me drag this table to the back room?"

"Sure, no problem."

The two of them got the table folded and each took a side to carry it back. Adam figured the guys must have had plans to go out because they weren't staying there to drink. None of them had asked him to come with them, which was fine because he would have said no anyway. They got the table into the clubhouse, leaning it up against the couch for the next time they played cards, and he turned around to head out.

"Hold up a sec," Michael said. He took a step closer and gave Adam a curious look.

"O-kay…"

"Hey, I want you to take this." Michael reached behind his back and pulled out his gun, holding it out for Adam to take. He didn't reach for it.

That was Michael's thirty-eight special, handed down to him from their father. Michael carried that gun with him everywhere. It didn't even have to be loaded. If he drew it, anyone who faced him knew very well how many bodies had fallen before it, and so just the sight of it alone carried enough weight in this city.

"Why?"

"Why?" Michael repeated. "Because shit's gonna go down soon and I want *all* of us to be prepared. Take this, do some practicing down at Miles' range on Bruckner Boulevard and make sure you're well acquainted with it." Michael opened the cylinder to show him that it was fully loaded before holding it back out for him again. "Miles will have plenty of practice ammo."

Adam shook his head, staring at the gun. After a heartbeat, he forced himself to take it. Michael patted him on the back.

"That's it. As long as we keep our cool, things will go without a hitch and Dad will be grateful."

He frowned, still staring at the gun in his hand. "And if the Perezes give us trouble?"

"Then we'll give 'em trouble right back."

He didn't like the sound of that, but Michael looked determined.

"All right."

"And, Adam? I know this isn't your favorite part of the job, but you being here means a lot."

"Sure." He looked away, suddenly worried that Michael knew somehow. Knew that despite him playing along and saying all the right things, he was planning on bailing as soon as this was all said and done. Michael couldn't know, though, and he resolved himself to play his cards close to his chest.

Michael was right. Adam *didn't* like doing this, and he never wanted to end up in another situation like this again. Ever again.

"Fine," Michael said, cramming his hands into the pocket of his jeans. "That's all I've got for tonight. You can head out."

Adam nodded. He checked the safety on the gun to be safe and tucked it into the back waistband of his jeans, making sure his shirt and jacket covered it up.

"Oh, and promise me you'll hit the range and get a little practice in with that thing. I don't want you to be rusty. Don't tell Billy, but I trust you with that way more than I trust him. I'll need you to cover my back."

"Okay, I promise."

"Good. I'll text you if I think of anything else."

"Fine. Night, Michael."

"Night."

Michael stayed behind to lock up as Adam headed for the door and down the hall. His mind felt jam-packed with the plan for next Tuesday. The route, the times, the guns…everything swirled in his head.

On his way home, though, walking the empty sidewalk back to the subway, his thoughts turned to Justin again. At least he'd get to see him one last time tomorrow night before everything went down Tuesday.

Chapter Sixteen

Nine-thirty Saturday night, Justin rang the bell to the employee dressing room at Eros and waited in the hall for someone to answer. He tapped his foot on the floor, trying to listen for the sounds of voices on the other side. It was quiet, though, and he worried that no one was there until the door flung open and someone peeked out.

It was a woman with a thin face and long straight black hair framing her slender features. He recognized her immediately as one of the twins but for the life of him had no clue as to which one.

"Oh, hello," she said. "Come on in."

"Thanks." He shuffled in past her. She was wearing a matching set of lime-green bra and panties and her shoes were a pair of strappy black heels that looked impossible to walk in at that height. He tried not to stare and averted his eyes to be polite.

"I've seen you around a couple of times this month, right?" she asked, squinting at him.

"Yeah, I just started a couple of weeks ago."

"That's what I thought. My name is Jillian. Nice to meet you."

"Hi, same. I'm Justin." He held out his hand and she shook it with a strong grip.

"Good to know." She started walking back to her station but glanced back. "So, you've got another appointment tonight? It's a slow one."

She wasn't wrong. He had never seen it so empty in the dressing room before. Besides them, there were only two others, a girl with glasses sitting at one of the first stations, and Jillian's sister in the back next to her spot.

"Yeah, tonight's my third."

"Oh, so you must be getting into the swing of things then, huh?"

"Eh, sort of."

"Well, if you ever have any questions, feel free to ask me or my sister. We've both been here for years."

"Actually..." He started, freezing by his station and twisting his hands. Jillian stopped and turned back with a curious look. "Can I ask if you've ever had someone by the name of Adam?"

"Oh yeah," she said, leaning against the wall between his station and Zelda's. "Both Lil and I had him before, but that was a long time ago. To be honest, I haven't heard of him being around much anymore. Why, do you have him tonight?"

"Yeah."

"He's an all right guy, if you're into that *danger* sort of thing."

"Danger?" he asked.

"Yeah, well, he's got a bit of a reputation, but here it doesn't mean much. He won't bother you any."

"Okay, that's good." Damn, he was apparently one of the few people in the whole city who hadn't known about the Creeds and their reputation.

"If you think of anything else, just let me know." She pushed herself off the wall and meandered back to her spot.

He sat to drop his bag and shrug off his sweatshirt. Both Missy and Zelda's spots were tidy and empty beside him. It was strange being there without them. Listening to the two of them talk and laugh had been like a safety blanket, but he knew where everything was by now and he could get ready by himself. It might have been nice though to have Missy to confide in, especially tonight, with Adam's promise looming in the back of his mind.

He grabbed his change of pants out of his bag and headed to the showers. Every stall door was crooked open and the only sound came from a dripping faucet somewhere in the back. He picked his usual stall at the back and got the water running, beginning his routine while the water heated.

"Breathe and relax. Breathe...and relax," he whispered to himself under the noise of the shower stream. The spray of soothing water ran over him and he closed his eyes and stood under the pounding force. The drum of water on tile echoed and reverberated in the stall, drowning out the world around him, and he stayed wrapped in the bubble of white noise to think.

This was probably going to be his last night here. After the internal debates, fears and motivations that brought him to Eros, this was it. Not only had he accomplished what he had set out to do and earned enough money to ensure that Jewels' surgery would be covered, but that burning curiosity inside him about the mysterious wonders of sex was about to be sated in every way. He and Adam had worked their way up and now it was the grand finale, the last frontier — and after that?

Well, after that, why would Adam keep wasting his money on him? Time here at Eros Elite wasn't cheap and he couldn't keep asking Adam to see him again. And sure, he could ask Morita to find him someone else, make this a regular thing. The money would be helpful when they lived week by week, but that wasn't what he wanted.

It was Adam. He was the reason Justin kept coming back. Getting close to him, giving himself up willingly and being surprised at the tenderness returned to him — that was what he wanted. Romance, in other words. *How greedy of me.*

He grabbed his bar of soap and started washing, but the thought of his parents crept in. Sometimes, if he tried really hard, he could remember them, but every day it was harder and harder to remember all the right details. He couldn't quite remember what shade of brown his mom's hair had been, or how his dad had looked if he smiled. He could remember the night they'd brought him over to Jewels. The sun had already set, and the last traces of orange had been gone from the sky. He remembered getting out of the elevator on the floor of her apartment, the same one they lived in now, and being so excited to see her.

She had always been full of love and patience when it came to watching him, and he'd loved those moments when she babysat. Back then, Jewels had still worked as a nurse at St. Anthony Hospital, a couple of years from retiring. Still, even after her shift, she'd found the energy to watch him, play games with him and feed him with a smile on her face. He remembered that night his parents had brought him over and the moment he'd realized that they were never coming back.

The police had found his parents, both dead in an apartment in Queens from a methadone overdose. The apartment had belonged to their dealer and while he had only gone to jail for nine years for possessing and selling drugs, Justin's parents were just plain gone. Jewels had been strong for him when he couldn't even imagine the pain of losing her only child.

Would his parents be disappointed in him for going through with this? Selling his body in a whorehouse to a stranger? At least he had decided to do it so he could step up and take care of the only family he had left. That was more than they could say they had done.

He hit the water tap and shook himself off before reaching for the towel and drying his chilling skin. The only change of clothes he brought with him were the pair of sweatpants he had gotten here. No boxer-briefs, no exotic panties, just the pants to cover his decency until he got to the room. Tonight, he was going to strip down nude before he crawled into the bed. If it was going to be his last time here at Eros, he was going to make the most of his hour with Adam.

Chapter Seventeen

The television in the guest room at Eros was playing the news, but Adam wasn't watching it. He stood in the back at the huge stretch of mirrors above the bathroom sink counter instead, leaning heavily on the marble surface. He had showered at home and wandered here after work, where the almost constant coming and going of delivery trucks had him busy all day. Of course, now he was exhausted, but he knew it was really because of the gang meeting last night. Sleep had been nearly impossible once he had lain in bed, running the plans for the trade over and over, all the while considering the possibility of his escape in the back of his mind.

He glanced at the parcel on the counter beside him. It was a thin package, wrapped in a sheet of newspaper he'd taken home from the grocery. He knew that it might throw a wrench into his whole plan, but that hadn't stopped him from bringing it.

He reached behind his back and pulled out the revolver tucked into the waist of his jeans. He double-checked the safety and turned it over in his hands, feeling the heavy, balanced weight of it. He glanced up at his reflection holding the gun and blinked at the sight of himself.

There he was, the thug, the gangster, the *monster* that everyone thought he was. The sight of him was bad enough on its own—he didn't need the revolver in his hands to make it any worse.

He pulled open the metal door of the safe underneath the sink counter. Just like a hotel room, the guest rooms at Eros Elite each came with a fireproof safe where clients could store their personal belongings while they indulged. He'd never bothered with it before, but there was no way he was going to bring his father's revolver into the same room as Justin. Michael might have felt more comfortable with its weight on his person, but to Adam, it was a ball and chain holding him down.

With the gun safely tucked away, he grabbed the package off the counter before heading into the front. The clock on the wall read nine-fifty-eight, so he picked up the remote to click off the television and tossed it onto the chair before he made his way out.

All was silent in the hall while knocked on the door and waited. Eros seemed like a ghost town tonight, but that was fine by him. *Less people to avoid eye contact with.*

"Come on in!"

He opened the door and stepped inside, almost freezing right in the doorway at the sight of Justin lying out on the bed and waiting for him. Tonight, he was gorgeously nude already, and Adam had to remind himself to shut the door behind him.

"Justin, you are something else, you know that?" he asked. He put the package down on the tiny side table by the door.

"Am I?"

"Most definitely," he confirmed. "Always full of surprises."

Justin's hands were placed on his chest, resting on Adam's side of the wall in a lazy pose, overlapping over his heart. The black velvet curtain draped heavily over his collarbone and shoulders. His legs were bent at the knee a bit and they were pressed together, making Adam's eyes drift up his pale, glowing thighs towards the sweet V of his groin and hips.

He synced his phone to the Bluetooth, flooding soft music into the room, and Justin's hands twitched, his fingers squeezing together and tapping on his collarbone. His body language screamed underlying tension that he wanted to ease away for him.

"God, you look a sight," he purred. "As much as those panties you had on last time were sexy, seeing all of you is still the best, sweetheart."

Justin shivered on the bed hard enough for Adam to see from a few feet away.

"Really?"

"Really really."

Adam had a feeling Justin wasn't used to getting compliments, especially such blatant ones. He couldn't help but think that it was a crying shame.

"Well, I just wanted to be ready for you."

The earnest way he said it made Adam's blood heat up. It was an intoxicating feeling, knowing that Justin wanted it — wanted him — that badly, and he was going to give it to him. He had promised after all.

"Can you do something for me, Justin?"

"Oh, sure. W-What is it?"

"I want to watch you touch yourself while I get undressed. I want to see the way you do it."

"You do?" he whispered.

"Yes. Please."

"Okay." His hands twitched again on his chest. "All right."

"Let me see it, sweetheart."

Adam started pulling off the sleeves on his sweatshirt. Ever so slowly, Justin started to move. He placed his left hand on the bed and clenched the sheets underneath him in a fist. He trailed his right hand downward over his sternum, his smooth stomach, and finally to the space between his legs.

He wrapped his fingers around the interested flesh there. Adam stared as Justin began toying with himself, giving his cute cock tiny tugs as he took in a deep breath and got into the motion of his hand.

Adam reached behind his neck and tugged his T-shirt up and off. He kicked his boots off next and began loosening his black jeans but didn't want to tear his eyes from Justin. He wanted to be fully undressed tonight. It wasn't as if Justin would be able to see his scars or anything, and he didn't want him to feel self-conscious as the only one naked through this new endeavor.

Justin's hand faltered on his cock, which was beginning to fill out nicely in his grip. His other hand curled tighter into the sheets. "Is this all right?" he asked.

Adam realized he had been staring and not talking, so he reached the foot of the bed, crawled up and let his mouth run.

"Absolutely, gorgeous. Tell me, how do you normally do it at home? Are you the kinda guy that likes to do it fast and business-like in the shower like a hit-and-run? Or do you like to take your time? Making an ordeal of it in the nest of your bed and coming hard across yourself without worrying about the mess?"

Justin squeezed his cock, easing to a barely moving pace.

"Sometimes...sometimes when I'm in bed and can't sleep, I'll make it slow."

"And what do you think about?" he asked. He placed both his hands on Justin's bony knees and pulled them apart, getting a lovely view of Justin's balls and small, rosy hole as he moved up higher between his legs.

"All sorts of things I guess, but...but mainly I like to imagine what it's like to go all the way with someone."

"You like thinking about someone fucking you?"

"Yes," he confessed. His hand kept an easy pace on his flushed cock.

"And what else?"

"Lately?"

"Yeah."

"Honestly?"

"Yes."

"You."

He smiled to himself. He bent one of Justin's knees higher and placed a kiss on the inside of his leg.

"What about me?"

"The sound of your voice," Justin said, no hesitation. Adam hadn't been expecting that answer. "And your hands. They're so big and warm all the time. They..." He paused for a second, maybe choosing his words carefully as his hand came to a stop. "They always feel really nice."

Adam placed another kiss a little higher on Justin's thigh, a sort of reward for the honesty.

"I'm glad. Will you let me open you up then, Justin? I believe I made you a promise last week if you're still interested."

"Yes, please. I want that."

"Then keep touching yourself for me, baby boy, and just let me take care of you."

Justin swallowed loudly. "Okay."

The pace of his hand picked up again, a lazy speed. Adam wanted to offset any discomfort that might happen as he stretched Justin open. Having him touch himself ensured that it would take the edge off and Adam could focus one hundred percent on his task.

He reached over to the side table and plucked out a brand-new bottle of lube. He made sure to coat the fingers on his right hand liberally. If Justin was as tight as last time, Adam was going to need it to ease into him. With his clean hand, he grabbed one of the throw pillows on the bed.

"Lift your hips up for me, sweetheart."

Justin picked his hips up off the bed and Adam slipped the pillow underneath him, lifting him at the best angle to work at. He put his hand under Justin's balls and gently touched his index finger to the tiny bud of his hole.

"You've got a beautiful asshole," he said. It made Justin laugh skeptically, his breath light.

"N-Now you're being ridiculous."

"I am certainly not," he defended. He stroked his finger over the little ring, admiring the way it twitched under the attention. "It's always so smooth and pink and happy to see me. If I had you in my bed for the night, I'd spend hours just tonguing it loose to watch it twitch."

"*Fuck*," Justin cursed. His fingers squeezed the tip of his ruby cockhead and Adam worked one finger inside him. The tight muscles of Justin's body clung to his digit and he set to loosening them with slick thrusts in and out.

"Soon," he teased. He set to kissing the inside of Justin's thigh again. The pale ivory of his skin was delicious, and Adam let himself waste a little extra time placing pink mark after pink mark along the stretch. "Do you do this at home too? Slip your fingers inside yourself as you jerk off?"

His second finger pressed tight against his first and Justin stretched open wider around them as Adam nudged them in.

"Hmm, yeah. Yeah, I do," Justin panted.

Adam's cock grew heavy between his legs, but he chose to ignore it and keep going.

"And have you done it thinking of me?" He curled his fingers upward to find that sensitive place inside Justin and was rewarded by a surprised gasp that threw him off mid-sentence.

"Yes, I—*ungh*—oh shit. Yes, yes. I really want it, Adam."

"Okay, sweetheart. Soon, I promise."

He worked his hand in rhythmic thrusting, spreading his fingers and scissoring the muscles looser. The soft noises Justin panted out were fuel for the fire and he wanted so badly to just sink his cock right in, but Justin needed more preparation than that.

Finally, he pulled his fingers back enough to try and nudge a third fingertip right next to the others. At the new stretch, Justin tensed up and stopped his hand.

"Keep nice and relaxed, Justin. Trust me, it will help," he said. Adam leaned down and swiped his tongue over the head of Justin's cock where it peeked out from his fist. Justin gasped and let out a slow breath, trying to relax for him. Adam pressed his fingertips forward again and very carefully began rocking them in little increments.

With a lot of patience and determination, he got all three fingers inside and he gave Justin a minute to adjust. He rocked his hand a couple of times, just barely sliding them in and out.

"Damn, Justin. You feel so fucking nice inside. I can only imagine how amazing it's going to feel on my cock."

Justin moaned and his legs squeezed Adam's sides. The feeling of Justin's bare skin against his was new and different, especially on his left side where the scars stretched all the way around to his back. Even before, when he had come to Eros twice a month just to look for a good lay, he had never gotten completely undressed during sex. Sure, the other person couldn't see him, but he still had to look at himself. The view of Justin's lean legs against him, though, was a lovely sight to see.

Justin stroked his cock in long, languid pulls. The tip was beginning to leak pre-cum in a shiny drop. Carefully, Adam slipped his fingers free from Justin's body, making him groan.

"I think you're ready. Just give me a quick sec." He snagged a condom from the open drawer and hurried to get it on, reaching around for the bottle of lube on the bed to get his cock slick the second it was properly on. He was hard as a rock, already sensitive at the blood-flushed tip from the erotic process of getting Justin stretched open. He used the extra lube on his fingers, working them back into Justin's body to get him even wetter.

"I'm gonna start pushing in. Okay, baby boy?"

"Yes, okay," Justin panted. It came out like a whisper and it was clear he was nervous.

"I want you to take a deep breath and let it out slowly when I start. Just keep breathing through it and it'll feel better in a minute, I swear. All right?"

"Okay."

"And promise me that if you need me to stop or slow down, you'll tell me."

"I will. I promise." Justin gulped. He let go of his cock and dropped his hands to the bed, squeezing the sheets in little pulses before he flattened them out to make himself relax.

Adam took hold of his shaft and angled the tip between Justin's legs. He rubbed the wet tip over his hole, enjoying the soft feeling of it and the way a little moan squeaked out of Justin.

"Breathe for me, sweetheart."

He crept his hips forward, feeling the resistance of his hole for a moment before the muscles gave to the pressure and the head of his cock slipped inside. The second it did, Justin's breath rushed out in a swoop. His chest hitched, locking up, and his hands squeezed into tight fists by his sides.

"Just keep breathing, Justin," Adam reminded him. He pushed in with a slow, steady motion without forcing the muscles inside him to adjust to the stretch of him too quickly. His words got Justin breathing again, and Adam let go of his shaft and moved in.

"You're doing so good," he reassured. He rubbed his hands up and down the length of Justin's thighs with massaging strokes before he reached up and held on to Justin's hip bones while he settled all the way inside finally, his hips meeting the soft curve of Justin's ass.

"That's it, Justin. That's all of me." His cock throbbed in the ridiculous tight heat of Justin's body and he had to force down the impulse to start fucking that amazing warmth. Justin's breath, however, sounded harsh and short on the other side of the curtain, and Adam caught the way he sniffled.

"Do you need me to pull out?" he asked. God, the last thing he wanted to do was make Justin cry.

"No! No, please, don't," Justin pleaded, clearing his throat. "Please don't go." He sounded so sad and Adam's protective instincts flared up with tremendous force.

"I won't, I promise. We'll just give it a minute. All right, sweetheart?"

He placed a hand on the center of Justin's chest, right over his pounding heart. Justin's hand flew up and clutched his, giving it a squeeze, but then he pulled back as though Adam's skin had scorched him.

"I'm sorry," he rushed out. "I'm sorry, I forgot."

At first Adam was confused, but then he remembered that he hadn't given Justin permission tonight to touch him. He didn't care though, not now in this moment when he clearly needed comforting.

"Don't be, it's all right." He placed Justin's left hand back on his heaving chest over his heart and held it there. His right, he brought to his own lips to kiss the line of Justin's knuckles.

"You can touch me, Justin. It's okay. I want it."

He nuzzled into Justin's palm, placing a quick kiss on the inside of his wrist where the warm skin was fluttering from the pulse underneath. He dragged Justin's hand down the side of his cheek, the line of his neck, over the delicate chain of his cross, and finally to the dead center of his chest where his own heart was tattooing a rapid pace.

Justin sighed out a moan and dug his fingertips into the muscles of Adam's chest. His ring and pinky fingers rubbed over the ragged line of scarring on his chest and it was a bit too much on the tender flesh.

"Gentle, sweetheart," he purred, rubbing the back of Justin's hand. "Nice and gentle here, okay?"

"Okay," Justin whispered. He touched lightly, but the heat radiating off his palm into the middle of Adam's chest was still wonderful and electric, and Justin didn't seem to be bothered by his strange requests.

He pulled his hand from Justin's chest and reached down between them to rub the slick, bloodless rim of Justin's hole stretched around him as he rocked his hips. He barely pulled out an inch before working it back in. Justin squeaked out a lovely whimper and his legs shook around Adam's waist, squeezing him as though Justin were trying to make sure he didn't pull away suddenly.

Justin's whole body seemed to melt into the sensation second by second. His tiny whimpers eased into soft, panting moans and when Adam finally wrapped his hand around his cock, he savored the way Justin's toes curled and his back arched into the touch.

"How does it feel?" he asked.

How does it feel? Justin's mind could hardly keep up with the barrage of new sensations sparking through his whole body.

He had never felt so opened and filled before. The burning stretch of Adam's cock had felt overwhelming, but it had gotten better like he had promised. The length of him was hot and stiff and rubbing against every good place inside him. Never mind the astounding duality of Adam's large and calloused hand pumping his cock in tandem with the rocking of his hips.

All he could do was latch his hands to Adam's broad shoulders, hang on and enjoy being shaken apart at the seams in the best way possible.

"Aw, fuck," he gasped. It was so hard to put coherent thoughts together. "God, it feels so *much*. I had no idea it'd feel like this."

"In a good way?"

"*Jesus*, yes. Oh God, Adam."

He slid his hands up to the corded muscles on Adam's neck. It was blissful to get to explore the feeling of Adam's body against his. Everywhere he touched was searing hot and packed with hard muscles. Everything about Adam seemed large and made Justin want to be pressed underneath his weight, taking everything he chose to give him.

"Dammit, Justin. You're so fucking tight and hot inside. I feel like I'm losing my mind," Adam groaned. "Do you think you could come like this on my cock, baby boy?" Adam's voice was deep and gravelly, and it made Justin shiver.

"Yes," he whined, wanting that with delirious force. He wanted Adam to bring him there. Wanted to succumb to the orgasm he felt bubbling in his guts. "Yes, please. I'm so close," he begged.

Adam squeezed his hip, slipping down just an inch to hold his thigh and ass to fuck into him at the perfect angle. His hand on Justin's cock was deliberate and skilled, as if he could read every hitch in Justin's breath and knew just what was going to tip him closer to the edge.

Justin stroked over the back of Adam's neck, over the fine short hairs at the base of his skull and then carefully back down Adam's chest. Justin hoped his touch was gentle enough. He had one chance to enjoy touching Adam freely, and he greedily took full advantage.

Adam's cock thrust in and hit his prostate with precision, shocking an uncensored, desperate moan from him.

"*Ohhh*, oh God, Adam. I'm gonna come," he warned. The combination of feelings was too much, too compounding. He felt the moment when his balls started to draw up tight, his abdomen muscles clench up, and every movement of Adam's cock and hand shot bolts of pleasure through his system, about to drag him under without a fighting chance.

"*Shit, shit, shit,*" Adam panted, moving just a little faster and losing his rhythm as Justin's body began to hit his peak. He kept jerking him off, pressing his hips into him deep and perfect.

Justin's orgasm crashed over him *hard*.

The pleasure peaked and knocked all the air out of his lungs. He lifted his head off the bed, almost curling in on himself, and he scrambled to cling to Adam, but his brain whited out through the tremendous sensation. Even the way Adam's cock kept thrusting in and out of him only amplified the pleasure and made him come harder than he ever had before. He barely even felt the way his own release sprayed across his stomach and chest in hot drops while Adam fisted his prick with demanding pulls before finally letting him go.

Adam cursed under his breath and pulled out, leaving a weird sense of emptiness that was jarring. He heard Adam rip the condom off and his hand made slick sounds as he fisted his own cock, finally groaning out when his own orgasm hit. He added to the mess across Justin's torso, and he almost wished Adam hadn't pulled out, even though his whole body felt like a livewire still.

"Aw, fuck," Adam moaned, coming back down. His grip on Justin's hip finally loosened and he reached for Justin's hand on his chest. He brought it to the side of his face again and placed a series of lazy kisses on the inside of his wrist. Justin smiled at the brush of Adam's lips on the thin skin and squeezed his other hand on Adam's shoulder.

"Sorry," Adam said. "I didn't hurt you at the end, did I?"

"No. No, I'm fine, I promise. More than fine, actually." Adam gave a quick laugh back and the hot air of his breath ghosted over his wrist.

"Yeah, me too."

Justin rubbed his thumb up and down the side of Adam's face, along the line of his cheekbone, and the five-o'clock shadow on his jaw was prickly on his palm. Getting to touch, it was too easy to imagine the handsome face he had seen the other day in the bookstore.

"This might be crossing a line," Adam said, speaking slow. "And I really don't want to fuck up a good thing but..."

"But what?"

"Would you actually want to go on a date with me? Like, a real one. Outside of here? Just once. I swear it doesn't have to mean anything."

Justin's voice caught in his throat. A date? With Adam Creed? Face to face, with no walls to hide behind? His heart fluttered from excitement. Adam said it didn't have to mean anything, but that was exactly what he wanted.

"Yeah. I would really like that."

"Really? Oh, thank fuck," Adam sighed, making him chuckle.

"Where would we go?"

"How about I show you a night out on the town? All the best places that I know are fucking great. Not posh, snobby places, but the real shit. Just good food, good drinks, and I promise you won't regret it."

Adam sounded so hopeful and the second hung in a long pause. Justin wished more than anything that he could see him now — see that sweet, earnest face he could picture just from the sound of his voice.

"Any promise of food and I'm in. I'd love to."

Adam laughed. "Perfect. I guarantee that you'll eat so good, I'll have to carry you home piggy-back style."

"Sounds like a plan."

"Awesome. Hold on one second." Adam jumped off the bed. Justin heard the shuffle of fabric and figured he must be grabbing his clothes. After only a second, Adam crawled up on the bed again, shifted close to him, and suddenly his hands landed on Justin's left thigh.

"Here's my cell number," Adam said. The pop of a marker cap snapped in the room and the tip of the pen touched the inside of Justin's thigh in tickling squiggles.

"Is that a magic marker? And where did you get that?" Justin chuckled, trying to hold still for him to write.

"It's a Sharpie actually," Adam laughed. "I've always got one in my pocket because of work."

"A Sharpie? Really?"

Adam finished writing and gave the delicate skin of his thigh a teasing pinch.

"Can't risk it washing away in the shower, can I?"

"Very funny."

Adam placed a kiss over where he had pinched and sat up.

"Can you call me tomorrow night?" he asked. "Around ten?"

"Sure."

"Perfect. There's something I need to do, but by then I'll have a plan."

"Okay," he said. He didn't want to pry and press him further about it. "Thanks for tonight, Adam."

"Thank you, Justin, and I'll be looking forward to your call tomorrow."

"Yeah, me too."

"Oh shit, I almost forgot," Adam said, springing up off the bed, and his voice traveled away. "I was gonna do this first, but whatever. I brought this for you. It's nothing really but I was out and... Anyway, I'll just leave it here on the bed."

"Something for me?"

"Yeah, it's kinda dumb but the thought popped into my head and, well, I don't know."

"Thank you."

"Don't worry about it. Have a good night, Justin," he said.

"Good night."

He took Justin's hand to press one last kiss to the back of it before he pulled back and headed to the door. It clicked shut and Justin let out a long breath that turned into a tiny laugh right at the end. Holy crap, he was going out on a date. For real. With Adam. It was a dizzying amount of information to process all at once, especially after everything that had just happened, but he felt light and bubbly inside.

He shoved the sliding wall up until it clicked into place at the top and sat up, wincing at the weird sensation in his backside. God, how was he going to walk or sit without pulling a face in front of Jewels tomorrow? He was going to have to pray that it had faded by then.

By his legs on the bed was a small, flat rectangle wrapped in newsprint. It was very lightweight and he turned it over to peel back the taped edges. He let the paper fall to the bed and his eyes went wide at the present in his hand.

It was a children's book, thin and printed with a creepy drawing of a screaming zombie-creature on the cover. The title read *Scary Stories to Tell in the Dark*, the same one Adam had asked if he had read their first night together. He also recognized it as the book Adam had picked from the shelf at his store. He had actually gone out of his way to get this for him and now, they were going to go on a date. Justin glanced down at his leg and there in scrawling digits of black ink was Adam's cell number.

As soon as he got back to the dressing room, he was going to store the number in his phone and tuck the book safely in his bag.

Chapter Eighteen

Just past nine o'clock, Adam walked up the front steps of Ginny's bar and pulled the wooden door open. The mild June breeze swept around him and he let the door close itself behind him. It was busy tonight for a Sunday, and music from the jukebox was blaring, on top of the television playing on the wall. The front tables and stools by the bar were stuffed with groups of twenty-something-year-olds hanging out and sipping bottles of IPAs. Some were sitting at the benches built into nooks by the front windows, leaning on throw pillows, and he tried to shuffle through them.

He caught the eye of the bartender and Frank tossed a nod of his head to him and finished pouring two glasses from the tap. Adam reached into his back pocket and pulled out a ten.

"'S'up, Adam," Frank said, sliding over to him and wiping his hands off on the towel tucked into the waist of his dark jeans. "The usual for you and Steve tonight?"

"Yeah, just get me two Coronas. He fucking loves that shit."

Frank chuckled. "Sure thing, coming right up."

He waited for Frank to pass him the bottles and glanced up as the bell over the door rang out to see Steve attempting to step in. It only took Steve a second before he found Adam. He finally got through the gaggle of people and straightened his suit jacket with a huff.

"Hey, thanks, man," he said, taking the bottle Adam offered him. "Jesus, it's like people don't know tomorrow's Monday or something."

"Yeah, who would *ever* go out on Sunday night to drink?"

Steve elbowed him. "Let's go see if there are any spots in the back."

The seats behind the pool table and jukebox were quieter, and the two of them managed to sneak into a booth in the corner under a dim ceiling lamp. Adam slid into the booth across the black leather seat and Steve tugged off his suit jacket and got settled in. He knew what he had to talk to Steve about and yet he had no clue how to do it. Steve started talking before he had a chance to figure it out, though.

"You'll never guess who I saw today."

"Really?" he said, taking a sip of his beer.

"Yeah, get a load of this. So, I closed up Eros, got down to the subway at Penn Station and hopped on the A-line. As I'm standing there, squeezed between two Brazilian women talking a blue streak in Portuguese, who do you think I saw all the way down at the other end of the car?"

"I don't know. Who?"

"Billy."

Adam leaned back and sighed. "He give you any trouble?"

"No, he didn't even see me." Steve picked up his beer and took a drink. "At least, I don't think so. He was with a couple of your guys. Um, the tall, lanky one and the meathead pretty-boy?"

"You mean Jones and Miller."

"Yes, yes, that's right. Anyway, they were vaping something and passing it around. Being kinda rowdy, but I couldn't really hear what shit they were saying. I ended up switching over to the F-line, but Billy and the guys stayed on. You know, toward Fulton Street? What do you think they're doing all the way down there?"

"Probably going to some strip club or something, but who knows with those idiots." He picked up his beer and took a long gulp. "Look, there's something I want to talk to you about."

"This has got to be good." Steve placed his bottle of beer back down on the table. "You look like you shot the sheriff and robbed the bank."

"Well." He hesitated. "I may have done a shitty thing as a friend."

"The kind of shitty like you slept with my sister and never called her back, or shitty like you slept with my *mom* and never called *her* back?" he joked.

"I'm trying to be serious here."

"Okay, okay. I'm listening."

"Well, um, last night... I may have asked Justin out on a date."

"You did?" Steve asked, his face turning sober.

"Yeah — and look, Steve, I get it. He's your employee and it wasn't my place to cross any business moral codes of right or wrong or anything like that — "

"By asking out one of my employees."

"Yeah, exactly. It's just... Honestly, man? There's something about him I can't get over. In these past few weeks, he's been in my head all the time and I had to ask."

Steve nodded as though he were processing the new information. "Well, it's about fucking time," he said, breaking out into a smile.

"Huh?"

"Why do you think I paired you two up? I've been waiting patiently. I completely called it."

"Oh, bullshit."

"Absolutely! I thought for sure you were going to ask him last week, but it looks like you got there eventually."

"You're really taking credit for this," he said, not bothering to phrase it as a question.

"Of course I am. Didn't I say a couple of weeks ago that I know your type? And you clearly like him."

Adam looked down at his beer, swiveling the bottle in tiny circles just to watch the liquid swirl.

"Yeah, I do. I don't know, he's just not what I was expecting."

"I'll take that as a good thing. You're always expecting the worse."

He scoffed out a laugh and took another sip of beer. He guessed he shouldn't have been surprised by Steve's reaction—that guy had been trying to set him up for years. There was still something nagging at him though.

He leaned in real close and Steve got the message and leaned in too so he could hear him whisper over the music.

"Michael's got us running a huge trade. Tuesday night to Newark. Some big-wig prick who's looking to start up a new channel of opportunity, if you know what I mean."

"So what? You worried about getting busted?"

"Naw, no more so than usual."

"Then what?"

"This is my chance, Steve. If I leave as soon as it's over, I can get states away before they even realized I'm gone."

"You still wanna do that?"

"Yes. I have to." He shook his head. "I don't have any other choice. I don't want to be doing this for the rest of my life. I don't want to be a fucking *criminal* forever."

"Then if you're planning on getting out of Dodge, why did you ask the kid out?"

Adam ducked his head. "I haven't thought that far ahead."

"I know how hard thinking is for you, but you'd better figure it out. Tuesday is the day after tomorrow, Adam. And you asking Justin out when you've got one foot out of the door sounds to *me* like you're trying to set yourself up for failure," he said, giving Adam a wiser-than-thou look. "You're scared."

"I'm not scared."

"Yes. You are."

"We haven't even had the date yet, for Christ's sake."

"Fine, but all I'm saying is to leave yourself open for possibilities."

He opened his mouth and shut it. Honestly, he had run through the idea that Justin would find out who he was and wouldn't want anything to do with him. It'd be easier. He had gotten plenty used to that song and dance over the years. It was the other possibility that maybe Justin would be different—wouldn't *care* who his family was—and *that* would be the wrench in all his plans.

For Christ's sake, he had packed anything important he owned days ago, gathered his whole life's savings in cold hard cash and researched most of the east coast for small towns renting out rooms.

Regardless, he found himself dying to know with growing intensity how his date with Justin was going to go.

"I'm willing to see what happens," he admitted.

"Good. I'd hate to see all my hard work and expertise go to waste."

"You're a riot, you know that, right?"

"So, are you going to have a shot of vodka with me? To celebrate?"

"I don't know about celebrating. I could still make a royal ass of myself."

"That's a really good possibility," Steve agreed.

Adam laughed and shrugged in resignation. "But I could definitely use a shot."

"Okay, good," Steve said. He slammed down the empty bottle and made a hurry-up motion while Adam finished his. "I'll cover the first round."

* * * *

Adam was at the bar counter, getting fresh beers and listening to Steve flirting with a pair of gorgeous cousins next to them. However, he was too distracted checking his cell phone as ten o'clock came and began to inch by.

Fuck, what if Justin didn't call? Maybe he'd changed his mind and decided against it. Maybe he had said yes and planned all along to ghost him. Every minute that ticked by on the digital clock felt like another nagging voice in his head chiming in, telling him how stupid he had been for thinking there was a chance.

He wanted so badly to meet him for real. He wanted to see what Justin looked like when he gave that breathy laugh that Adam loved to hear. How would his smile look? Or how would his lips feel if he kissed him?

He was about to check his phone for the umpteenth time when it vibrated suddenly in his hand. He almost didn't believe it at first, but after the second of shock wore off, he rushed to check the screen. A number he didn't know lit up and if it was a spam call, he was going to lose his mind.

"Be right back," he said, nudging Steve's arm. He pushed out onto the quiet sidewalk and fresh air to escape the noise inside before he hit the button to answer.

"Hello?"

"Hi, Adam? It's Justin."

Oh, thank fuck. He un-hunched his shoulders and took in a breath of relief, relaxing in the orange glow of the metal streetlamp next to him.

"Hey, I'm glad you called."

"I hope I didn't keep you waiting. I had to wait for my grandma to get ready for bed." His voice was just as cute and shy like it was in person. Damn, it was nice to hear it again.

"It's fine. Don't worry about it."

"All right, good." Justin laughed, soft and timid. "So, uh, did you come up with a plan yet for our date?"

Adam smiled, shuffling his weight from one foot to another.

"As a matter of fact, I did," he said.

"When were you thinking?"

A part of him didn't want to wait. He was so friggin' curious to meet Justin, it was making him crazy imagining what he looked like. Tonight wouldn't work, but he came to a compromise.

"What about tomorrow night? At like nine?"

"That would be okay with me."

"I had an idea for dinner, but I want it to be a surprise."

Justin chuckled and it was a light, amused sound. "Should I be worried?"

"Only if you have an allergy to shellfish."

"Well, I'm in the clear there."

"Awesome, then I think you might enjoy it."

"Okay," he agreed. "I'm game."

There was that streak of bravery that didn't seem like it would exist in such a quiet, polite kid, yet was pleasantly surprising every time it came out.

"Then how about you meet me in Times Square. You know where the Hard Rock store is? There's an Armed Forces Recruiting Station right in front of it. I'll be there waiting at nine."

"All right. I think I know what you're talking about. I'll be wearing my red sweatshirt so you can find me."

"Perfect. I'll have my eye out."

"So, I guess I'll see you tomorrow night then?" Justin asked.

A selfish bit of him wanted to keep Justin on the phone but Steve was inside and he didn't want to hold Justin up.

"Yeah, I'm looking forward to it."

"Me too. Goodnight, Adam."

"Night, Justin."

The line clicked and he lowered the phone, staring at it. Steve not only was fine with him asking Justin out, but had been actively hoping it would happen.

A taxi honked at a car double-parked in the street down the block and he glanced back up, shaking himself from his thoughts. Now, he was going to go back inside, drink a couple more beers, walk home eventually when drinking lost its appeal and try to get some sleep. Before he went inside, however, he made sure to save Justin's number on his phone.

Justin hung up the phone and squeezed it tight in his hands before blowing out a long breath of relief through his mouth. He had squirrelled himself away in his bedroom and sat at the foot of his bed, gathering the courage to hit the call button. Now that it was over, he flopped back down on the bed, his arms splayed out to the sides, and blinked up at the ceiling. His heart was still racing from the excitement.

He could still feel Adam everywhere—his naked body hot and pressed tight against his, his hands running over every inch of his skin, even *inside* him still. His breath would still get short and his cock half-hard thinking about it, and it happened all day long despite him struggling not to daydream about it.

He really hoped he wasn't going to fuck tomorrow up. If he had been able to live through three whole appointments with Adam at Eros, then he'd be able to survive an actual date, right?

To add to his nerves, Adam wanted it to be a surprise. Justin felt like he'd had a lifetime of surprises already in the past three weeks, but something about Adam had him constantly pushing himself. It was the easy way he nudged him a bit past his normal comfort zone, little by little. It only made every interaction with him that much more exciting. So, while he had zero idea what he and Adam were going to do tomorrow, he had a feeling that it wouldn't be anything too crazy.

Or, at least that was what he was going to tell himself, so he'd be able to sleep through the night.

Chapter Nineteen

Once two o'clock in the afternoon the next day rolled near, Adam crept his way out from the back room of the grocery store and glanced around to check the coast.

Maria's Grocery had been a staple for the community for over twenty-five years since the Ramirezes had moved to Manhattan, and Adam considered himself gifted every day to have a stable, reliable job that let him work in peace.

He typically tried to avoid the front of the store at all costs, but now it was already after the lunch rush and he had to find Maria to talk to her. He crept out from the back, peeking around, and spied her short frame by the deli counter across the store, fussing over a rack of bread. However, blocking his way was Sidney Devlin. The twenty-four-year-old was a snarky kid who wore a sneer like it had been born on his mug. He was sweeping in the middle of the shelves, so Adam turned left and went down the next aisle to avoid him, skirting past the canned fruit, canned vegetables and canned meats stacked in neat piles.

Maria was rearranging the packages of buns and rolls in front of the glass counter of deli meats and pre-made dishes.

"Um, Maria?"

"Yes, oh yes?" she said, finally noticing him, and she tried to straighten out her achy back as she stood. Maria was a petite woman of seventy-nine who spoke with a thick Spanish accent but tried to use nothing but English in the store. She shuffled over and patted his arm while she straightened out her white sweater. "Please, please, Adam. Move this shelf back for me. Please. I am too old to move such things."

"Oh, sure, Maria. Like this?" He reached down and pushed the leg-high metal shelf of bread to the right, flush against the counter.

"Yes, yes, yes," she said, waving her hand to the right, and he inched it farther until she seemed to be satisfied and stopped waving. "There, it's there. Thank you, Adam."

"Any time," he said. Sidney peeked his head around the aisle, the broom seemingly forgotten in his hands. He caught Adam watching him and pretended to be straightening out the boxes of instant rice nearby.

"You are so strong. We need you up here more often," she said.

"Yeah, well, I wanted to ask you something."

"Yes?" She leaned down to restack the buns again.

"Do you think it'd be all right if I left an hour early tonight?"

"Seven-thirty?"

"Yeah."

"Not eight-thirty?"

"No. If that's okay for tonight."

Maria's husband, Santos, was in his usual tall-backed, wooden chair behind the deli counter. Santos Ramirez was eighty-one years old and filled with so much piss and vinegar that he would probably live to the age of a hundred and fifty, just out of spite for the world. He got up and leaned an arm on the top of the glass counter.

"What could you need an extra hour for?" he asked. "Can't it wait?"

"Hush," Maria hissed. She hated when Santos tried to act like the boss. *Everyone* knew that Maria really wore the pants in the relationship. It was her name on the side of the building after all. She turned to Adam with a knitted brow.

"Is something wrong?" she asked.

"Oh, no. No."

"Then what?" Santos asked.

"*Hush!*"

"No, it's fine," Adam said. "I actually have a date tonight."

Santos barked out a laugh. Maria hissed at him again and tried to slap his arm, but he just shooed her away and leaned back, still chuckling. Even Sidney scoffed out a chuckle from the safety of his aisle. He wasn't bothering anymore to pretend like he wasn't listening in. God, Adam couldn't stand that asshole.

"You stop right now," Maria told Santos.

"Why? The *Phantom of the Grocery* only bothers to come out when he wants something," he said, gesturing at Adam.

Spanish started pouring out of Maria and Adam thought he recognized a few curse words, but his

Spanish was rusty. She put her wrinkly hands on her hips and switched to English.

"And he works three times the hours a week that *you* do, you old man."

Santos said something in Spanish, frowning and shuffling back to his chair. She must have laid into him pretty good for him to just roll over without a few more minutes of their usual bickering. At least he had that going for him.

Maria turned back to him and gave him a smile and another pat on the arm.

"We will be fine tonight. You may leave early for your date."

"Thanks, Maria."

"This is a very special occasion!" she insisted. "You don't want to be ungentlemanly and keep her waiting."

"No, of course not." He tried to keep the smirk off his face. There was no way he was going to correct her and shock her poor, sweet, Catholic heart.

"Are you excited?" she asked. Maria always loved asking him about his personal life.

He *was* excited though. Maybe more like a weird combination of excited, anxious and deadly curious.

"Yeah, I am," he replied. "I think she could be something special."

Maria beamed. She leaned in close to whisper like this was the hottest gossip. "You know, I could tell. You have a different aura today."

"Do I?"

"Yes, yes," she insisted. "Now have a wondrous time tonight. Don't let Santos keep you for even a minute past seven-thirty. You hear me?"

"Yes, ma'am."

"Good, good. We'll see you Wednesday like usual then." She turned around and headed up to the registers. She passed Sidney who promptly went back to sweeping the floor with astute diligence. He didn't tell her that he had no intention of ever coming back, not after the deal went down tomorrow night. As shitty as it was just leaving the Ramirez family high and dry, he couldn't risk explaining where he was going. Too many dangerous people knew he worked here already, and Maria had been too kind to him over the years. He watched her go and made his way to the back room again.

Now he just had to find enough things for him to do to pass the last couple of hours as quickly as possible.

Chapter Twenty

That night, Justin left work for home at seven on the dot. Despite the busy, bruising and painfully long commute back to his apartment, his thoughts didn't linger on any of it. He was far too distracted as the hour of nine loomed ahead. The clock was ticking, and he had just about an hour to get mentally and physically ready before he went back out. He kicked off his shoes inside by the door and heard shuffling in the kitchen, so he rounded the corner and found Jewels right there at the linoleum countertop.

"Hey, Jewels."

"Hi, honey. How was work?"

"It was okay. Went by too slow," he said. He pulled out a stool at the island in the middle of the small space and sat down across from her.

Their kitchen was more like a kitchenette attached to a nook just big enough to fit a dining room table for the two of them, although the table had become more of a catchall for mail, groceries and jackets. They usually ate their meals together in the living room, Jewels in her recliner and him on the olive-green loveseat so they could watch television.

"Would you like something to eat?"

"Actually," he said, choosing his words. "I'm headed back out in a bit."

"You're going out again tonight?" she asked. She uncapped the jar of mayonnaise and grabbed a butter knife from the drawer.

"Yeah."

"With the same person from Saturday night? And the Saturday before that?"

He could guess where she was going with this.

"Yeah..."

"Ah, I see. And does this young woman have a name?"

He blushed and ducked his head. He shuffled in his seat, staring at his lap. Jewels was the sweetest lady he had ever known, so he bit the bullet and told her the truth.

"Actually, it's a guy. His name is Adam."

He let her process the information as she spread mayonnaise on the slices of white bread, but it didn't take her long to continue the investigation. "Tell me he's at least a gentleman," she said.

He huffed out a laugh in surprise. Of course, that would be her first concern. "Yes, Jewels, he is."

"And is he handsome?"

"Oh my God," he groaned, trying to contain a laugh but doing it poorly.

"I'm just asking!" she defended. The cold cuts were forgotten on the counter as she waited for an answer. He shook his head and bit his lip. If it was possible, his face was burning up even more.

"Yeah, he is," he confirmed. Jewels smiled and returned to placing slices of meat in an orderly fashion on her sandwich.

"You know," she began, "I appreciate you telling me, and I want to make sure that you know I'd support you no matter what." She leveled him with a serious look, and it warmed his heart hearing her sincerity, even if he already knew without her having to say it.

"Thank you."

"It's true, no matter what you choose in your life, honey. All I ask is that you please, *please*, promise me that you'll be careful. That you'll be safe," she pleaded.

He knew that she was thinking about his parents and about all the bad decisions they had made along the way, how each bad choice led them further away, where she could no longer protect them. His heart broke thinking about how she must worry the same thing might happen to him, how one day he might not come back home, and an officer would come to tell her he wasn't *ever* coming home.

"Jewels, I don't want you to worry about me. I promise, I'll play it smart."

"Okay. That's all I can ask for. He's going to feed you, right? I don't want you skipping out on dinner. I can make something really quick," she insisted.

"It's all right, Jewels. Thank you, but I think dinner is in the plans somewhere."

"Okay, okay. If you say so. Are you excited?" she asked.

He fiddled with the sleeve of his shirt at his wrist. "Yeah."

"What's wrong?"

"I guess I'm still a little nervous. It's *technically* our first date. *My* first date even."

"Oh well, I've had many first dates in my day."

"E-Excuse me?"

"Don't judge," she said with a chuckle. "This was before I met Art." Her husband. He had passed away from a severe heart attack before Justin was born, so he'd never actually met him, although Jewels always spoke of him fondly.

"My advice to you," she said, "is to just be yourself and to not put so much pressure on your every little move. If you can't have a good time like a pair of friends first, then it won't work as a relationship down the line. Being friends is the first step to being boyfriends."

He blinked at her, stunned in silence. It made sense in a way. Just because he and Adam had already had sex, it didn't mean that their date had to have some crazy level of expectation over it. They were just gonna hang out and get to know each other from the *same* side of a wall this time.

"Thanks, Jewels. I think I get it."

"Good, and anytime, honey. Oh, and also trust me when I say you don't have to give it all up on the first date."

"Oh my God," he said, hiding his face in his hands. Oh yeah, it was already far too late for that.

"I'm just saying," she added. She grabbed her plate to bring it into the living room and he eyed her sandwich when she walked by.

"Do you have to fast at all for tomorrow?" Her surgery was scheduled for two tomorrow afternoon, but they were going to have to be there by noon to check in and get into prep.

"Yes," she said, "but not until midnight. I'll be all right."

He watched her settle down into her recliner and got his feet moving again. He had a bunch to do in not a whole lot of time.

Chapter Twenty-One

Dressed in his nice red and black-checkered dress shirt, some fitted black jeans, his not-*so*-old pair of Converse and his usual red hoodie, Justin ventured out toward Times Square. Just up ahead would be the Armed Forces Recruitment Station, a metal-plated stand in the middle of the square a little bigger than a newsstand.

The second he would reach Forty-Third, he'd be able to see it perfectly through the crowd. The nervous excitement inside of him was boiling up, bubbling to the surface and making his palms sweat. Yeah, he had technically already seen what Adam looked like, but it was the idea of just the two of them, face to face, that was thrilling and scary at the same time.

He paused on the edge of the sidewalk on Forty-Third in the tide of pedestrians. Across the street, standing by the side of the station facing the Hard Rock, was Adam. He looked even more handsome than Justin remembered — his chiseled jaw, muscular frame, his dirty-blond hair and the beginning shadow of stubble on his face. It was surreal to see him stand there and put two and two together that *he* was the man who Justin had let take him apart and share one of the most intimate moments of his life. Seeing Adam there across the way, he couldn't deny to himself that he had a crush on him.

Like, a big crush.

Adam was scanning the crowd. He turned and when his eyes locked on Justin's from across the street, Justin knew that Adam realized exactly who he was. A smile tugged on his face, his eyes sparkled, and the blood rushed to Justin's face as he timidly returned the smile. He made his legs move from his spot and weaved his way through the crowd. Once he was closer, Adam dragged his gaze up and down, taking in the sight of him.

"Hi, Justin?" he said, reaching out for a handshake.

Justin reached to return it and his skin tingled from the warmth of Adam's broad hand.

"Yeah, hi. Adam, right?"

Adam beamed at him. "Yeah, it's nice to finally meet you."

"Same." Adam dragged his eyes blatantly up and down his frame again and the heat in his face only got worse. He coughed and ducked his head to try to hide his blush, but it must have been obvious.

"I'm sorry," Adam said. "I don't mean to stare, but you are even hotter than I imagined."

Justin snorted out a laugh without meaning to and tried to play it cool.

"Well, if there's a nice reason to be stared at, that's it. I could say the same thing about you."

Where did that come from? Did he honestly just tell Adam that he thought he was hot? To be fair, he *did* think that, but he hadn't been planning on blurting it out right off the bat.

It made Adam laugh. The corners of his eyes wrinkled and it made his eyes sparkle in the flashing of neon around them.

"That's good to hear. Do you have a last name, Justin?"

"Yeah, it's Turner."

"Well then, Mr. Turner. Now that we are officially well-met, would you mind being my company for dinner this evening?"

"I'd love to. But where exactly are we going?"

"Actually, it's one of the best places in Manhattan." Adam turned around and pointed up to a giant spinning sign on the side of a huge building with an oversized cartoon lobster plastered on both sides as it turned.

"Lobster Leo's?"

"Hell yeah! Have you ever been?"

"No…"

"What? Really? Well then, this is the perfect surprise. You're in for a treat, trust me."

Despite living in the city his whole life, Justin had never actually gone inside that over-the-top themed restaurant. He enjoyed how sincere Adam sounded though. If he thought it was fun, then why the hell not?

"Sounds good to me."

"Then let's go. I reserved a table for us and everything." Adam made a grand sweeping gesture with his arm and followed behind him as they wormed their way through the people toward the glass doors of the restaurant.

They walked into what appeared to be a waiting area with a large staircase against the back wall leading upstairs. A maître d' station stood right in front of them and a young guy with a headset gave them a smile.

"Hello, party of two?"

"Actually," Adam said, "I called earlier. Adam, for two."

"Oh, yes. Good evening, Mr. Creed. If you don't mind waiting for a second, I'll let upstairs know you're here."

"Thanks, Kevin."

Kevin, the maître d', nodded and started tapping on the tablet in front of him. He reached for the walkie-talkie on his hip and said something Justin couldn't hear in the noise.

The waiting area was crammed full of other people. He and Adam squeezed themselves into the back corner near the staircase. Justin tucked himself against the wall between the corner and a machine that squashed pennies down with cartoon pictures of sea critters. He leaned his back to the wall and Adam stepped into his space to make room for a party of six trying to walk by them and up the stairs.

Adam was so incredibly close, almost pressed right up against him so that their chests were brushing. He was a couple of inches taller than him, blocking him in completely from the rest of the crowd, and the moment hung in thrumming tension. He glanced up to see Adam giving him a soft smile. Oh no, he was even more handsome up close like this, and he could smell his lovely cologne again. If it weren't so loud in here, he was sure that Adam would be able to hear the pounding of his heart this close.

"Sorry, it can be a bit of a zoo in here," Adam said. Kevin the maître d' was calling names out left and right and throngs of people were coming and going, up and down the stairs. How big was the restaurant up there? Could there really be that much space if the waiting room down here was so tightly packed?

"It's all right," he assured Adam. "A busy place means it must be pretty good, right?"

"I like to think so. Plus, it gives a great opportunity to people watch."

"I can imagine. Especially with all these tourists."

"Exactly. You're never gonna see the same people twice. Take that guy over there for example," Adam said, nodding just past the penny machine to a middle-aged gentleman standing with two teenage boys who were both eyeball-deep in their iPhones.

"What about him?"

"Um, have you ever seen a more fabulous fanny pack anywhere?"

Justin snorted, covering his mouth with his hand. The guy did have a unique fanny pack that appeared to be pearlescent and changed colors in the light. It fit perfectly under his spare tire and right over his shorts.

"I don't think so," he agreed. "I sort of need one now that I've seen him pulling it off."

"That's what I was thinking!" Adam dramatically whispered.

"Creed, party of two!" Kevin called out. Adam whipped his head around and he backed away so he could sneak out. It was strange hearing Adam's last name. Justin imagined all mafia gangs to be sort of like Marsellus Wallace from *Pulp Fiction*. Nothing but fear of a name and people bowing at his feet like scared mice just so they didn't wake up falling off a tall building.

He followed Adam's lead and they climbed the stairs, but he was surprised to see the waiting wasn't over. At the top of the stairs started a queue that snaked in front of them with fake sea-weathered boards for railings to corral the ten people waiting at the top.

The line moved quickly as a second maître d' with another headset asked for the number of each party reaching him, grabbing the appropriate number of menus and silverware sets. This restaurant was a well-oiled machine and before Justin had come up with any small talk, they were already at the front of the line.

"Hey, Adam. Two tonight?" the young African-American teenager asked. He had short hair that was dyed lavender purple and grabbed the menus.

"Yes, sir."

"All right, man," the guy said, sounding surprised and giving Justin a once-over. A waitress came flying around the corner and took the menus from the young guy. She didn't say anything, but Adam followed her and Justin tried to keep up.

"Here you go," she said, placing the menus on the table of the booth in the corner. "Your waitress will be right over for you."

"Thanks," Adam said. He held a hand out for Justin and let him sit down first.

The booth was roomy, and he stepped up to slide in. Dividing walls separated them from the other empty booth next to them, and a dazzling collage of seafood-themed decorations and paintings was plastered on the wall next to them. The glow of the billboards outside gave the table a cozy, mood-lit space filled with purples, greens and reds as the signs changed.

"What do you think?" Adam shrugged off his leather jacket and underneath he was wearing a black button-up made of soft-looking cotton. The sleeves were rolled up to his elbows and a glint of a gold chain peeked out from where the top button was undone on his shirt.

Justin remembered how the chain had felt under his fingers the other night while Adam had rocked inside him with easy thrusts. He also thought he could just see the edge of a pink blotch on Adam's chest. Maybe it was a birthmark, but either way, he didn't want to get caught staring and blushing like an idiot.

"It's uh, certainly a lot to take in, but I'm sort of loving it."

Adam beamed. "Well, just hold on. It gets even better." A waitress came rushing over with a pad of paper in one hand and a half-smile creeping onto her face.

"Hey, Adam," she said. "It's been a while. How's it going?"

"It's going good, Sam. I'm actually taking my friend Justin here out for a glamorous night on the town," he said.

"So, you brought him *here*?"

"Hey!"

"I'm just kidding. Have you ever been here before, Justin?"

"No, I haven't."

"All right! Let me give you the official Lobster Leo's welcome then. Adam here knows the spiel, but he can just hear it again."

"Like I mind — it's my favorite part."

"Good evening and welcome to Lobster Leo's. We've traveled the seven seas to bring the most delicious of Neptune's treasures for the whole family to enjoy. It's our job to make sure that you're happy as a clam!"

"Oh, wow," Justin said.

"So, can I start you guys off with anything to drink?"

"Do you mind?" Adam asked, turning to Justin and raising an eyebrow.

"No, I'll let the pro take the reins."

"Ha, okay. Thanks." He turned to Sam with a wicked grin. "I'm thinking tonight we want the full grand-tourist experience."

"The *grand* one?"

"*Oh yeah*. Like, start us off with two Coronaritas and whatever the fuck that thing is with all the shrimp sticking out of it?"

"You mean the Shrimp Stacker?"

"Yes! We'll take that to start, please."

"Good choice this evening, sirs. I will be right back." With that, she zoomed off.

"So, you come here often?" Justin teased.

"Yeah, you caught me. I've been known to haunt the bar some nights, drinking beer and eating popcorn shrimp."

"Do you know *all* the wait staff by now?"

"Well enough to call and wish each of their mothers happy birthday accordingly."

"Oh really?" Justin laughed.

"Yes, sir."

"Then what's *his* name?" he asked, nodding his head at a guy over Adam's shoulder.

"Oh, that's Eric. Lovely guy. Excellent craps player. You don't want to sit at a table with him unless you're prepared to lose a couple hundred."

"Really? Hmm... What about *her*?"

"You mean Vanessa? She can really knock the drinks back when she wants to, but I think it has to do with the fact she's taller than half the WNBA. She does roller derby in her spare time and I'd hate to be one of those poor folks going up against her."

"I think you're making this up."

Adam gasped in a fake, dramatic breath. "Why, I never."

Justin laughed, but tried to stifle it as Sam came flying back over, balancing a tray on one arm.

"Here you guys go." She lowered two heavy plastic glasses down in front of them. The drink inside was light green and chilled on big square ice cubes, but the shocking part was the whole bottle of Corona beer tipped upside-down in the drink, resting by the neck in a plastic holder clipped to the side of the glass. She also put down a standing metal cone lined with red-checked paper and stuffed with skewers of fried shrimp jutting out of the top.

"Do you guys know what you'd like?" she asked, pulling out her pad of paper.

"All set?" Adam asked him.

"Yeah."

"Okay, then fire away."

"Um, I'll have the landlubber's macaroni, please."

"Sure thing, honey. And for you, Adam?"

"I'll get the Baton Rouge shrimp, Sam. Thanks."

"No problem, you two. I'll go put that in right now."

Justin pulled his drink over and it weighed a ton with the bottle of beer sticking out of the top. He took a timid sip with the straw, but it was better than he had been anticipating. It was sweet and a little sour, and right at the end he could feel the burn from the alcohol sliding down his chest.

"So," Adam said, "do you have your own place here in the city?"

"No. I live with my grandmother, Jewels."

"And what's she like?"

"She's really great. Sort of has this tendency to just tell you how it is, but she only does it because she wants what's best for you. After being a nurse for almost her whole life, it's got to be that motherly instinct she's honed to a craft. She raised me since I was just a kid and I don't know what I'd do without her."

"That must be nice. You know, having someone looking out for you like that. Someone supportive."

"What about you?" he asked. Andrew had mentioned Adam had a father and brother, but he didn't know if he was playing a dangerous card bringing them up.

"Naw," Adam said. He took a sip of his drink. "I mean, I've got my two older brothers and my dad, but they're not nearly as sweet as your grandmother sounds."

"Okay. Fair enough."

A waiter who wasn't Sam came over, balancing two huge plates in his hands.

"Good evening," he said. "Who ordered the mac and cheese?"

"Oh, that would be me," Justin said, moving his drink out of the way.

"And for you, sir." The waiter put Adam's down as well. "Enjoy."

"Thanks," Adam replied. He looked at Justin and huffed out a laugh at his shocked face. "I told you it'd be enough food that I'd have to carry you out of here."

"You weren't kidding."

They both tucked in and Justin hummed out a happy sound at the taste of the food. They ate in silence for a moment, but he used the quiet to try to come up with something to say. Luckily, a thought popped into his head.

"Oh, um, I read the book you gave me."

"Already?"

"Yeah, well, it didn't take too long. But, um, I actually really liked it."

Adam smiled, nodding. He didn't say anything else about it, and Justin wondered with painful curiosity what was running through his head. Adam tilted his head to the side and squinted at him as though *he* were trying to read Justin's thoughts.

"Can I ask you a serious question?"

"Okay. Sure."

"Why did you go to Eros?" he asked. It was blunt and felt like a slap to the face, but Adam kept going. "I mean, I get it. It's a great opportunity for the girls who usually work the corners to step their game up, but for someone like you? I just don't see it."

Justin paused, staring down at the table. He felt ashamed to say the reason, but he still told the truth.

"I needed the money."

Adam was silent and Justin dared to look up. His face was serious, and his voice was quiet.

"Are you in any trouble? Someone bothering you and Jewels, maybe?"

"Oh, no. It's nothing like that." All he could think about was Andrew telling him how Chris's dad owed the Creed family a lot of money. This kind of thing might be commonplace in Adam's world, but not his.

"You swear?"

"Yeah, yes. I swear," he stammered. "It's Jewels. I found out last month that she was sick. She needs a third stent in her heart, and she's got an appointment for the surgery. Tomorrow actually. But I knew there would be no way we could afford it. I just... I considered my options and did what had to be done."

Adam stared at him with a serious face.

"Okay," he said. "I believe you." He reached for a shrimp and popped it into his mouth. "All right, your turn."

"My turn for what?"

"Well, I asked you a serious question, now it's your turn. It's only fair."

"Oh, um, okay." He wrapped his hands around the plastic cup of his drink, spinning it on the coaster as his mind raced.

Should he ask Adam about his family? Was it rude to bring up someone's mafia family? He couldn't tell Adam that the girls at Eros had been gossiping about him, or that his friend had dished out the information like it was New York's hottest tabloid news. Besides, he realized that he was more curious about something else.

"Okay then," he said, gaining the courage. "Why do *you* go to Eros?"

"Turning my own question against me, huh? That should be against the rules."

"No way—you didn't state any rules."

"All right, all right. Well, I guess I go because it's easy."

"Easy? No offense, but look at you."

"Look at me?" Adam chuckled. He picked up his drink and took a sip.

"I-I just mean, I find it hard to believe that plenty of people don't think you're good-looking enough. That's all."

"Well, thank you," he said. He didn't seem to be upset by his awkward phrasing, but he didn't seem to agree either. "I guess you'd be surprised, Justin."

"I hope I didn't go too far," Justin whispered, picking at his pasta.

"No, you didn't. I told you to ask me a question, didn't I?"

"Okay, because I have to admit I'm glad it was you Morita decided to pick for my first night there at Eros."

Adam smiled at him. "Yeah. Me too."

"That's good." He laughed nervously, but Adam's warm laugh as he joined eased his nerves.

"So, Justin," he said, ending the serious streak. "What was your favorite story from the book? Mine was *The Viper*…"

Chapter Twenty-Two

"God, I don't remember the last time I ate that much," Justin said.

"Well, good. You looked like you could use a good meal."

"Hey," Justin defended, bumping his shoulder into his as they walked down East Sixth Street, just off the F-line.

"I mean nothing by it. Just that you should have a full banquet every night so you can get nice and fat."

Justin giggled and Adam stole a glance at Justin's blushing ears and neck. Maybe that Coronarita had been enough to get his blood flowing.

"Thanks, but I think I'll try to keep my figure until at least my mid-life crisis."

"Okay, but I hope you've still got some steam left for our next stop."

"That depends. Are you going to tell me where we're going?"

"Actually, we're already here," Adam said. He came to a halt and Justin stopped a second after, looking up at the sign hanging above the sidewalk. "Wanna get a drink?"

Justin glanced back at him. His stunning face broke out into a surprised grin. "Okay, sure."

Adam hopped up the step and held the door to Ginny's open for Justin to walk in. It was thankfully quieter tonight than it had been yesterday, and the dark, cozy bar was playing slow rock from the jukebox for the few patrons.

He watched Justin look around at the antique-style bar with its mirror-backed counter and taxidermy animal heads on the walls. Frank was behind the counter again tonight, deep in a conversation with Ron Andrews, and didn't even notice them as they came in.

"Here, let's sit back there." He led the two of them past the counter and around the pool table to his usual booth in the corner. Justin sat down and Adam tugged off his jacket to toss it onto the seat. "I'm gonna get us something to drink. Any preferences?"

"Oh, um, I don't know. Sorry, I don't usually do this," Justin apologized.

"That's fine. I've got you. Just hang tight a second, okay?"

Justin unhunched his tensed shoulders and the timid smile on his face was so painfully cute, Adam almost said as much just to make his pink cheeks rosier. He took pity on him instead. "Be right back."

He left Justin to settle in. Frank and Ron were done, and Frank was leaning against the back counter, typing on his phone.

"Hey, man. Can I get two Coors?"

Frank glanced up and smiled, placing his phone down. "Sure, no problem. You with someone tonight?"

"Yeah, actually. Back there." Adam nodded with a tilt of his head and pulled out his wallet.

"Oh yeah?" Frank asked. He leaned past him and stole a glance at Justin in the booth, checking him out with a wary eye. "You swear he's legal?"

"Absolutely. I would never pull that shit with you, Frank. Not after serving my sorry ass for all these years and doing it well."

"Damn straight, and I trust you. Wanna tab?"

"Naw, I doubt I'll need one tonight." Adam dropped a twenty on the countertop. "Thanks again." He grabbed the bottles and turned back to the booth. Justin had taken off his hoodie and his fitted flannel shirt was perfectly matched with his ivory and pink skin.

"Here you go." Adam slid into the booth across from him.

"Thanks. So, is this another one of your haunts?"

"Yes, sir. My work and apartment are both nearby so I'm not a stranger."

"I wish I've been to even half the places you have. I feel like I've lived here my whole life but barely seen any of it now."

"It's a huge city. Don't sweat it. We could go somewhere brand-new every night and still not see half of it in months."

"I guess you're right." Justin picked up his beer and took a sip.

"And I bet you could show me a thing or two as well."

"Maybe," he said, glancing around the bar. "But you know, it's not too shabby here. I'm really enjoying the mounted taxidermy."

"Of course you would, cuter-Vincent Price."

Justin snorted, almost choking on his beer. Adam loved when he laughed that hard.

"You really think I'm cuter than the master of horror?" he teased between giggles.

"Only a little," he said, earning a kick to his foot from Justin under the table.

"You sure know how to sweet-talk a lady."

"Sorry, sweetheart. My forte is more dirty talk than sweet talk."

Justin laughed again, looking down at his lap. If possible, his adorably pink ears flushed even darker and his blush crept down the length of his neck to his collar. He looked at the pool table near them.

"You wanna play a round?" Adam asked.

"Oh, I don't know how," Justin said.

"That's fine. I'll show you. It's really not that hard. I'm sure you'll get the hang of it."

"Um, okay, if you think so."

"Come on," he urged. He stood from the booth, carrying his beer with him, and Justin followed him. He put his beer on the wooden edge of the pool table, grabbed two cue sticks and handed one to Justin, who took it with a nervous eye, then racked up the balls. Justin watched like he was taking notes and it was adorable how hard he seemed to be studying.

He tossed the triangle frame back on the hook on the wall and chalked the end of his stick. Done with that, he tossed the chalk to Justin who managed to catch it and repeat the process with his own pool stick.

"Now, the rules aren't too difficult. I'll break to see who's got stripes and who's got solids. You want to use the cue ball," Adam said, pointing to the one white one, "to hit all of your balls in first, *without* hitting the eight ball. Here, just watch."

He leaned down and lined up for the first shot. He pulled back and nailed the cue ball straight on, ricocheting it with a clack against the others. Pool balls spilled out in every direction and the striped 14-ball sank into the corner pocket.

"Okay, so I'll be stripes, since I got that one in. Basically, I'll try to aim for those, you aim for solids and the eight ball is last. You get that in by accident, then I automatically win."

"All right, I think I get it."

"Here, why don't you give it a shot, just to get the hang of it? We won't count this as an official tournament league game."

"I appreciate that."

"Just for you," he said with a wink. "So, go ahead. Try to find a solid to sink."

He picked up his drink and pretended not to be ogling while Justin inched around the table with laser focus. "No, no, like this," he said. He stepped behind Justin and placed his arms around him, reaching for his hands on the pool stick and sliding them to the right spots. He leaned down and Justin bent with him, pressed against the pool table's edge with Adam tight against his back.

Justin turned his head toward him and Adam caught the way Justin stared at his lips before flicking his gaze up to his eyes and away. Justin cleared his throat and Adam leaned in closer, just to whisper in his ear and make him squirm even harder. "Just make sure you hit it with enough force to make it do what you want. Don't be afraid to really nail it."

Justin's breath was heavy, but he focused down the length of the pool stick toward the cue ball. Adam nudged him to tug the stick backward, and Justin followed his direction with undivided attention.

"Ready?" Adam asked. He let go of Justin's hands.

Justin shivered hard against the line of his body, but he kept his focus. Adam dragged his gaze over Justin's profile, along his pink cheekbones, past his blushing ears and all the way down his warm neck to where his collarbones peeked out from the front of his shirt.

"Then whenever you're ready…"

He held his breath and waited for Justin to make his move. The stick rocked for a second and darted forward, smacking the cue ball perfectly and sending the orange five-ball into the farthest pocket.

"Hey! There you go!" Adam backed up and let Justin have his space again. He looked shocked he had managed to do it, but he smiled up at Adam after a second.

"I guess I had a good teacher."

"Well, at least a good *enough* teacher. I've never actually won a game of pool in my life," Adam said, leaning against the heavy wooden edge.

"Are you sure you're not just saying that to ease me into a false sense of security before you make a scandalous deal and sweep the floor with me?"

He burst out a laugh, caught off guard. "Well, if I was, I would say I'm not, right? And besides, what sort of scandalous deal do you think I'd make?"

"I'm not sure, but I bet it'd sound tempting."

"Absolutely. I'd make it too good to refuse."

Justin chuckled. He decided to give him a break, despite how much he enjoyed riling him up.

"Okay, hotshot. You got one in, so you get to go again."

"All right. Let's go."

* * * *

Adam ended up *just* winning their first round, but like he'd thought, Justin got the hang of it and won by a margin at the end of their second. He pretended to be deeply hurt by the slaughter, but Justin was ruthless and showed no pity to his disgraced honor.

"You know, at least you finally won *a game* of pool," Justin said.

"Ouch. I knew I should have never revealed my ancient techniques. I was destined to be overthrown."

"Don't take it so hard," he said. He bumped his shoulder into Adam's and Adam was tempted to wrap his arm around him and keep him there, but Justin had already swayed back before he got the chance.

"Do you want another drink?" he asked, although he thought he already knew the answer.

"Oh, I don't think I need it."

Adam dipped his head and nodded but glanced up at him. "You know, my place is just a few blocks up if you'd like to go there and talk? Maybe get a glass of water."

Justin blushed again. Adam was certain that he was about to find a way to politely decline, but he surprised him.

"Yeah, sure. I'd like that."

"Really?"

"Yeah."

"Okay cool. Then let's blow this place."

Justin grabbed his hoodie off the booth and slipped it back on while Adam got his jacket. As they walked out, Frank looked up from his phone to give him a wink, and he flipped him the bird behind Justin's back, making Frank snicker.

His apartment was only seven short blocks north, and the two of them fell into an easy stroll while they slowly made their way up. The sidewalks were almost empty and a passing car or two bumbled by in the now-quiet city. He glanced over at Justin, who was fascinated by the exotic store fronts and tiny markets that they passed, and Adam's gaze drifted down to where his arm swung by his side. Without letting himself overthink it, he reached over and took Justin's hand in his own, lacing their fingers together.

Justin whipped his gaze down to their hands and back up to Adam's face. Their eyes locked for a moment, and Adam swore it was that same electric feeling in his spine that he had felt when they'd held hands over Justin's chest last time at Eros. Justin bit his lip and smiled, squeezing his hand right back.

As reluctant as he was to admit to himself, Adam couldn't help but feel that maybe, just *maybe*, he had managed to stumble into something that had the potential to be great. Everything about Justin seemed to get better and better, and Adam knew he had to take at least a tiny step of faith, if not a leap, like Steve had said.

Their hands swung between them as they walked a little closer together, up through the cozy streets of the East Village. He made some more small talk, mainly trying to see if he could get Justin to laugh again. Thankfully, it wasn't too hard after some drinks, but Adam still took pride every time he managed to land a joke and get one of those breathy giggles to grace his ears.

They passed Tompkins Square Park. The scenic patch of green in the concrete surroundings was quiet and empty now as it was approaching midnight. Orange glowing streetlamps lined the edge of the park and they strolled under their warm circles of light. A couple of people passed by them on the sidewalk, but no one gave them a second glance.

When they got to the last block to Adam's apartment on the corner of East Thirteenth street, they walked past a gap between closed storefronts.

"Hey, fuckface!" someone shouted down the hardly lit alley beside them. Two men were leaning against the bricks. They were both smoking joints and the bigger one who had yelled had a bottle wrapped in a brown paper bag dangling from his hand by his side.

"Aw, Jesus," he sighed. He dropped Justin's hand from his.

"Do you know those guys?"

"Yeah, unfortunately. Just stay behind me," he whispered. Justin peeked around his shoulder to watch.

"What a small fucking world it is, right?" the other, smaller, man said.

"Hey, Michael. Hey, Billy."

"You looking to get fucked up tonight?" Michael smiled, flicking the end of his smoldering joint. "Billy and I were just pregaming before heading over to Jones' place."

"Looks like he's already got some company to me," Billy said. He tossed his smoke to the ground, crushing the roach under his boot.

"And who might we have here?" Michael drawled. Billy laughed beside him, but Adam didn't find any of this funny.

"Don't worry about it," he said. "And sorry, but I've got other plans tonight."

"Plans, huh?" Billy asked. Adam's blood began to boil as Billy raked his eyes up and down Justin. "Like these kinds of plans?" He dropped his hands and started thrusting his hips, pretending to hold someone still and fucking them. "Are you gonna share, Adam?"

"Don't you even think about it, Billy. I'm not joking."

"What?" he sneered. "You too good now to share your whores with your bro? Maybe, you can fuck him while I see if his mouth is as good as one of Jimmy Vincenzo's gals."

Billy took another step closer, but Adam immediately swung his fist, connecting it with Billy's chin with a resounding thud. Billy stumbled backward and just managed not to fall to the ground next to the dumpster.

"Hey! Hey!" Michael shouted. He stepped up to Adam, slapping a hand on his chest and blocking him from Billy, who was cursing up a storm.

"Goddammit, motherfucker! You're such a goddamn fucking asshole, fuck!"

"Take him home, Adam," Michael growled. He looked over Adam's shoulder toward Justin. Adam glanced back and saw a steely look on Justin's young face, staring right back at Michael with clenched fists by his sides.

"Now," Michael ordered. "Before someone else sees you." He stared at him and he didn't have to mention their father out loud, only imply him with that angry glare. "You're crossing a line."

"Oh, am I?"

"Yeah."

"Being out with him?"

"Yes, now get the fuck out of here, before I let Billy take some of those swings he's been itching to take."

"I don't need you picking my fights for me," he said. He turned his attention to Billy, who was fuming but also hiding behind Michael with a pissy look on his face. "And I swear to God, Billy. You better stop talking shit unless you want to eat it."

"I'd love to see you try," Billy sneered.

"Just get the fuck outta here," Michael said, pushing him back. "And I'll see your sorry ass tomorrow. Don't be fucking late."

He stepped back to Justin, who wasn't afraid to take his arm and lead him away from those two assholes. They got back to the sidewalk and he turned to make sure they weren't being followed. Michael and Billy were done with them, though, and he was surprised when Justin's hand reached over to his and broke him from his angry thoughts.

Justin held his hand in a strong grip with a look of determination. It was just as brave as the one he had given Michael, and Adam's heart melted a bit more seeing it again.

He pulled his hand free from Justin's but only so he could wrap his arm around his waist and tug him near while they walked. Justin smiled and tucked himself in closer, his arm around Adam's back, and they made their way the last bit to his place.

Chapter Twenty-Three

Justin followed Adam up the stairwell of his apartment building. The fluorescent light bulb on the second-floor landing was flickering, the spastic flashing casting shadows throughout the bare concrete walls and up through the center of the stairs where he could peek over the handrail and look up all the way to the ninth floor. They only went as far as the third though, and Adam tugged the metal fire door open for him.

He hadn't really known what to expect, but he certainly hadn't imagined a place like this. The building was old and barren, devoid of any decor besides the worn-thin maroon carpet and the stained, peeling wallpaper. Even his own apartment building, shitty as *that* was, looked better than this.

Adam pulled a set of keys from his pocket and unlocked the janky doorknob of the door at the end of the short hallway. He held it open with an apologetic half-smile on his face.

"Sorry, it's um, not really much to look at," Adam said.

He hated to say it, but that was the truth. Neon-pink light flooded into the tiny living room from the one window across the space. Shades of pink glowed on every surface—the gray fabric of the couch, the neutral white walls and the old ivory carpet. Adam flicked a switch next to the door and one standing lamp in the corner by the couch lit the room in an orange bubble. Justin inched inside a bit more and looked around.

The furniture was basic and the walls were blank, but there was a collection of Adam's things arranged around that gave the apartment a smidgen of evidence that it was lived in—a set of mismatched weights on the floor by the sofa, a bookcase against the left wall. Besides a pile of magazines on the bottom shelf, there weren't any other books. A bureau on the other wall had a boxy television sitting on top with myriad odds and ends and knickknacks surrounding it, including a bong standing on the corner, something Justin recognized from all the cop shows Jewels loved.

Truth be told, the place looked more like a hide-out for someone on the run to crash in. It gave him the impression that Adam didn't want to be here, even if he was.

"It's all right," he said, trying to be polite. "Have you lived here long?"

Adam dropped his keys on a side table and shrugged off his leather jacket to hang it on a hook on the wall. He crammed his hands into his jeans pockets and looked around like he was trying to see his place for the first time too.

"Uh, yeah, kinda. It's been almost three years now, I guess. I wasn't really planning on staying here for that long."

"Oh."

"But make yourself comfortable," he said, gesturing to the couch. "I'll get you a glass of water."

"Thanks. Can you point me towards the bathroom?"

"Sure. It's through the bedroom door over there, just to the right." He pointed to the cracked-open door behind him.

Justin spun and walked over to push the creaky door open. Light from the living room spilled in and he could barely make out the shapes of a bed and a set of drawers. The bathroom door was right next to him and he found the light switch on the wall and walked in.

He turned around and unzipped his pants, the alcohol already filtering through his system. He looked at his reflection in the mirror as he soaped his hands after and paused, surprised to see the rosy flush on his cheeks from the drinks. His hair was wind-swept and once his hands were dried, he immediately tried his best to comb it back down with his fingers. He didn't want to be, but God, he was nervous. He thought that Adam and he had really been hitting it off well. He had managed to attempt some flirting and Adam had returned it right back with that gorgeous smile that made Justin's hands sweaty every time he flashed it.

It had all been going so well until those two guys in the alley. For a second there he would have bet money that Adam was about to get into a full-fledged brawl. *Michael and Billy.* That was what Adam had called them. Whoever they were, it was clear that tensions were high between them.

He felt a pang of guilt realizing it was because of him. Adam had defended him, though, and he should apologize to him once he got back out to the living room. He checked himself in the mirror one last time just to make sure and took the plunge to head back out.

Adam watched Justin find the bathroom light and step inside, and he let out a long breath and shuffled his way into the kitchen. He got the cold water running and reached over to the cabinet to pluck out a glass from the shelf. After a second thought, he grabbed one for himself as well.

He was going to have to apologize for what had just happened. *Fuck Michael and Billy.* Why the *fuck* did they always need to butt into his life and mess it up like they did to everyone else in the city? It was lucky for Billy that Michael had been there to stop him, because Adam's patience with him was nonexistent and he wouldn't have pulled his punches.

Jesus, how the hell was he going to be able to make it up to Justin? That was, if he wasn't too freaked out for Adam to fix it. He wouldn't blame him — who would? Getting into a fight with his shit-faced mafia brothers in the alley was a fantastic way to ruin a first date.

Adam heard the bathroom door open and took the glasses into the living room. Justin gave him a small smile that, despite how sweet it was, didn't make Adam feel any better about how bad he had fucked things up.

"Oh, water," he said. "That's perfect."

"It's the least I could do. Here." He handed him the glass and sat on the couch, and Justin took it with a quiet thanks and joined him. The couch was a hand-me-down from Steve's old apartment, but it was still roomy and long enough to stretch out on. Justin sat close, though, his knee almost touching Adam's. The warmth radiating off Justin's smaller body this close it was an entrancing feeling.

"Look, I really need to apologize for Michael and Billy."

"How do you know them?" Justin asked.

"They're my brothers I mentioned."

Justin's eyes widened. "Oh, okay."

"Sometimes I really hate them. I mean, I *know* that they hate me, but that doesn't make anything they said fucking acceptable."

The tension thrummed as Justin's face fell.

"Hey," Adam said, trying to get Justin to look at him again. "Don't listen to a word they said. They don't know what they're talking about."

Justin tried to give him a smile, but it was painfully obvious how fake it was. "It's all right. It's not like they were wrong. Technically, I *am* a whore now. I'm the one that chose to go there. To Eros."

Adam shook his head hard. "Only so you could help someone you love," he replied. The words poured out of him but he couldn't stop, not when Justin had to understand. "What you did was something noble. It was courageous. Don't you ever fucking think less of yourself for that."

"You really think so?"

"Yes," Adam said with full sincerity. He took Justin's glass from his hands and placed both down on the rickety coffee table in front of them so he could reach for Justin's hands where they were resting limply on his knees.

Justin sucked in a soft breath. Adam squeezed Justin's fingers and ran his thumbs over his knuckles, trying to relax him.

"I admire that courage, Justin. Sometimes, with all this shit in my life, I'm so fucking scared I don't know how I'm ever gonna get by. But you, you're a breath of fresh air in all this bullshit. I mean that. Justin," he said, steeling himself for what he didn't want to say. "My family? They aren't *good* people."

Justin's eyes were trained on his and a look of recognition Adam had suspected would come flashed on his face. He didn't care about that, however, because while he knew Justin had to find out who he was eventually, he was…different. He was sweet, earnest, but more importantly, he deserved the truth.

"All of us have done terrible things," Adam admitted.

Justin's face fell into a look of worry, as though Adam's words were breaking his heart, but he only held his hands tighter, moving even closer. Adam couldn't stand it. He had to slip a hand free to cup the side of Justin's face. He stroked his thumb over the delicate line of Justin's cheekbone where the skin was warm and pink and so very soft.

Justin's eyes fluttered with the touch and his breath hitched in his chest. Adam held his breath and waited for the moment when Justin pulled away, but it never came. Justin leaned into it instead and glanced up under his eyelashes, waiting.

"*I've* done terrible things," Adam continued, "but please believe me when I say that…that I don't *want* to be like them."

"Then that already proves that you aren't," Justin replied. "I've heard things about your family from almost everyone it seems in the past month, but I can't bring myself to feel what they feel. The person *I* know isn't the same one everyone thinks they know." He shook his head, almost to himself, before he spoke. "Maybe I'm naive, but I feel nothing but safe when I'm with you."

"I would never try to hurt you," Adam rushed to say. "And I would do everything to make sure my brothers never lay a finger on you."

"I know," Justin whispered.

His eyes were lingering on Adam's lips and Adam guessed that Justin didn't realize he was doing it, but the gaze was blatant and loud. Holy fuck, when was the last time anyone had looked at him like that, full of unbridled hunger and lust? Had Justin even been kissed before? Who was he kidding — the answer was probably no. More than anything else in the whole world, Adam suddenly wanted to close the last bit of space between them, to bring them together completely and be his first kiss, but it felt too precious to take without permission.

"Justin? Could I kiss you?" Justin's pulse fluttered under Adam's palm where it rested on the side of his neck.

"Yes," he whispered. His chest was rising and falling as his eyes searched Adam's. The gaze was intense and Justin broke it, dropping his eyes down to their laps where they sat almost pressed together on the couch. It was clear he was too nervous to make the first move, but that was all right with Adam.

He leaned almost all the way in, leaving just the tiniest hint of space to ease him into it, to make sure he wasn't caught off guard. Before he could seal the deal, however, Justin moved forward the final inch and brought their lips together in a burning press.

If he'd thought that holding Justin's hand earlier had been electric, then this was a whole fucking lightning bolt crashing onto his head and all the way down his spine. The press of Justin's lips was a little off, but packed full of hunger, so Adam used his hold on the side of Justin's neck to show him how their lips could lock together perfectly. When a tiny hum snuck out of Justin, Adam took the sound as encouragement to swipe his tongue along the seam of Justin's lips and prompt him to open up for him.

It was clear that Justin was trying his best to follow his lead. He was inexperienced, but a fast learner. When Adam's tongue found his, twisting them in a slick glide, Justin reached up to clench the front of his shirt at the collar and try the motion again with his own tongue. It was slick and burning hot and wove against his while he eased Justin in the motion of it.

Their lips made wet sounds through Justin's soft panting and Adam tried to breathe without breaking the increasingly excited, urgent kisses. God, even the taste of the very air leaving his lungs was sweet and addicting, and Adam had a hard time making himself pause long enough to let Justin get used to the give-and-take as they made out.

It had been so long since he had really kissed someone. Like, really *really* kissed. He pulled back a smidge, just so he could nibble a teasing bite on Justin's bottom lip. It wasn't strong, but it was enough to surprise a teeny gasp out of Justin that Adam used to tilt his head to the other side and re-slot their lips back together.

Justin was clinging onto him, moaning a happy humming when they reconnected. The sound of it stoked Adam's fire just right, and he had to make himself pause for a moment. He used his hold on Justin's neck to keep him far enough away so he wouldn't be tempted to never stop kissing him.

Justin's eyes fluttered open and he gave Adam a questioning look through his half-lidded eyes.

"*Fuck*," Adam groaned, and Justin huffed out a breath of a laugh as though he completely agreed. A high blush burnt hectic rosy spots along the slope of his cheekbones. It looked perfectly matched with his alabaster skin and blown-wide chocolate-brown eyes. He looked too tempting to resist.

"Do," Adam said, slowly and with a hint of a smile, "you wanna take this over to the bedroom?"

Justin took a shaky breath in and he blinked before ducking his gaze again. Adam immediately wished he could suck the words back in because he never knew if he was pushing a little too far and would scare Justin off. He was about to open his mouth and backpedal to fix things when Justin nodded.

"Yeah, I do."

"All right," he said. "Then come here, sweetheart."

He grabbed Justin's hand in his, twining their fingers together before he stood and prompted him to do the same. He didn't rush right to the bedroom, though. Once Justin was standing, Adam tugged him tight into his space with a quick little pull. He snaked his arms around Justin's lower back and their bodies slotted together. Justin's smaller frame nestled right against his, and he slid his hands upward to wrap around Adam's neck.

Adam kissed him again, bringing the intensity back up to where they had left off. It was too easy to get lost in the wonderful feeling of kissing Justin, but he also knew how to multitask.

With his hold around his back, he shuffled backward with inching steps. At first Justin stumbled but then matched his steps one at a time while Adam focused on kissing that adorable half-smile off his face.

Together they inched back safely, and he directed them with skill back through his open bedroom door, flicking the light switch on the wall without even having to look, and stopped them at the side of his bed.

He had one moment to regret not having straightened the sheets before he'd left earlier, but the thought went right out of his head when he sat on the edge of the mattress and tugged Justin down onto his lap.

The way Justin seated himself easily on the top of Adam's thighs told Adam that he was still enjoying where this was going. Justin confirmed Adam's theory by holding Adam's stubbled face with both hands and kissing him again.

Adam hurried to push Justin's sweatshirt off his shoulders and down his arms, Justin helping him. As soon as the sweatshirt hit the floor, Adam went for the top button of Justin's flannel shirt. He pecked his lips a couple more times, but once the first button was undone, Adam latched his mouth to the line of Justin's collarbone.

Justin moaned, clutching the back of Adam's head, and Adam tasted Justin's smooth, hot skin. His hands worked downward, button by button, and his mouth worked upward, licking and nipping along the slope of his neck. Justin panted in his ear, squeaking out a keening gasp when Adam found a particularly sensitive place near his hairline behind his ear. Adam sucked hard on the spot, lapping at it to soothe it afterward. As much as he loved hearing the sounds he could pull from Justin, it seemed like there were a trillion freaking buttons on his shirt and it was a miracle when the last one popped free.

"Thank fuck," he sighed, slipping his hands under the fabric and over Justin's shoulders to send it to the floor with the sweatshirt.

Justin's skin was beautiful. It was creamy and silky and too inviting not to touch. Adam ran his hands down Justin's shoulder blades, down the muscles of his back and around to the jut of his hips where they peeked out from the black denim waistband of his jeans. He pulled Justin flush against him and even through the fabric of his own shirt felt the heat pouring off him.

Their lips reconnected and, damn, Justin was already getting good at kissing, a true natural. He slipped his hands down from Adam's neck, eagerly reaching for the button at his throat to do the same thing to his shirt, and Adam's heart skidded to a stop.

"Wait, hold up," he whispered, pulling back so he could gather his thoughts. He wrapped his hands around Justin's to make him stop before he undid the first button and his stomach flipped in fear, making him feel sick.

"Is something wrong?"

"It's just, um, I really like you, Justin, so I'm gonna be honest. It's sort of a mess under there."

"A mess?" Justin asked, furrowing his eyebrows together in confusion.

"I mean like, the skin's not so pretty to look at. It's probably for the best if the shirt stays on."

"So..." Justin said. "You're telling me, it's like that time in *Nightmare on Elm Street Four*, when Freddy's chest turned into the melty, screaming faces of the souls trapped inside him?"

Adam huffed out a laugh, dropping his head and shaking it for a moment before he looked back up. "It might as well be."

Justin smiled softly at him, still so very close that it was maddening not to lean in and kiss those warm, soft lips again.

"Well then, I've already seen *that*," he said, shaking his head. "I'm not going to be afraid, Adam. I swear."

It was sweet to hear him say that, but it was a different thing altogether believing him. That old, defensive feeling that had been ingrained deep in Adam for years was not easy to shake, but he prayed — prayed *hard* — that this time it was going to be different. He had to leave himself open to the possibility despite how scary it was to do so. Otherwise, he might miss something great right in front of him.

"Did you..." Justin started, trying to school the smile off his face but failing. "Did you mean it when you said you like me?"

Adam laughed again. "I believe I said I *really* like you."

"Good." Justin leaned in and took another quick kiss, getting braver by the minute. He pulled back and raised an eyebrow. "So, may I?" His hands still held the front of Adam's shirt, waiting for the go-ahead.

"All right," he said, barely audible. He dropped his hands from Justin's and rested them around his back to keep Justin close in his lap. Justin leaned in and touched his lips to Adam's again, so Adam tightened his grip more and stroked up and down the hot, smooth skin of Justin's back, making him sigh against his lips and pull back to resume the unbuttoning now that he had permission.

He popped each button free from the cotton, revealing first the muscles stretched across his chest and lower, but all Adam could focus on was the gnarled mapwork of scars that were unveiled with every new inch. He watched Justin's face as he got the last couple of buttons done, but when Justin looked back up at him to help push the fabric off his shoulders and down his arms, he didn't look shocked, or sickened, or dripping with pity. He looked more concerned with how Adam would react, as though he were nervous about pushing him even after all these weeks in which Adam had been the one pushing him.

"Is this okay?" Justin whispered, resting his hands on Adam's pecs where the thin gold chain glinted on · his chest. His right hand just overlapped onto the scars stretching down from Adam's left collarbone. The touch was gentle, but not because he seemed reluctant to touch — he seemed like he wanted to but was holding back.

"Yeah," Adam agreed. He pressed their foreheads together and stole another quick kiss, but Justin pulled back to speak again.

"Does it hurt?"

"Sometimes. It usually just feels too much." It was hard to explain, that overload of sensations that the scars picked up on, both good and bad. Justin must have figured out what he meant, though, because he nodded his head against his.

Adam slowly brought his mouth back to Justin's, gentle and sweet. Justin wrapped his arms around Adam's neck and the feeling of Justin's heart pounding under his burning skin was exquisite as their bare chests finally touched. It was intimate in a way he had never truly allowed himself to experience, and he gripped Justin's hips tighter, rubbing the knobs of his hip bones just to hear that pretty sigh sneak out of him again.

"God, you're gorgeous," he purred between kisses. He raked his hands up Justin's back, making him squirm again in his lap.

"Damn. So are you, Adam," he gasped. He squeezed the corded muscles in Adam's neck and shoulders. His hips were starting to rock in small nudges and Adam's cock throbbed in his jeans when Justin rubbed his ass down against him.

It felt great, but he wanted more. He scooped an arm under Justin's ass and hoisted him up, to drop him onto the mess of his sheets and lay him down.

Damn, Justin looked a sight on his bed. Getting Justin in bed at Eros was one thing, but he liked him *way* more here in this setting. Justin shifted on the warm gray sheets and gulped quietly while Adam dragged his gaze over his body. He was hard in his jeans, the stiff outline of it visible under the dark denim, confirming that Adam wasn't the only one affected here.

He ran his hands down Justin's legs and he reached to pull the sneakers off him, tossing them to the floor without looking. He kicked off his own boots and crawled up over him, slipping a knee between his legs and slinking up close enough so he could reach Justin's lips for another kiss. Justin arched up into the press of his body above him. His hips bucked and his cock rutted against Adam's hip with tiny wiggles, so Adam slid his right hand down the smooth plane of Justin's stomach to massage the line of his erection through his jeans.

"*Oh, God,*" Justin gasped. He squeezed the back of Adam's neck and tipped his head back on the pillow.

It was such a shame that he hadn't gotten to see the lovely faces he could pull from Justin when he'd touched him before, but it was worth the wait to see them now. Adam didn't have to look to pop open the button of Justin's jeans and tug down the fly to pull out his trapped cock, so he didn't. Instead, he kept his eyes on Justin's face as it shifted into surprised pleasure the moment Adam's palm squeezed him tight.

Justin shivered in his arms and moaned, hard in Adam's hand, so much that Adam felt the blood pumping from his pulse in the engorged flesh. He started to take it nice and slow, tempted to spend the rest of the night like that. It was an enticing thought, and he ducked his head to suck on that teasing spot on

Justin's neck he had found earlier. The hot, needy sounds panting out of Justin grew twice as desperate from both Adam's hand and mouth working together to make him lose it.

He pumped his hand along Justin's length with lazy movements. He multitasked by leaving a wandering line of rosy spots up and down his neck. Each little mark glowed warm pink, but he tried his best to keep them from bruising, even if he wanted to bite hard enough to leave a mark like his own personal brand on Justin's stunning skin for days.

He focused hard on leaving one last good spot on the crest of his left collarbone when Justin's chest hitched.

"Adam," he whimpered.

Satisfied with his handiwork, Adam nipped the teased skin with his teeth for good measure and glanced up at Justin's face.

"Is this okay?" he asked.

"Yes." His chest was heaving through the pleasure and his hips undulated like he wanted to be able to fuck up into Adam's tight fist.

"Can I keep going?"

"Yes, please," Justin begged. It was music to Adam's ears, so he dipped his head lower than before and took Justin's pebbled-hard nipple into his mouth and sucked.

Justin's body bucked hard, a gasp tearing from his throat. Adam hadn't forgotten how very sensitive Justin was there and he used the knowledge to his advantage now. Adam stopped moving his hand on Justin's cock and instead gripped the base in a tight fist and focused one hundred percent on nibbling the hard bud of flesh on Justin's chest between his teeth.

"Oh, holy fuck," Justin gasped, twitching under his body again.

He let go of Justin's cock and kept working his mouth, sneaking his hand lower and rolling Justin's balls in his hands for a second before tracing a circle over his hole with his index finger. He teased the tight furl of muscles but didn't try to push further. Justin squeezed Adam's shoulders, digging his fingers in hard enough that Adam felt the sting of his short nails as Justin wiggled and tried to spread his trapped legs further.

Adam searched his face to find any hesitation. "Do you wanna…" he asked, leaving the question hanging so he could try to judge what Justin was thinking.

Justin blinked at him, his mouth parted slightly to catch his breath. He closed it and swallowed before he nodded, too shy to answer out loud. Adam leaned down to kiss him, but he kept it short. He wanted to hear him say it.

"Are you sure, Justin?"

"Yeah," he whispered. He licked his dry lips and Adam traced the motion of his tongue with his eyes.

"Okay." He nodded, pecking Justin's lips again. He shimmied up and reached over for his tried-and-true, half-empty bottle of lube that he kept stowed in the bottom drawer of his nightstand under the mess of check stubs and pieces of old mail.

Before he opened it, he tossed it to the sheets and reached for Justin's jeans instead. He snuck his fingers under the waistband and Justin lifted his hips to help. Adam didn't touch his own jeans. Not yet. He crawled closer again and Justin reached up to wrap his hands around his neck to pull him back down over him. He twined their legs together, but he used his knee between Justin's to nudge him and spread his legs a bit more for him to work.

He had to steal another kiss — it had been too long since the last one. While he did, he felt around on the sheets next to Justin for the bottle. He broke the kiss, but Justin didn't let him get too far away. He leaned up to place a kiss to the side of Adam's neck and started trailing a line of his own down the slope of skin over the muscles with little nips and tantalizing swipes of his soft tongue.

"Fuck, that feels good," Adam praised. "Keep going, Justin."

He hummed out a sound and kept kissing, exploring the taste of Adam's skin, but Adam had things to do and was in a hurry to do them.

He used his one hand to pop the cap on the lube open. There was a flaw in his plan though — he was going to need two hands, and right now he was using his other arm for balance.

"Dammit," he cursed. "You're gonna have to help me out here."

Justin pulled back and gave him a questioning look before he noticed the bottle in his hand.

"Oh," he said, taking the bottle from him. "Sure."

"Thanks, sweetheart. Just give me a bit to start."

He squeezed some lube out into his cupped fingers, warmed it in his hand then smeared it over his fingers.

Justin closed the bottle cap with a click and placed it down on the bed, all the way off to the left and hopefully out of the way. When he wasn't looking, Adam used his now slick fingers to slip his hands between his thighs and find that tight ring of muscles again. He rubbed over the hole in sudden little circles, gliding the rough pad of his index finger over the smooth skin, and Justin twitched and whipped his head back toward him.

He took it slowly. It was so different having Justin's eyes on him while he touched him in the most sensuous way, easing him open with the gentlest rocks of his finger and working his way in deeper. He brought their pace down, kissing barely there pecks of lips between Justin's shaky breaths. He didn't want to rush. He couldn't get enough of seeing that sweet, pleading look on Justin's face as he willingly gave himself over to him. The moment seemed like more than just sex — more as though it were something terrifically fragile and precious that Justin was letting him have.

He nudged his middle finger against his index and pressed the tips back into the warmth of Justin's body. They sank inside with the slick help from the lube, but Adam noticed how tense the muscles were and how Justin's fingers squeezed into his shoulders a little harder.

He felt so very wonderful inside, soft and hot and *tight*. Adam knew how amazing it was going to be pushing his cock inside, and right now he was rock-hard in his jeans. He scissored his fingers, spreading Justin open more. As desperate as he was to bury himself inside that fantastic ass, he had to put the effort in beforehand. It was going to be worth the wait. He pressed three fingers together and chased the hitching breaths that left Justin's lips with a searing kiss. Justin met it with force, as though Adam were his lifeline.

"Damn," Adam gasped, dragging air down deep into his lungs. "I don't know how I'm not going to blow my load the second I'm inside you."

That surprised a gorgeous laugh out of Justin. The muscles deep inside him clenched down on Adam's fingers. He didn't stop moving his hand, working his fingers in diligently, and Justin's smile melted back into a look of arousal.

"Are you ready?" Adam asked.

"Yes," Justin whispered, nodding. "I'm ready."

"Okay, just hold on a second for me, sweetheart."

"Okay."

Justin let him pull back and Adam jumped up off the bed and undressed. He knew full well that Justin was staring—he could *feel* his eyes on him. It wasn't a bad feeling though. He was hard still, his cock lying stiff against his abs, and he liked seeing that look on Justin's face.

He shoved his pants and boxers down in one go, too eager to wait a second longer, and crawled back up to Justin. He spread Justin's legs and pulled him closer, getting into position. He leaned over to his nightstand and snagged a condom, but Justin reached out and stopped him.

"No," he breathed. "I want to be able to feel your skin."

Adam's heart twisted with a weird lurch. Where the fuck did this kid come from and how had he fallen into his lap like a mysterious gift? All Adam knew was that he wanted to make this as good for Justin as possible. He wanted to give him anything he desired.

He snagged the bottle of lube and hurried to get his painfully hard cock slick.

"You still good?" he checked.

"Yes."

"Okay." He propped himself up with his left hand and cherished the way Justin wrapped his arms around his lower back and squeezed his fingertips into the muscles. He snaked a hand between their bodies to adjust his cock, rutting along the slick crease of Justin's ass for a distracting moment and making him gasp. "Hold on, sweetheart. Breathe for me."

He lined up the tip of his cock and pushed forward slowly, gradually. This time he got to see the look on Justin's face as the sensation of being stretched that far open flicked a hint of pain across his face.

Adam closed the space to kiss that look away, trying to distract Justin from the feeling with every little trick he could think of — licking the roof of his mouth, nibbling on his bottom lip — whatever it took as he pushed all the way forward.

Justin moaned against his lips when his cock bottomed out. The noise was throaty and loud, a reassuring sound like music to his ears. His cock throbbed and flexed in the glorious heat of Justin's body but he still gave Justin a minute to adjust to the fullness, kissing along his neck anywhere he saw fit. Justin raked his fingers up Adam's back and through the short blond hairs at the back of his skull, his breath loud in their small bubble of space.

Adam didn't need to ask to know when to start moving. He felt the moment when Justin's body slowly began to relax underneath him, the muscles unclenching as his body got used to the hard press of Adam inside. He took the cue and readjusted himself, keeping some of his weight off Justin's smaller body and trying not to press him too far in on himself. Justin shifted his legs and locked them behind Adam's back.

His first couple of thrusts were gentle. Justin's body was still so very tight around him, and his gaze flicked from Adam's face to where their bodies were joined together. All the usual flirting and dirty talk flew clear out of Adam's head at the sight of Justin's trusting chocolate eyes staring into his. He had no words for what he was feeling—he could only try to bring Justin apart along with him.

He kept his mouth close to Justin's, swallowing the panting and soft moans that squeaked out of him. Between the lube and the amazing angle, his stiff cock slid in and out of Justin's body with sinful perfection.

Justin became ravenous as they kissed. Adam shifted his arm and cupped the back of Justin's neck with a steady grasp, keeping them locked together where they could breathe in each other's air as they kissed.

Fuck, he was already right there near the edge. He couldn't help it. *This* wasn't how he got to have sex, and he was quickly unraveling from Justin's heavenly sounds alone. He tried some well-aimed thrusts, staccato and just a bit harder, jolting the breath out of Justin with shocked gasps.

Justin broke their kiss and threw back his head as his orgasm peaked. He didn't warn Adam that it was happening, just moaned loudly before the sound cut out entirely. He squeezed his legs tighter around Adam's sides and where they were hooked around his back. Justin's body shook and the first pulses of cum striped his stomach with the rocking of his hips.

Groaning, Adam picked up the speed, just a little, fucking through the rippling muscles of Justin's orgasm where he was so incredibly tight and fluttering around him. It felt so goddamn good, bringing him closer and closer to his own end. It was the fucked-out moan Justin gave, the way he let his whole body relax underneath him so he could keep going, that was too perfect and pushed Adam over the edge not far behind him.

The air punched out of Adam's lungs with a groan and he dropped his head to Justin's chest. He buried himself as deep as possible inside Justin and his cock flexed in the tight heat, flooding the still twitching hole.

He kept bucking his hips in tiny thrusts to ride through the waves of amazing bliss and he bit one last nip to Justin's collarbone.

When the world flooded back in, he cracked his eyes open again and glanced up to see Justin watching him. His breathing was heavy, and he looked at him with sweet awe on his flushed face. Adam dipped down to kiss him breathless, reluctant to part in any way, not even when the sweat on their skin began to cool. He eventually had to pull out or he risked getting hard again. It had been a while since he had gone twice in a row, but it seemed all-too possible having such a sexy body underneath him as a temptation.

Very carefully, he inched back and watched Justin's face for any signs of discomfort, but he only sighed out a soft breath when Adam pulled out and let his legs back down on the sheets so he could stretch out. The smooth curve of his pale stomach was dotted with the pearly drops of his release, completing the thoroughly debauched look on him that Adam greedily drank in while he sat back on his heels and caught his breath.

"Don't you dare move a muscle, gorgeous. I'll be right back."

"Okay, sure," Justin said. He gave a soft laugh, his eyes warm and sparkling. Adam liked how giggly he seemed to get after he came. It was too cute. Justin drew his knees together like he was suddenly shy, like Adam hadn't just been very acquainted with the lovely space between his legs.

He leaned down to drop a last kiss on one of Justin's knees and made himself get up, trailing his hand down Justin's calf and off his ankle. As soon as he got a warm, damp hand towel, he was going to take his time cleaning him off and maybe kiss him silly to hear that laugh again.

Chapter Twenty-Four

Justin lay loose-limbed and sprawled out in Adam's bed. He was sore now and a little sticky still between his legs despite Adam's careful help, but he was also so very tired and in no hurry to get up yet. Adam's sheets were incredibly smooth against his bare back and legs, way softer than his own at home. He wondered if regular cotton sheets were too rough against Adam's skin. That would explain why the bedding seemed to be the one thing in this apartment that Adam actually spent good money on.

Adam himself was currently just as lazy. He had lain on his side and practically draped himself over Justin, curled up and resting his head on his chest. It was sweet and Justin let him settle down, placing his arm around Adam's shoulder and tracing the warm skin there in wandering squiggles with his fingers. There was the lightest dusting of golden freckles spilling across his broad shoulders but they were very faded, like they didn't get to see the sun.

He bit his lips and ghosted his fingertips over the hard line of Adam's trapezius muscles in his neck. Jesus, he seemed to be packed with muscles everywhere. Just by touch alone, he had been able to tell at Eros that Adam was built, but finally getting to see the chiseled definition of muscles in his arms, chest and stomach was so much better. Yeah, he knew that Adam didn't like what he saw when he looked at his own body — that much was obvious from the pained dread that had been plastered on his face when Justin had tried to undress him, but Justin hadn't been lying that it didn't bother him.

It was the opposite in fact. Adam had looked stunning tossing him down onto his bed, and even more breathtaking holding him close and pushing inside him with an easy thrust of his hips that had stolen Justin's breath away. He hadn't been able to tear his eyes from him.

The scars weren't the only ghosts haunting Adam. Despite him telling Justin not to dwell on it, Justin couldn't stop replaying the tense moment earlier when Adam had squared up to Billy. The hard glint in Billy's eyes, the clench of Adam's fist, Michael's booming voice when he separated the two of them...it was impossible to shake from his mind.

"Can I ask you a question?" he whispered. He didn't want to break their peaceful, quiet moment, but he had to ask.

Adam hummed and it breezed over Justin's chest. He didn't bother moving, so Justin blinked up at the ceiling and gathered the courage to speak.

"If it's not too rude of me to ask...why did you say earlier that Michael and Billy hate you? They're your brothers. What could be so bad that they'd hate you?"

There was a heavy silence between them. Adam was lying on his right side and Justin saw the edges of scars along the left of his ribcage before they faded to his back. He watched the way Adam's muscles flexed with every breath. He thought maybe he had pushed his luck, but he was proven wrong when Adam finally spoke.

"I killed our mother," he said.

Justin's breath froze in his lungs. He didn't know how on earth to respond to that. Adam continued, though, without prompting. He spoke slowly and carefully, just over a whisper so Justin could hear.

"It was a long time ago. I was just a baby. We had this place in the Upper East Side. Some apartment in one of those fancy-ass buildings. Dad was away. In Atlantic City, I think, and it was just the four of us." He paused and Justin let him find his words without rushing him.

"In the middle of the night, a fire started in the living room. I don't know how, but it spread fast. Mom got Michael and Billy from their beds and out into the hall, but she went back for me. The nursery was all the way in the back of the apartment." Adam scoffed out a sound and shook his head against his chest. "It was a fucking death trap. When the firefighters finally got there, they found her burnt corpse curled over me in the corner. She hadn't been able to get out and she died trying to protect me from the flames, even though I've still got these scars to remind me every day that..." Adam's voice broke for a second and it sounded harsh in his throat. "That if she hadn't gone back for me, she'd still be here."

Justin shook his head on the pillow. "Yeah, but then *you* wouldn't be. She was your mom, Adam. She chose to save you because you were her baby. It sounds to me like she loved you more than anything."

Adam sniffed and pressed his face harder into Justin's chest. Justin felt wetness on his skin, and he realized that Adam must be crying. He didn't comment on it, but he still had more to say.

"And I'm sorry, but it's bullshit if Michael and Billy blame you for that. It wasn't your fault. They can't hold you responsible for that. *You* can't hold yourself responsible for that."

Adam shifted, rubbing at his face for a second before he leaned up. There was a serious, almost-pained look on Adam's face still—in his eyes as they locked with his—and Justin could tell that he hadn't opened up like that in a while. It was something that Adam had pushed so far down that it clawed and cut while dragged into the light of day again.

Adam hesitated, but only for a heartbeat, before he spoke. He sounded cautious, as though it was too important to mess up. "If you really meant it earlier, about why you ended up at Eros, then I want you to know that I would be more than happy to give you all the money you need."

Justin was shocked. He knew it had to be obvious on his face from the way Adam immediately tried to explain.

"I just mean that, after the past few weeks and tonight... I just don't know if I can stand the idea of sharing you now that I've had you like this."

Justin's heart skipped a beat, pounding double-time once it started up again.

"I don't want anyone else," he replied. He spoke the truth without overthinking it for a second. A weird emotion that Justin couldn't name flashed across Adam's face, but in the end, he seemed to be upset.

"Then there's something that you've got to know," he said. Justin held his breath. "I'm leaving tomorrow night. There is something that I have to do that I don't want to, but afterwards I'm taking my things and leaving Manhattan."

The previously elated feeling in Justin's chest punched out like he had been socked by a knock-out swing. Left in its wake was a shocked ache that throbbed in pain with the beat of his heart.

"Leaving...for good?"

"Yeah," Adam said. That new ache became a stabbing sensation in his chest as Adam's words sunk in. "I'm getting out of here. I've been planning on it for a while now and it has to be tomorrow night."

"Oh... I..." he tried to say, but the air was caught in his windpipe. Oh God, this was really happening, even though everything in his being screamed that it *couldn't* be, not like this. After getting this far and getting this close to Adam, he was just going to vanish? It was like a nightmare.

"Oh no, Justin, please don't be sad." Adam reached his free hand up and cupped the side of his face with a warm, comforting stroke. "I'm telling you this because I want you to come with me."

"Wait, what?"

"Come with me," he said. It was soft and hopeful. "I don't care where we go — it could be anywhere you want. I've got plenty of cash, we'd be set for a couple of years easy."

He blinked at Adam, completely at a loss for words. It sounded like an old-school love story, two fresh lovers running off into the sunset and leaving every problem in the dust when they went. It would be like some grand, mysterious adventure where the ending was in the wind, but that was okay as long as they had each other.

His life, however, wasn't some dead-end where he had nothing to lose and could slip away into the night without a trace. There might not be any reasons left for Adam to stay, but Justin still had Jewels. Not only was she sick and mere hours away from a serious surgery, but he couldn't imagine abandoning her.

He could *never* do that to her. As much as every new piece he discovered of Adam swept him away, Adam was asking the impossible from him. Leaving was the one thing he could never do. He swallowed down the ache in his throat as his pounding heart tried to stab its way out.

"I wish I could say yes," he whispered, "but I can't leave Jewels. Not after everything she's done for me. Not when it's been us against the world for so long."

Adam nodded slowly. He traced the side of Justin's face along the ridge of his cheekbone and down the line of his jaw. He tried to enjoy the tender touch, but it was overwhelmed by the terrible feeling that he had just given up something capable of growing into more than this curious, physical relationship. He had wanted so desperately to find out. It was so unfair that it was about to be ripped away from him.

"I guess," Adam said, "if I had someone like that too, then I wouldn't want to leave either." At least he seemed to understand, not that it really changed anything. A thought popped into Justin's head—a last resort of hope—and he had to risk saying it.

"I know I can't ask you to stay if you've made up your mind, but if you could, if it's possible at all, just think about it? I get that there's a lot of bad blood here. Billy and Michael made that pretty obvious. I get it. But maybe there's another way?"

It sounded pathetic, but he wasn't willing to give him up so easily. Adam made him laugh, he didn't sugarcoat bullshit and he looked at him like he was something *worth* looking at. He wasn't about to let that slip away if he could help it, but chances were he was too little too late. If this was what Adam had planned for a while, then what sway did Justin's option offer?

Adam slipped his hand around to the back of his head and leaned in for a kiss that, despite the burning sadness in his chest, he was still happy to reciprocate. Kissing Adam was proving to be his new favorite thing, maybe even more than the mind-blowing orgasms.

The kiss was sweet and lazy, as if Adam was tasting him like a refreshing sip of water in the middle of an Indian summer. Adam's lips were soft and gentle against his, parting just a hint so that he could taste him again. The ache in his chest and the icy dread in Justin's veins even melted a little from the tempting heat of Adam's affections. It was impossible to thaw entirely, though, especially when the nagging voice in the back of his head whispered that he wasn't going to be getting any more of these. Not when Adam was leaving tomorrow.

When Adam finally trailed the lingering end of the kiss off, he pulled back only an inch.

"If you can't leave, then I get it. I'll think about it," he said.

"Really?"

"Really. I promise."

Justin surged up and locked his lips back with Adam's. He wove his fingers through the short fuzz of hair at the base of his skull and Adam returned the energy two-fold, pressing the whole line of his naked body against Justin's so he could feel every searing, muscular inch of him. They kissed until they finally needed to breathe.

"Can you stay?" Adam whispered. Justin wanted so badly to say yes, to stay here in his bed where they could lie and kiss all night. They could never have had this sort of intimacy or time at Eros and he was being greedy, but he couldn't help it. It was new and addicting, and Adam made it so hard to resist but Justin had to, even if it felt like almost saying goodbye already. If he walked out of here tonight, there was the very real possibility that it would be the last he saw or heard from Adam ever again. Still, he had to be responsible.

"I wish I could, but I really should be back. For Jewels."

Adam nodded. He stroked the side of his face for a moment, stealing another kiss that was too short in Justin's opinion.

"Then let me at least call you a taxi," he said.

"You don't—"

"Please," Adam interrupted. "It's already super late. It would make me feel much better knowing you're not walking home."

He knew that Adam was thinking about his brothers. To be honest, Justin didn't want to run into them again if by chance they were still around. He wasn't stupid, and he knew that Michael and Billy didn't like him or the fact that Adam was with him. Maybe accepting his offer was the best choice. It had to be past two in the morning already and he *was* exhausted. A ride home would be kind of nice.

"Okay," he said. "Thank you."

"Of course. Here, I'll let you get dressed and I'll call a cab."

Adam shifted away, letting him get up and grab his clothes from where Adam had tossed them on the floor.

"I'll be right back," Justin said, slipping over to the bathroom with his armful of clothing, and Adam tossed him a smile. Justin caught the way Adam's eyes flicked over his nude body one last time, and he tried not to blush.

He cleaned himself up as best he could before hopping into his clothes, but he'd still have to crawl into the shower at home. He just prayed that he wouldn't wake Jewels up. Thankfully if he was quiet enough, she would never know just how late he got back. Never mind the fact that she would know in an instant exactly what he had been up to if he came home at three in the morning and took a late-night shower. He wanted to spare himself the embarrassment.

The ache in his chest morphed into a weird brew of doubt and hope. Adam had said that he would think about it, but would he really? Should Justin just accept the fact that more likely than not, Adam would be gone by tomorrow night? It was the little butterfly of hope that made him want to protect and foster the idea. It was all he had.

Once he was dressed, he checked himself in the mirror. At first, he didn't notice anything out of place, besides his hair which had to be combed neat with his fingers, but at the last second, he caught the hot-pink splotch on his collarbone where Adam had kissed and sucked hard enough to leave a mark. Oh great, now he had to pray that Jewels didn't see that either, but he knew better. There was almost nothing he could hide from her. Well, it was too late to worry about a hickey now.

Adam was waiting for him when he got back out. He had gotten into a pair of gray sweatpants and nothing else. More importantly though, he had left his chest bare where Justin could still see the shapes of scars in the dim light. It took effort on his part not to stare, but because so much gorgeous muscle was in plain view as Adam's sweatpants hung dangerously low on his hips.

Adam got up from the couch and met him in front of the door to the hall. He got right up into his space and reached out to pull him even closer, snaking his hands around Justin's lower back. Justin snuck his arms between Adam's and held him right back, tilting up his head for Adam to lean down to press another kiss to his lips.

"Your cab's downstairs. It's already taken care of," Adam said, although Justin knew he meant that it was already paid for.

"You didn't have to."

"I know," Adam said. He gave Justin one of those coy smirks that he was quickly coming to love, and he leaned up on his toes to kiss it off Adam's face.

"Thank you."

"Can I text you tomorrow? To see how everything is going?"

"Yeah."

"Okay, good." Adam gave him one more kiss that was too short for Justin's liking, but it would have to do. "I'll talk to you tomorrow then, Justin. Have a good night."

"You too," he replied.

Adam watched him the whole way to the stairwell at the end of the hall. Reaching the metal fire door, Justin turned back, and Adam gave him a soft smile that he returned.

The taxi was idling at the sidewalk just like Adam had said, and Justin opened the back door and got in.

He was kind of grateful that he hadn't gotten one of the overly friendly drivers who liked to talk a client's ear off because the night was slow and they were bored. Today felt like one of those days where a whole week's worth of events had been crammed in, and more was yet to come. He had a couple of hours to sleep ahead of him, but after that it would be time to bring Jewels to the hospital for her surgery.

Everything in the past month had led him up to this day and now that it was finally the early morning, he figured that sleep would be hard to find. He also couldn't shake the terrible feeling that he might never see Adam again, and that weighed down on him with the rest of the dread building. No, sleep was not going to be easy at all.

Chapter Twenty-Five

Miles McCarthy was a long-time friend of the Creed family — his father, Brendan McCarthy, had been one of Shawn Creed's oldest friends. After Brendan had passed away six years ago, Miles had taken up the family business that made enough money to keep the McCarthys well off, even without the extra 'side deals' that Miles sometimes made with the Creeds. While the McCarthy's owned a meat-packing plant in the Bronx that delivered products to almost a tenth of the businesses in Manhattan, it was one of their older warehouses along the East River where Adam turned up, to practice shooting like he had promised Michael.

Miles's place was just a couple of minutes' walk from the Creeds' warehouse and had a nicer facade to it. Instead of metal plating, the outside was solid cement painted an Easter-pastel shade of green. Quaint as it looked, the building was almost strong enough to stand the blast from a bomb, and those thick, heavy walls made for great soundproofing. Adam jogged up the brick stoop with its wrought-iron handrails and rang the doorbell.

He waited for a couple of minutes and was about to press the button again when the door swung open. Standing there with a smile beaming on his face was Miles.

"Well look who it is!"

"Hey, Miles, how's it going?"

"I could ask you the same thing! When was the last time I saw your ugly mug, huh?" Miles laughed. He was almost as big around as three regular-sized men, just like his father had been, and his laugh was deep and jovial. If Miles grew out his red goatee and dyed it white, he'd be able to play one of those mall Santas if he wanted to.

"I don't know, a good few years at least."

"You've got that right! Come on in, come on in," Miles said, stepping back so Adam could walk inside into a drab hallway. The floor was covered with aged white tiles that needed a good waxing and that barely reflected the strips of fluorescent lights lined down the hallway ceiling. The metal door sealed shut behind him and Miles started walking them down the hall, talking over his shoulder.

"You know, Michael still comes down here to shoot about once a week. He said that he was going to get you to come by, but I didn't believe it until I saw your text with my own eyes."

"Yeah, well, you don't want to get too rusty, you know?"

"Amen to that. Always be prepared." He turned back to look at Adam. "Is that what the Boy Scouts say?"

"Um, sure? Something like that, at least."

"Yeah, and it's a good way to live life, my friend. Here we go." He pushed through a set of metal swinging doors halfway down the hall on the left that led into a long barren room. It might have once been another meat-packing floor, but the only signs of heavy industrial equipment having been there were small holes in the ground where they'd been bolted down into the cement and skid marks where they'd been dragged out.

The far wall across the way had a stack of cement blocks, stacked neat and tight. They were a dozen feet across and a foot taller than Adam. In front of the blocks stood two rows of equally large wooden pallets, four or five deep, to catch and slow any bullets before they reached the cement. The front pallets were painted with fading bullseyes, their rings of red, blue, and white paint dotted with bullet holes, and eventually Miles would replace them with new pallets and paint fresh ones.

In the middle of the room stood an ancient oak table so heavy that it would fall through the floor if it was on the second story of a house. It made the perfect place to stand behind and shoot, and Adam remembered how their fathers would rest their ashtray and beer cans on it while they took their turns shooting.

"So, you got something to shoot with or are you looking for a rental?" Miles asked.

"Naw, I've got Michael's piece actually."

Miles gave him a look, his eyebrows rising in interest. "The thirty-eight special? Your dad's old snub nose?"

"Yeah."

Miles whistled. "Boy howdy, that is one nice gun, let me tell you. I always get so envious when Michael shows it off. I don't know of a gun more cherished around these parts than that one."

Adam just hummed a noise in agreement. Miles wasn't wrong—Adam's father's gun was almost as famous as the man was himself. He had given it to Michael two years ago and it might have well been a twenty-four-carat gold crown with how much of a big deal his brothers had made it. Billy had seemed pissed that it would never be his, only Michael's, the eldest. Adam couldn't have cared less though. Even having it now made him feel like he was just Little Baby Adam Creed, playing pretend with his father's prized possession. He couldn't wait for tonight to be over so he could get it away from him as soon as possible.

"You need some ammo?" Miles asked.

"Yeah, if you don't mind. Nothing crazy, I don't really plan on staying that long."

"No problem-o." Miles reached under his spare tire and unclipped a set of keys from his belt loop. They clanged in the echoey space and Miles shuffled to a row of locked metal cabinets along the far wall. "I'll just leave a box here for you and you can feel free to stay and use as much as you like. If you need anything, just holler. I'll be down the hall near the end. The guys are coming by for a game, so we'll be there."

"Sure thing. Thanks."

"Anytime," he said, and off he went. He hooked the set of keys to his belt loop and they jangled on his way out and down the hall.

Adam dropped the box of bullets on the table with a sigh. He reached behind his back and carefully took out the gun from his waistband. It *was* a beautifully crafted piece. The weight of it was perfect and balanced, the grip fit just right in his hand and the stormy metal on the sides was crisscrossed with etched lines that were rough and grating under his fingers. It was loaded already, so Adam reached for a set of shooting earmuffs hanging from a hook on the side of the table. Settling them on his head, the ambient hum of the world around him blinked out into dead silence.

He sighted down the line of the revolver and past it to the painted circle on the wall all the way at the end, thumbing the safety off. He took a deep breath, braced his arms and pulled the trigger. The sound was striking, even through the headset. The recoil of the gun was strong but not unfamiliar, and he held steady through the force of it with skill that came from practice.

He took another breath in and let it out as he pulled the trigger again. And again.

Each blast of gunpowder was powerful, the bullets sending chips of wood flying when holes exploded in the pallets. The smell of smoke drifted up, but he didn't stop, shooting through the rest of the cylinder. When the final bullet hit its mark, he set the safety and lowered the gun back down, breathing slowly and easily. He placed the revolver on the table, slipped the headset off to rest around his neck and stepped around the table to get a closer look at the wall.

A new pattern of holes popped out against the red and blue paint. The grouping was tight considering that it had been years since he had shot, but it definitely needed some improvement.

"Fuck me," he sighed, running his hand over the small crater-like holes. Shooting at a wall was one thing, but aiming a gun at a person and pulling the trigger? Expecting the same results? He didn't know if he was capable of that. Maybe that made him weak, or afraid like Billy had said, but it was the truth.

He backed away from the wall and went back to the station behind the table. The box of bullets was old, but the paper still held together well enough. He lifted off the top and took the casings out to begin loading bullets back into the cylinder one by one, taking his time with it.

The longer he thought about it, the more he realized he *was* scared. Not only that, but he was letting the fear win. He was going to run away, cowering under the dark shadow of his father, when what he really should be doing was listening to what Justin had said. Maybe there was another option. If Justin was willing to accept him, then he owed him what he said he'd do. He was going to try to think of a different way. Maybe, just maybe, he could get what he wanted without running away with his tail between his legs. It just took someone braver than he was to convince him.

He clicked the cylinder back into the gun and undid the safety, getting back into position. This time, he took longer sighting down until he was happier with his aim. He braced his stance and pulled the trigger.

BAM.

Sawdust exploded as the bullet struck. The image of Justin, nude and arching into his touch, flashed through his thoughts for the hundredth time since last night. He remembered the warm glow of Justin's ivory skin writhing under his body...

BAM.

...and the sound of Justin's shocked moan in the shell of his ear when Adam's cock had bottomed out. Adam's blood pounded in his ears from the striking gunshot.

BAM.

How was he ever going to forget the cute whimper that had moaned out of Justin as he'd caught his breath through the force of his orgasm?

BAM.

Or the way he himself had never come so hard in his life, his body craving every inch of Justin against his like he was oxygen and Adam was a man drowning?

BAM.

Justin kissing his lips, soft and slow, while their heart rates inched back down.

BAM.

The cylinder was empty. He had to come up with something, and he knew the one person standing in his way — the one person who pulled all the strings like he was just another puppet on a stage.

He was going to have to talk to his father.

Getting some air suddenly felt like a great idea. He didn't bother to go check the target. The last thing he cared about was seeing how he'd done. He emptied the gun and reloaded it, tucking it away at his back and leaving the headset and the box of ammo there on the table.

Outside on the raised cement loading dock Adam tugged out his cell phone and started a text to Justin.

Hey, it's Adam.

He paused, thinking it over, and typed out another sentence, sending it as well.

How's it going with Jewels?

Was that stupid? He cursed himself for not thinking about it harder before he hit Send. Maybe he should have asked how Justin was doing before he went right in about his sick grandma. It was too late to take it back now, though, so he stood there, waiting and trying not to look at his phone. He took another breath in deep and held it in his chest, counting to five in his head and blowing it out. Like a blessing, the phone vibrated, and he unlocked the screen. It was from Justin.

We're at the hospital now. She's still in the operating room.

Oh. Well, he guessed he probably should have figured that out. He texted back a response.

And how are YOU doing?

His phone buzzed again right away.

I don't know…
It's hard just sitting here, not being able to do anything.
I can't stop worrying about everything that could go wrong.

He hated the idea of Justin sitting there upset. He needed to hear his voice.

Can I call you?

It was terrible standing there waiting. He paced in a line, back and forth, scuffing his boots on the cement dock. After a painful, long couple of minutes, Justin answered.

Yes.

The second he got permission, he hit the Call button and waited as the phone rang. A peal of laughter from the men inside drifted out through the back door, but he was listening for the click of the line.

"Hello?"

"Hey, it's me," he said.

"Hey."

"So how long has she been in the operating room?"

"Only a half an hour," Justin said with a dejected huff of a laugh that sounded more strained than he probably meant it to. "It could be a while still, but at least the waiting room has *Dr. Phil* playing silently in the background for me to blink at."

"What if I came by?" he offered. "I could help keep you company while you wait. Maybe it will make the time go by faster."

There was a long pause from Justin's end and Adam worried that maybe he was reading the situation wrong.

"You would really do that?"

"Absolutely. Just tell me which hospital and I'll be there in a jiffy."

"It's St. Anthony Hospital, over in Kips Bay."

"Okay, I'm headed over."

"Thank you," Justin said, sounding apologetic.

"No problem. Just hang tight and I'll be right there."

"Okay, I'll see you soon then."

"See you soon," he said. Adam hung the phone up and opened the back door to head inside, but only so he could find Miles and tell him he was bouncing. He was in a hurry.

Chapter Twenty-Six

Justin sat alone in the waiting room of St. Anthony Hospital's cardiovascular surgical wing. Everything around him was sterile and depressing. The dark, muted silence made his head spin with a million thoughts. Heart surgery in its very nature seemed foreboding and scary. He had done the research, both on his phone and from whatever books he could find at work on his breaks. Heart stent surgery had progressed by miles in the past two decades. Reassuring as that was, this still wasn't Jewels' first rodeo. This was her *third* stent, and even he wasn't going to lie to himself that the margin for things to go wrong didn't get higher and higher after her previous other two.

He just couldn't imagine his life without her.

Jewels was his support system, his only family, and his *everything* since he'd been old enough to realize he loved her as though she were his mother. She could die right there on the operating table and take her last breath before he got the chance to tell her again how much he loved her.

Jewels wasn't anyone's grandmother here. She was just another ailing human body who would be put under a surgeon's blade and it would either heal or fail. It didn't matter how kind or honest or loving she was. There was nothing she could do, and there was nothing he could do, and *that* was the most terrifying thing of all.

Jewels had given him sweet look of understanding that made his heart break even more. How could she be so strong when it had him so scared?

As if that weren't enough to worry about, Justin also couldn't stop thinking about Adam. When his phone had gone off and he'd seen it was a text from him, it was like a godsend. Adam had not only texted him but offered to come see him. Even the sound of his voice, smooth and low like a gentle seduction, still sent shivers down Justin's spine to his toes. Just hearing him talk had made Justin's heart twist in agony, but having him offer to come so he wouldn't have to be alone?

But what if Adam was just coming to say goodbye? How would he ever live through that with his heart shattering into spiky little pieces as it was? He couldn't lose Adam, not like this, before things ever had a chance to begin. And he couldn't lose Jewels, not when she was such a fighter and his entire world.

He couldn't stand to lose anyone else in his life.

The door to the waiting room clicked open and the sudden sound of it almost made Justin jump out of his skin. He whipped his head up and there was Adam. Their eyes met and he stood without thinking, stepping forward and meeting him halfway across the room.

Adam's arms came out and Justin's breath left him as he fell into them. Adam wrapped them around his back and hugged him tight. He pressed his face into the soft material of Adam's T-shirt, and it was as if a simmering pot had finally come to a boil. All the emotions that Justin had been trying to hold back swarmed to the surface, making his stomach drop. His eyes and nose prickled as the tears tried to start, and a cold wave of ice water flooded his veins. He took in a hitched breath and the lovely warmth of Adam's cologne filled his lungs and made his head swim.

"Hey, hey," Adam said. He reached up and stroked the back of Justin's head before holding his shoulders and pulling him back, just an inch, so he could search his face.

Justin immediately felt a wave of embarrassment. How foolish of him to get so worked up—he just couldn't help it. He hadn't known that all those feelings would suddenly explode inside of him like an awakening volcano. He shook his head to try to force them back down into the Pandora's box they'd come out of.

"Hey, it's okay," Adam reassured him. He cupped the sides of Justin's neck with a tender hold, studying his face. "Did you get any sleep at all last night?"

Justin scoffed a sad sound. He had tried and failed miserably.

"No offense, pal, but I can tell," Adam said, a smile tugging at the corner of his lips, and Justin chuckled. He took in a deep breath and nodded.

"None taken."

Adam's hands were warm on his neck. Adam caressed the sides of his cheek with the rough pads of his thumbs, and Justin shivered at the intimate contact. He wasn't used to such affections in a public place, even if they were the only two people in the waiting room.

"How about," Adam began, "we head down to the cafeteria for a couple of minutes?"

"The cafeteria?"

"Yeah. The nurses have your cell number, right? They can call you when Jewels is all set. And I have a feeling that you could use a cup of coffee and a twenty-minute distraction."

The thought of leaving this depressing, morose room was better than great. This was the very last place he wanted to stay, even for a minute longer.

"Yeah, actually. I think that'd be nice."

"All right, good. Let's get some caffeine in you then."

Adam stepped away but placed a hand on his lower back to lead him to the door. His hand was warm and large, burning through Justin's sweatshirt to his skin. It was grounding, and he already felt better the second they stepped out into the hall.

* * * *

The cafeteria at St. Anthony Hospital was on the northside of the building's ground level and was the busiest place in the whole hospital by far.

"I'll get the coffee," Adam offered. "Do you want to go find us a seat?"

"Sure, I can do that."

"Awesome. How do you take it?"

"Um, just black, please."

Adam smiled. "A man after my own heart."

Justin laughed, tugging the sleeves of his sweatshirt. Heat began to burn his neck and ears.

"I'll go grab them and be right over," Adam said, still smirking. His eyes crinkled, making them sparkle, and Justin pushed down the bubbly feeling in his chest.

"Okay, thanks."

He found a small table for two in the back corner, sitting himself down near the window so he could sunbathe in the speckles of light breaking through the canopy of a narrow, droopy willow next to him.

He pulled out his cell phone to rest it on the tabletop. The screen lit up, flashing the digital clock. It was already three. If everything had gone according to plan, the surgeon would be wrapping up and Jewels would be heading into recovery.

He caught sight of Adam at a register, pulling out his wallet from the back pocket of his black jeans and handing the cashier a couple of dollars. He said something to the woman and nodded to her as he picked up the Styrofoam-lidded cups and walked away. Justin tried not to squirm in his seat. Adam got to the table and placed the coffees down, sitting in a plastic chair across from him.

"Careful, these things are still friggin boiling," he said.

"Thanks. I'll let it sit for a minute."

"Good thinking." Adam turned his head and glanced out to the courtyard. "I've never been here," he said. "Have you?"

"No, not to the cafe. Jewels used to work here and sometimes brought me when I was really little, but usually to the children's wing. Her friend Amy would watch me and let me play with the toys."

Adam chuckled and nodded. The moment was left hanging in an awkward pause, but Justin didn't know what to say. Adam glanced back at him and seemed to study him again with one of those drilling looks Justin still wasn't used to getting.

"Look, Justin," he finally said. "I just want you to know that I've been thinking about what you asked me last night. About staying."

"You have?"

"Yeah. You see, months ago? I decided to get the fuck out of here. You know who my family are, the sort of things they do daily and not even blink an eye." He paused until Justin nodded. "So, I decided to get out of the city, but what I really wanted was to get out of the game. The problem is getting out without getting hurt."

Justin shook his head hard. "I don't want you to risk getting yourself hurt."

"I'm not talking about me," he replied. "After last night? With Michael and Billy? I don't want any of this shit getting close to you." He reached over and took Justin's hands, holding them on the tabletop with a tight squeeze. "So that's why I can't tell you exactly what I'm going to do. I can't do that. Just believe me that I've got an idea, and hopefully after tonight, it'll be over."

"Tonight," Justin said, trying to absorb all of this at once. Clearly something big was tonight, something that scared Adam enough that he had been about to run, and Justin didn't even want to imagine what it could be. A dozen different plots from mafia movies ran through his head, each more sinister than the last.

"Yeah, tonight," Adam sighed.

Between them, Justin's phone rang on the table. It buzzed and spun, and he had to make his body unfreeze and pick it up. The caller ID read *St. Anthony* and he hit Answer.

"Hello, Mr. Turner?"

"Yes, that's me."

"This is Sarah from St. Anthony Hospital calling."

"Yes?" he asked. The forgotten dread came back two-fold.

"I just want to let you know that the procedure went smoothly. Julia is in our recovery room and in about fifteen minutes, we're moving her to a bed upstairs for a couple of hours for some monitoring, but she should be able to go home later tonight."

"Oh, that's great."

"Yes, she did wonderfully. If you'd like, you can make your way upstairs to wait for her. It's going to be room five-thirteen on the fifth floor."

"Thank you, yes. Room five-thirteen," he sighed. "I'll be right up."

He hung up the phone. Adam raised an eyebrow at him.

"Everything okay?"

"Yeah, the nurse just said she's out of surgery. They're going to keep her for a couple more hours, but I can head up and wait for her in the room."

"That's great news. I won't keep you then."

"Wait, Adam," he said. He reached out and held Adam's wrist, stopping him from getting up from the seat. "This obligation that you have tonight, just tell me. Is it the dangerous kind?"

Adam blinked at him, the muscles of his jaw clenching for a second. "Potentially."

"Could you get hurt?"

"Look, Justin. It's possible, but I'm going to do everything in my power to make sure everything goes well. It should be clean-cut. Nothing crazy."

Justin wasn't convinced. He knew it wasn't as easy as that. "I'm still going to worry about you."

Adam's eyes softened. He dropped his head for a moment before he leaned in closer across the tiny table, pulling his hand from Justin's and cupping the side of his face. Justin met him halfway and tried to breathe steadily. Adam had a way of sending his heartbeat off kilter, though. Their foreheads touched and he didn't let the fact that they were out in public bother him. It felt like just the two of them in the whole city of Manhattan, for a single moment.

"Justin, these days I've got to spend with you this month were the best I've had in a *long* time."

"Me too," he whispered.

"And I told you last night that I don't think I can share you now. I really meant that."

The words sunk in and slid down Justin's spine into a warm pool in his gut. It still sounded just as appealing as it had last night.

"Are you asking me to go steady? Like from an eighties high school movie?"

Adam laughed hard. "Yeah, I guess I am. I'd give you my letterman jacket to wear if I had one."

That made them both laugh. Justin ducked his head, shy, and knowing full well that he had to be blushing like crazy. The laughter died down and Adam took both of his hands in his again, rubbing his thumbs over the back of them.

"Is that a yes then?" he asked.

Justin huffed out a chuckle. He thought it was obvious, but he still answered, daring to look Adam in the eyes. "Yes."

"Good."

Adam closed the space between them and kissed him hard. It was chaste but still felt like the best one yet. If it could have lasted all day, it still wouldn't have been enough, but it had to end and Adam finally pulled away, sitting back in his chair again. He squeezed his hand one last time.

"Come on, let's get you out of here."

"Okay, yeah," he agreed. His head was spinning but he was happy, and more than anything, he was relieved. Jewels was out of surgery and he'd get to see her soon, not to mention how Adam seemed to have a plan. Things were starting to look up and he allowed that little bit of hope to grow.

But when they got back out into the main hall, Adam stopped and spun around. "I'm gonna head out," he said. "I've got to get ready for tonight."

Justin nodded, although the curiosity was killing him.

"Wait to hear from me tonight then," Adam said.

"When?"

"No later than midnight. All right?"

"Okay."

"I'll text you."

"I'll be waiting for it," Justin replied.

Adam leaned in a gave him one more quick kiss, too fleeting, but sweet nonetheless. Adam pulled back and Justin let him, standing there in the hall in front of the busy cafeteria as people moved around him. He watched as Adam left through the gentle stream of people and around the corner, and finally turned to find the elevator and head up to Jewels' room.

Chapter Twenty-Seven

Back in his apartment, Adam let out a long sigh and flicked on the switch, looking around. When he had moved in three years ago, he had seen right off the bat what a dump the place was. It hadn't been a problem though. It had been somewhere away from his family, all to himself.

He stepped past the stuffed backpack and duffel bag resting where he had left them days ago after he'd finished packing. They were all set and ready to go the second he was.

It wasn't like he had a crazy number of things, but he had still managed to get both bags stuffed. Mainly it was clothes, stuff like a couple pairs of newer jeans, T-shirts, boxers and socks. All the basics and necessary toiletries. He had also carefully packed an old four-by-six photo of his mother in a flat pocket of the backpack. Besides her cross, it was the only thing left of her. Arguably as important as the photo had been to pack, though, was the money.

He had squirreled away the cash over the years in a fireproof safe under his bed with steady determination. He had counted it twice before packing it away underneath the stacks of clothes in the bags, so he knew that exactly ninety-one thousand, three hundred and ninety-five dollars in bills were inside.

Where he was planning on going with his life stuffed into two bags after tonight's deal was done? He didn't know. He would probably find a motel somewhere after everything was done, but that was fine. He'd have a bed, a shower and a quiet place to call Justin and talk. He couldn't stay here though, not when Billy and Michael knew this was his place. He didn't want them turning up. Chances were, they were not going to be happy with him after what he had planned.

He rubbed his hands over his face, scratching the stubble that was already growing. He looked over to the kitchen and the digital clock on the microwave read four-thirty.

"Fuck," he cursed under his breath. He still had a good couple of hours to kill before he headed out to the warehouse. His stomach grumbled, loud and demanding, reminding him that he still hadn't eaten yet. Well, at least it would kill some time.

He strolled into the kitchen, but his feet felt like lead. He snagged the loaf of bread from the counter and the jar of almost-empty peanut butter from the shelf above the microwave. He tried to focus on the simple process of making a sandwich, he really did, but it was impossible to clear his mind and meditate.

The steel of the gun at his back seemed to be bone-chillingly cold, like it refused to warm up from his body heat. It was like a constant reminder — a whisper in his ear every time he wasn't expecting it — that if he had to use it tonight, it would be with full intent of protecting his life. Maybe even Michael's or Billy's too. It was a thought filled with enough dread to almost make the idea of eating hopeless. He had to push through it, however. He needed something to keep him going for the rest of the night.

It didn't take long to get the sandwich down and unfortunately, he was back where he started, staring at the empty kitchen and completely at a loss for what to do next. Watching television would be pointless — he was far too restless to be able to sit there.

Pull-ups were mindless yet better at keeping him distracted. He flew through his first set of ten, and, at some point, he stopped counting the rest, because even that felt like a slowly ticking clock. He continued until his muscles and skin on his palms started to really burn and he needed a breather.

The sun was getting closer to the horizon. It couldn't just be his hopeful wishing.

Taking another deep breath, Adam grabbed the bar and started all over again. He forced himself to work twice as hard this time, picking his speed up. All that bubbling anticipation turned into one simple, single-minded goal that was something he *could* do now, but as nice as it was to get out, it only tired him out faster.

He dropped back down, his boots thudding on the floor, and he stormed off to the bathroom with a sigh to wash up with some cold water. It was bad when working out still didn't help him blow off steam.

He needed a smoke.

As it turned out, a smoke turned into two and he walked around the apartment building's block twice. At least when his feet were moving, it didn't feel like waiting, so he made a point to make a second lap when the first one went by too quickly and a third when the second still didn't cut it.

The sun that had been still strong, if not low, by the time he gotten home was now struggling to stay afloat. The streetlamps were starting to turn on, lights from store windows and open doors spilling out onto the sidewalk.

At least dark meant that it was finally almost time. He got back around to his apartment building and went inside this time. The nervous energy thrumming under the surface of his skin grew and the voice in the back of his head reminded him that this was the last time he'd ever step inside this apartment.

On the top of the beat-up kitchen table was an unsealed letter-sized envelope with the name *Kastos* written on it.

Adam slipped six crisp hundred-dollar bills inside the envelope and tucked the flap in. Hopefully that would fix any hard feelings his landlord Mr. Kastos might feel about the sudden evacuation. With that last task out of the way, there was nothing left to do. He was packed, the apartment taken care of, and it was now or never. He took his key out of his pocket and tossed it on the tabletop where it landed with a *tink* right next to the envelope.

There was no sadness or painful nostalgic memories of this place, except maybe from the night before. As nice as it had been to have Justin's lovely company in this shithole, he had no intentions of bringing him anywhere near this crap apartment again.

Things were only supposed to get better from here. Well, at least that was what he hoped for. He grabbed his bags from the floor, slung the backpack over one shoulder and carried the duffel by its straps.

He turned the light off and took one last look around at the soft pink light glowing through the room. As he locked the door and stepped out, he prayed that this Chapter of his life was as good as over. For his *and* Justin's sake.

The door clicked shut behind him. First step done. Two more huge hurdles left.

* * * *

The night was shockingly warm and crystal-clear. The moon was almost full, and it made the dirt and gravel road that led down to warehouse seventeen-C light up like a beacon. Adam pulled his phone out to check the time.

Eight-fifty-three. Perfect.

The last thing he needed tonight was Michael up his ass about being late. If he was lucky, Michael would be too focused on their mission to be in a bitchy mood. It was a big 'if' though.

Instead of heading to the door and ringing the bell, Adam took a detour and hooked a right around the far side of the warehouse. Jones' old blue Ford pickup was parked in its usual spot against the side of the building, meaning Jones and Miller were already here. Those two traveled everywhere together, and chances were Billy had come along with them.

He slipped by the car and kept going to the fenced-in trash pit standing behind the warehouse. A huge built-in fence door, wide enough to back a truck into, stood latched closed, but the padlock for it was unlocked and dangled on a link of fence near the door.

He stepped inside and re-latched the door behind him with a creaky groan from the rusting metal hinges.

When the wind blew, the plastic lining flapped and fluttered, but now the night was still and everything was quiet. He turned around and crept beside the dinged-up blue dumpster and took a knee.

He hoped that the foot gap that was between the dumpster and the warehouse wall would be the perfect place to stow his bags. There was no way his brothers, or Jones and Miller even, would go looking back there, not tonight when they were about to leave. It wasn't like they were staying and getting shitfaced like they usually did.

To be safe, though, he walked out from the trash pit and snagged the padlock hanging on the fence. He locked the door and gave it a pull, just to be safe. Ninety grand wasn't something he was willing to take a risk with. He would just have to nonchalantly ask Michael for the key later. It would be no big deal.

With the deed done, he hurried back around to the front of the warehouse and buzzed the door. The intercom never went off, but the metal door flung open and Michael poked his head out.

"Good, you're here. That's everybody."

Adam followed him inside and could hear Billy and Miller talking before he stepped around the corner and saw them all in the middle of the warehouse, standing around two SUVs with tinted windows and sleek black paint that were parked inside.

Both the cars faced the side of the warehouse where a huge mechanical garage door stood. It was wide enough to fit the backs of two eighteen-wheelers inside so they could unload. Now though, Shawn Creed's two black Mercedes-Benz SUVs stood almost packed and loaded to go at the door. The older 350 model was going to be Jones and Miller's car and it looked like it was done being packed. The swanky 550, though, still had its trunk popped open and a few packages sat stacked on the ground nearby.

Peter Jones and Eliot Miller leaned up against the towering metal shelves.

Billy sat nearby on a huge wooden crate that was big enough to fit two grown men inside. Adam recognized the stamp on the side as Rich Davis', the guy who supplied them with fresh weed from Maine. As Adam followed Michael farther in, Billy glanced over at them. The look of pure annoyance that flashed over his face at the sight of Adam wasn't unexpected, but it was still obnoxious.

Billy went back to saying whatever he had been telling Miller and pretending that Adam didn't exist, so Adam sat himself down in an empty folding chair. He caught a glimpse of a purple and yellow bruise high on Billy's cheek from behind the strands of his hanging hair. He didn't feel sorry in the least.

"Okay assholes," Michael shouted. "Everyone's here so get fucking ready."

Billy stood up from the crate with a scowl painted on his face.

"You don't have to bark at us like we're fucking dogs, Mike."

"Oh, just shut it, Billy," Michael said, exasperated.

"Don't tell me to shut it! And why does Adam get to drive?" he asked. Adam rolled his eyes but didn't say anything. Michael shot him a look, though.

"What?" Billy demanded, pissy.

"Adam gets to drive," Michael explained, "because he can actually drive in a straight line."

"What the fuck does that mean?"

"It *means* he's usually not fucking hammered like you are, so just goddamn deal with it!"

"This is bullshit," Billy sneered.

"I don't give a crap. He's driving. You're going to be my backup." It was a sad compromise, like a parent giving a child a made-up role just to make them feel important. If Billy noticed though, he didn't seem to care. He nodded, still frowning, and crammed his hands into the pocket of his jeans and turned to walk away.

"I'm gonna go take a shit," he mumbled.

"You better not be doing any lines in there, I swear to Christ, Bill!" Michael shouted after him.

"Go fuck yourself," Billy retorted, flipping him the bird without a look back.

"Don't you fucking test me tonight!"

"Relax! I'm just taking a shit! Jesus Christ!"

The doors flung open and Billy shoved his way out to the back hall, still cursing under his breath.

"Such a goddamn asshole," Michael grumbled.

Jones shot Miller a look over the rim of his glasses and Miller gave him a nervous grimace back. Adam wasn't the only one who hated when Michael got angry. It wasn't just the pushy, testosterone-soaked strutting and growling he'd do like a rabid dog, but Michael's anger could fly completely out of hand if it reached that point. It was like a bolt of lightning, the strike of a viper or the flick of the switch on an electric chair. As much as Adam didn't like to think about such things, he was shocked that Michael hadn't killed anyone yet when he got like that. Or, at the very least, hadn't killed *Billy* yet considering how often Billy pushed his buttons.

"Hey, Mike, uh..." Jones started, cramming his hands into the pockets of his flannel jacket. "Could we just smoke a cigarette outside real fast before we go?"

Michael sighed and bent over the back of the trunk, resting his hands on the bed and hanging his head for a moment. Jones shifted his weight from foot to foot and it was so quiet, even the sound of his ratty sneakers scuffing the concrete floor was intensely loud.

"Fine," Michael said. He picked himself back up and rested his hands on his hips. "Just make it quick."

The two of them didn't hesitate a second to make their escape. Adam contemplated following them just to get some air, but Michael turned to him.

"Will you help me put the rest of these goddamn boxes in here?" he asked, sounding exhausted. The kettle that had been close to boiling had lost heat, and Adam felt a little sorry for him.

"Yeah, sure."

"Thanks."

Adam stood and walked over to grab one of the four boxes still left. The boxes themselves were recycled wooden boxes of plaster of Paris, their outside labels still intact. There was indeed powdered plaster inside, but only enough to bury the bricks of cocaine wrapped up in neat stacks. Each box had to weigh twenty pounds, and it was insane to think about how much money each box was worth as Adam slid it into the trunk.

Eight boxes, forty kilos and four million dollars just waiting to be made in exchange. It was no joke. Michael grabbed another box to place it right next to Adam's in the trunk and the two of them finished off the packing in no time. Michael didn't close the trunk, though, after he slid the last one in place.

"Hey, look," he started, breaking the moment of silence in the empty room. He leaned against the trunk, half sitting, with his right leg kicked out and his hands on the bumper. He was staring at the ground. "I just wanted to say sorry about last night. Mainly for Billy being such a fuckhead."

Adam let out a long sigh. He paced over to the folding chair he had been in, but he didn't sit. He wanted to tell his brother to cram it, but Michael spoke before he got a chance to say as much.

"You know I don't fucking care what you do. I mean, like who you're fucking."

"All right, Michael. Whatever."

"I'm just saying while *I* don't fucking care, it's not about what I think, and I know *you* know that."

He put his hands on his hips and spun to stare at Michael right back.

"Yes. I do. Thanks."

"Whatever," Michael said with a dismissive shrug. "I'm just trying to do something freakin' nice and apologize for that jackass ruining your date."

Adam shook his head. He hadn't expected to be having this conversation, not after last night's scuffle. Normally, the Creed men threw a punch and never apologized. It was strange to hear something kind coming out of Michael's mouth.

"Thanks, I appreciate that."

"No problem," Michael said, brushing it off. He raised an eyebrow. "He *was* your date, right?"

Adam gave him a look that screamed '*watch your step*', but of course, Michael didn't take it seriously.

"What? I'm just fucking curious, all right? Can't I make small talk with my little brother? What was his name?"

He wasn't biting, though. "Don't even."

"What?" Michael said again, his voice full of amused teasing. Adam didn't respond. Instead, he took a seat again and dropped his head into his hands, elbows on his knees, sighing.

"Fine, fine, I'm just going to forget about it completely. I swear. Although," he said, shaking his head and laughing, "for a second there last night, that kid looked like he wanted to sock me a good one. He's perfect for you."

Adam whipped his head up and looked at Michael. He was smirking, his eyebrows raised, and Adam couldn't help but huff out a laugh.

"Yeah, I think you're right," he teased back.

Michael laughed and nodded, finally letting the subject drop which Adam was thankful for. As innocently as Michael tried to play it off, Adam didn't want him or Billy to have *anything* to do with Justin. He would keep them on separate planets if he could.

The door to the back hall flung back open and Billy's Timberlands echoed off the floor. He looked around and raised his arms up in question before dropping them down to his sides.

"Where the fuck are Jones and Miller?" he asked.

"Ripping a butt outside," Michael said. "Why don't you go grab them? It's time to go."

"Fine." Despite the sour attitude, at least Billy's eyes looked clear and his nose didn't seem to be running. *Thank God for small miracles.* He walked across the room to the front door and shoved it open with a great push.

"Hurry the fuck up, you two!" he shouted out. Michael shook his head and stood up from the back of the car to slam the trunk shut. Jones and Miller came bopping in and they chatted as Jones pulled the car keys out of his pocket and hit the button on the key fob to unlock the car.

"Come on, everybody, let's go," Michael said, shouting over them and looking around the warehouse one last time.

"Yeah, let's fucking get it done!" Miller cheered, and Billy nodded.

"Let's hurry the fuck up so we can get back and get wasted."

"Yeah, yeah, yeah, you idiot," Michael grumbled. He shoved past Billy and swung open the passenger-side door. He turned his head toward Adam. "Come on, man. Let's go."

"Yeah, hold up, I'm coming."

God, he wished he had the time to call Justin now, even for just a minute. It had only been a couple of hours since he'd seen him but still, he wished he could hear his soft, easy voice. He loved the way the tender, breathy sound of it soaked under his skin and made his blood warm.

He thought for a moment about sending a text and pulled out his phone. For a second, an even crazier thought was there but then he immediately shoved it back down. If he *had* been on the phone, it might have just slipped out, uncontained and honest in the spur of the moment. In a shocking slap of reality that he hadn't been expecting from himself, he had wanted to say the 'L' word. He had wanted to tell Justin how much he cared about him and how badly he wanted them to have a chance to be together.

Thank God he hadn't sent it, though. A text was not how he wanted to tell him. He would, later. As soon as he was done and free and tucked away somewhere quiet where he could call Justin and hear his voice.

"Come on, man, get in the friggin car!" Billy shouted. He slid inside the backseat and slammed the car door shut with stupid force. Adam tucked his cell phone back into his jacket pocket, headed over to open the car door with a slow breath out and climbed into the driver's seat.

Chapter Twenty-Eight

Justin felt that he could finally let out a long, deep breath of relief when they unlocked the door to the apartment and Jewels shuffled in past him. The afternoon had crept by at a snail's pace and even though it was only eight-thirty at night, it felt as if three whole days had passed since the sun had come up that morning.

At least he'd been able to sit with Jewels once she'd been brought up to her room. When they'd rolled her in on a hospital bed, she'd been awake and chatting away with the young male nurses who were pushing her in. The sight of her up and talking away had melted the rest of the lingering fear right from Justin's chest and 'relieved' didn't quite seem to cut it—it was something much happier than relieved.

The afternoon had still dragged on as they waited for the official okay to go.

All the two of them had been able to do was sit and watch the boxy television bolted up high on the wall. It had only picked up the public channels, but had been better than nothing. Sitting there had been like another round of torture, a psychological pain that had nagged and nagged. This time it had been the worried waiting for Adam that had hung over Justin's head with a mix of conflicting feelings.

There was such an exciting swell of happiness that came from the thought of Adam being his. Justin knew he wanted that more than anything else now. He had never imagined a person, never mind a man as overwhelmingly handsome and thrilling as Adam, would find him attractive. Not just attractive even. Adam thought that he was gorgeous and stunning. Just remembering the way he had purred such words against his lips last night made Justin's heart skip and his cock throb in his jeans.

It was impossible to be completely happy, though, not when Adam was out somewhere, doing something so dangerous that he couldn't tell Justin what. How could Adam say that after he was done tonight, the two of them would be free to see each other? His brother, Michael, had said that Adam had crossed a line being with him.

What did Adam have up his sleeve to be able to promise that they could be together? Justin had no idea, and the waiting and curiosity compounded together to make him painfully restless.

Jewels settled into her cherished recliner with a long and well-deserved sigh.

"If we never do that again, it'll be fine by me," she said. She tugged the crocheted afghan off the back of her chair, and Justin helped her unfold it and drape it over her lap.

"Yeah, I agree. How are you feeling?"

"Not too bad. Just a little tired after such a long day, but it's nice to be home."

"Let me get you a glass of water," he offered, starting to head for the kitchen.

"Justin, sweetie? Come here for a second."

His heart sank into his stomach, but he stepped back over. He got to the side of her chair, but it felt like he towered over her as she sat. So he knelt beside her, reaching a hand up to the arm of the chair when she tried to reach for his. She folded his hand in hers and her skin was soft but thin over the bones of her hand when she squeezed.

Her face looked older too. The little wrinkles around her face seemed to have deepened in just one day. Maybe it was just the somber look on her face combined with the toll of surgery on top of it. Either way, it was clear that she had something on her mind that was itching to get out.

"I know that today was tough on you, sweetie," she finally said.

He couldn't help but let out a huff of a laugh. "Tough on me? I'm not the one that went through heart surgery."

Jewels laughed, strong and loud like she always did. "That's true, but that doesn't mean it wasn't hard on you too."

He was quiet. He *had* been nervous, and scared beyond belief, but he hadn't wanted her to see that.

"I know," she continued, "that life has dealt us some tough cards. And I know that when so many people you love leave you, that it can make getting close to someone new scarier. We both learned that the hard way."

A hard lump formed in his throat, caught right above his chest where his heart was thumping. He couldn't talk, but he nodded slowly.

"The terrible truth is, Justin, that I won't be around forever either."

"Jewels…"

"Hold on, let me finish," she said. "That's just how it works. I don't make the rules. Mother Nature does. But I want to tell you something that I've been meaning to for a while. The truth, the *real* truth, is that in the end we all lose the people we love. But that should never mean that we *stop loving*. We should never stop looking and giving and receiving love, because in the end, that's what makes it all worth it. All the pain…" She shook her head in a gentle motion. "All the pain is far overshadowed in the end by the love."

Hot tears were burning at the corners of his eyes and he swallowed hard to move the lump in his throat, but it was painful and too stubborn. Jewels' eyes were wet-looking as well, but she kept talking.

"And while I have done and seen and loved a lot in this world, the one thing that I regret more than anything else is the death of my daughter. She…" Jewels' voice wavered, and he wanted to tell her that it was okay, but his own voice was lost.

"She had been filled with such happiness. I wish you could have seen her happy, Justin, I really do, because she was so beautiful. But in the end, she died unhappy. Unhappy and chasing that happiness in a needle."

The tears finally did spill over his eyes and he had to drop his head. He didn't want her to see, even though he knew that she *had* seen. It was too sore a spot inside him that her words stabbed at, and it was too much to look at her as she kept speaking.

"So that's why when I got you, Justin, you were the one ray of happiness in my life again. And I want, more than anything else in this world, for you to know that you should never stop striving for what makes you *truly* happy. You will always have my support, no matter what. And one day, I know that you'll find someone who will fight in your corner and strive to find happiness right alongside you. That's what friends, family and loved ones are for."

The tears were still sneaking out and he tried to force them down, but he looked back up at her. He rubbed the wetness off his face quickly with the back of his free arm, using the old sleeve of his hoodie to get most of the tears off. He tried to give her a half-smile but her face broke into a huge grin and she laughed softly.

"So, no more crying, honey. Not today. Today was a good day overall, right?"

"Yeah," he said, trying to slow the racing of his heart and brush all those depressing thoughts away. She was right. Today had been pretty good overall. The thought of Adam leaning in and kissing him in the hospital cafe, asking him to be his, swam into his head for the hundredth time and that giddy feeling bubbled in his chest again.

"Yeah, it was. Adam, uh, today…he asked me to be his boyfriend."

Her mouth dropped open for a second before she broke into a huge grin.

"He did?" she whispered. She tried to tuck her smile away, but if Justin had to say, she looked sort of proud.

"Well, well, well then. And I'm guessing that you told this handsome gentleman yes?"

He tried to swallow his thumping heart down. As mortifying as it was, at least Jewels seemed to be loving this drama as it unfolded.

"Yes."

"Well, today *was* a good day then, huh?"

He laughed again. "Yeah, I'd say so."

"Then how about we put a movie on and tuck ourselves in with some snacks? I feel like I've been asleep all day and I'm not quite ready to go to bed yet. Plus," she added, "it's been a while since we watched something together."

He couldn't say no to that. He knew in the back of his mind that it would be almost impossible to focus on anything with the nagging worry of Adam flashing through his head every other minute. It was as if his phone was burning a hole in his pocket while he waited for it to buzz. Either way, at least a movie might help pass the time, so he nodded.

"Yeah, sure, Jewels. I'll go grab us something from the kitchen, and you find us something good to watch."

"All right, can do," she said. He headed out while she turned the television on and started flipping through the channels.

Chapter Twenty-Nine

Adam pulled the SUV out of the warehouse and Jones kept a short, neat distance behind him while they headed out. The barren streets around the industrial waterfront were silent as the cars passed, the gravel crunching under the tires. He turned them off Elm Hill Ave and toward the expressway. It was quiet inside the car while he merged onto the highway and took them the short distance over the Robert Kennedy Bridge down to Manhattan. They were going to take the long way over to Jersey. The long, *long* way.

Normally, FDR Drive, the parkway that ran down the eastside of Manhattan along the East River, was a hot mess during the day. It cleared up considerably though by the time nine o'clock rolled around, and he felt like they were moving at a good clip.

Michael seemed to have his head on a swivel as Adam drove. Certain cars or trucks passed by and had him craning his neck around to get a good look inside, as though he were expecting someone he recognized at any moment. Adam wasn't stupid. He knew that

Michael was keeping an eye out for anyone following them, but he also hadn't noticed a single person beside Jones and Miller trailing them, who never got too close or too many cars behind. Either way, he wished that Michael would relax a little. Agitated energy was pouring off him and the restlessness was only going to get Billy worked up again.

By the time they had driven down the whole length of the city and were hooking up around Battery Park at the very southern tip of the island, Michael finally leaned back in his seat.

"You know, we're making great time, and I don't see a single one of those Perez fucks."

Billy leaned forward in the back seat. "I told you, Mike. They would never have the balls to fuck with us."

"Maybe, but I still didn't want them sticking their fucking noses in our shit like they love to do. You know how Arlo Perez *dreams* he could be in the same league as Dad."

Billy scoffed. "Yeah, but after we caught his guys poaching our spots at St. Mary's, I haven't seen one of them even close. Maybe we scared 'em back up to Claremont where they all came out of the woodwork to begin with."

"I wouldn't hold my breath," Michael replied, shaking his head. "Arlo might have a lot of young-blood junkies working for him, but they've got more stupid than brains. Sooner or later they're gonna try to push us out."

"Well, good-fucking-luck." Billy slumped back in his seat.

Adam had never gotten into a confrontation with anyone from the Perez gang. He sort of made it a point to avoid most of the shit Michael and Billy did all day long, but he had heard his brothers talk about the fast-rising Latin-American gang leader and his lackeys on plenty of occasions. He still remembered the night two months ago when he had found his brothers back at the warehouse. Michael had sported a massive black eye like a prize-fighter and Billy had been amped and rambling about the coolest fistfight that had gone down in St. Mary's Park.

Defending a couple of spots for selling coke was one thing, but transporting *four million dollars* in product was another thing altogether, and Michael wasn't dumb enough to let some measly wins around the neighborhood make him cocky and let his guard down.

"Just keep your eyes peeled for me, yeah?" he asked Adam, his voice full of careful warning.

"Yeah," he agreed. "Of course."

The next few minutes went by in silence. He didn't mind—it let him focus on driving. He took the turn at Watts Street to loop around for the Holland Tunnel. A sign on the side of the street warned that all hazardous materials were restricted in the tunnel, and that vehicle inspections were subject to happen beyond this point. A cold wave of ice flooded his veins, but Michael next to him looked as uninterested as possible. A police officer in a yellow safety vest was on the corner, leaning against one of the cement barrier blocks next to a police booth. Even *he* looked like he couldn't care less, staring blankly at car after car with a hundred-yard gaze. Adam drove past him, down into the yellow-lit cement tube, and watched in the mirror as Jones passed right by as well.

The tunnel was a long stretch beneath the Hudson River. The two lanes of traffic whipped through, and Adam took them smoothly as the evenly spaced bulbs on the ceiling passed by in hypnotizing patterns of flashing lights in the dark. It would have been nice to just get all the way through and finish up the last stretch of the journey toward Newark in quiet peace, but of course, he was never that lucky.

Billy shifted in the back and leaned forward. "Hey, guys. Check this out."

He glanced back in the rearview mirror and caught Billy pulling a gun out of the back of his jeans.

"Oh, what the fuck, Billy."

Michael whipped his head around and did a double-take. "Where the hell did you get that piece of shit?" he asked.

"What the fuck are you talking about? This thing is goddamn cool!"

"It's a fucking mistake, that's what it is. Is that a *Skorpion*?"

"Yeah, man," Billy grinned. He spoke with a sort of amused reverence, twisting and turning the monstrosity of a gun in his hand. Headlights flashed and bounced across its glossy, polished, blue-tinted steel. "It's the Skorpion machine pistol. This thing came right from Kyoto. The boys and me went down to Fulton Street the other day and I picked myself out the nicest thing there. Isn't it fucking gorgeous?"

"Jesus fucking Christ. Are you brain dead?" Michael yelled at Billy. "Do you know how much more fucking trouble we'll be in if the goddamn police see you with that piece of shit while we're moving *this much product*?"

"What are you talking about?" Billy asked, playing dumb.

"Having a fucking handgun is one thing, but your stupid ass could put us away for a decade, easy!"

"Relax, relax," Billy said.

"How am I supposed to relax when you keep being a fucking idiot?!"

"Okay, okay," Adam interjected. "Billy, put that thing away before you shoot it off in the car. I'm trying to drive over here, for Christ's sake."

"What the hell is wrong with you guys?" Billy scoffed. He tucked the gun away again, even if it was with a scowl on his face.

"Just cool it back there," Michael said. "And I better not see that fucking thing again for the rest of the night, Bill. Especially when we get to the garage. You pull that out while I'm talking to Moretti and you're gonna get us all blasted."

"Come on, I'm not that fucking dumb."

"Yeah, well, you really make me wonder sometimes."

"Oh, fuck off."

"Yeah, yeah," Michael grunted. He shifted in his seat and his temper was back to a simmer again by the time they got out of the tunnel and through Jersey City. He just stared ahead with steely eyes, scanning the highway as they cruised along. Finally, he broke the heavy silence.

"Adam, you're going to be taking a left after we go through the station. After a set of lights up ahead sometime."

"Okay, sure." He kept his eyes peeled as they drove, but he glanced up to the rearview mirror from time to time to check on Billy. He was sulking out the window, his gaze lost out on the lights and signs of towering building after building. Newark wasn't too different from Manhattan, just smaller in general, and Billy seemed entertained enough with the busy view to keep himself distracted.

Adam turned onto Raymond Boulevard that ran along a river and right through the tunnels of traffic that stretched out next to the humongous train station. Buses and cars went under the heavy cement epicenter of a building and under arches that read *NEWARK PENN STATION* in big, fading letters.

"Look over there." Michael pointed up ahead. "See that sign on the left? That's the hotel. Right before the entrance should be the garage."

"Yeah, I see it."

"Good, get us over there."

Billy made a scoffing sound in the backseat. "This place is a fucking dump. Just like the city," he said.

Michael nodded. "Everywhere's the same, Bill. It's all a fucking dump."

No one argued with Michael's pessimistic, sage advice and he turned to Adam again when they approached the set of lights before their destination and stopped at the red.

"Okay, when we get in there, just head up. I'm gonna tell you where to park. And I want the two of you to both sit as still as fucking statues. No talking. No moving. No going to pull out your fucking cell phones, you hear me?"

Adam nodded and Billy grunted an affirmative.

"If these guys get even a little nervous, we'll be in big fucking trouble. So, I mean it. You got that, Billy?"

"*Yes*, okay?"

The light turned green and Adam brought them up to the garage entrance, turning left and driving them up the ramp to get them inside. The place was desolate. He took the car around the corner of the first level of the garage, Jones' headlights flickering around the corner behind them as they went up the next ramp. On the third floor, three cars were parked together in the back corner. Michael shifted in his seat again, looking dead ahead. "Stay cool, boys," he said. He gestured toward the cars. "And bring us up right by them. Back just a bit. That's perfect."

Adam turned the SUV into a space the row behind a sleek black Lincoln Continental. He turned his headlights off, so they weren't pointed directly into the backseat of the Lincoln and Jones swung into the spot right next to him and did the same to his lights.

Two silver vans, flashy Mercedes models nonetheless, flanked the Lincoln. All three cars had New Jersey plates. After a few seconds, both the driver and passenger-side doors of the vans opened and four massive men in matching black suits got out. Adam caught the way shoulder holsters peeked out from under their open jackets when their beefy arms swung while they walked.

Three of the goons shuffled into a line behind the Lincoln. The fourth walked over and opened the back door for a middle-aged man to step out. Adam had never met this Moretti guy, but he wasn't surprised in the least by the man who got out of the car.

Moretti wore a tailored suit that looked like it had been woven out of strands of silver. Sparkling cufflinks of crystal and what was surely white-gold flashed at the wrists of his pristine white dress shirt peeking out from the sleeves of his jacket.

His face was lined with age but was too tan, like he spent ample time in a tanning bed when he wasn't out making million-dollar deals in an hour or two. His hair was dark and swept up in a pompadour like an old-timey greaser, but the sides at his temples were silvered. The mustache and goatee on his face was already completely gray.

Michael turned to Adam and gave him one last look.

"Cover me, all right?" he whispered.

"Yeah," he said. The hard press of the gun at his back against his spine reminded him that it was there, waiting patiently, ready to help at any second if he wanted it. He didn't want it, though. He wanted it off his skin and away from him forever. Soon, very soon now, and it would be.

Michael got out of the car, walked right up to Moretti and said something, probably introducing himself. Moretti shockingly reached out and shook Michael's hand. He had to know Michael as Shawn Creed's eldest son. There was just no way a man like him would shake some lackey's hand. Moretti opened his mouth to speak but he was too quiet to pick out the words, even with the spacious garage to amplify the sound. Adam wished he had left the window cracked so he could hear.

Moretti's face barely moved. In an eerie way, he reminded Adam of his father. He was statue-like in a manner that only came with having so much money he never needed to lift a finger or break a sweat. No matter who he spoke to, it would always be to someone beneath him. Adam wondered if this man also had a family. Did he have some trophy wife with as many kids he could trick her into pushing out? Did he raise his sons to do his dirty work for him too?

Moretti gave a stoic nod and Michael whipped around. He gestured to Adam. *Pop the trunk.* Adam reached to press the button and both he and Jones opened the trunk but made no other move. Two of

Moretti's bodyguards flanked off from their formation and went to work hoisting the boxes of cocaine out and over to their own vans. Michael stood in place, watching the men work. No one moved a muscle except for the guards.

Only when the very last crate was in place in the back of the vans did Moretti nod to the guard on his right. He reached into the backseat of the Lincoln and stood back up, carrying two simple black briefcases in his hands. He brought them up to Moretti, who glanced at them and gave a final nod. The guard then stepped forward and handed them off to Michael who took them with a thanks that Adam could hear now that the trunk was popped open.

Moretti's voice was still a soft mumble, but he must have been pleased, because he spun around and slid back into his car. A guard closed the door for him and the rest of them got back into their vans as if it were a choreographed routine. They started up their cars and, in perfect formation, pulled out from their spots and headed back down the garage, their tires squealing on the garage floor as they turned the corner and disappeared.

Michael uprooted himself from his spot and walked over to Jones' car. He threw one of the briefcases into the back and shut the trunk with a slam. He did the same to their car and still no one said a word until Michael opened the passenger door and fell back into his seat with a huff.

"Get us out of here."

The way back up to the Bronx was supposed to be easier than the way down. None of that bullshit of driving the whole length of Manhattan where traffic could be a living hell, suddenly and without mercy, on even the quietest seeming of nights.

All they had to do was head straight north out of Newark toward I-95. Once there, it was nothing but fifteen minutes of easy driving through New Jersey to the George Washington Bridge and across the river into the Bronx, Jones and Miller a perfect three-cars behind, cruising along just like every other good-doer. They were approaching the halfway mark when Billy spoke.

"Hey, Mike. Let's go out later."

Michael didn't bother to turn his head to answer. "No."

A flash of headlights in Adam's rearview caught his attention. A mustard-yellow car, a Jeep Wrangler most likely by the shape of it, moved from the far-left lane and across all four lanes of traffic to the right, without any blinker.

"We should be going out and celebrating!" Billy argued. "After the haul we just made?"

"No. Like I said, we're hanging low tonight. And probably tomorrow night too."

"But *why*?" Billy moaned.

Adam watched as the Jeep swerved back out of the right lane, through the middle and all the way to the left again. It passed by Jones' car and hung back, driving side by side with it for a moment.

"Why?" Michael asked. "Because you think it's a good idea to go flaunting around the city after we just made an important and delicate arrangement? With a guy who could pay a dozen different men to put a sniper's bullet through your dumb skull?"

"What, you really think Moretti gives a shit with what we do now? He's got Dad's supply, who fucking cares?"

"Can you really not keep it in your pants for just one night?!"

The Jeep floored it again, zooming past Jones. It was coming up hot on Adam's left side but got stuck behind a tan convertible taking it easy in the fast lane.

"Is it so fucking terrible to want to have some fun?"

"You're impossible."

"Hey," Adam said.

Billy and Michael ignored him.

"*I'm* impossible? You're the one that acts like he's got a pole up his ass."

"Only because you're constantly getting into fucking trouble."

The Jeep was almost beside them now, inching even closer. Adam could just make out the shapes of two people in the front, but the windshield was heavily tinted, well past any legal shade, and it was impossible in the dark. The motion of another car behind the Jeep caught his eye. It was another Wrangler, this one white, and it pulled into the left lane right behind the first one.

"Our whole friggin' livelihood is trouble!"

"Guys!" Adam shouted. Michael, who had been leaning back to yell at Billy, whipped his head around at the sudden shouting.

"What? What is it?"

"I think someone's following us."

The blood drained from Michael's face and his eyes turned hard. He started scanning the cars around him, his eyebrows furrowed. "Where?"

"Two Jeeps. On the left. They're coming up fast."

"For how long?"

"I don't know. I just saw them a minute ago."

"*Fuck.*"

The yellow Jeep glided right up beside them.

"Who the fuck are they?" Billy asked.

"I don't know, I don't know," Michael snapped.

The Jeep started pulling ahead at a normal clip, past them.

It got a car-length ahead and Adam eased back on the gas to let it get some distance away. He started to get hopeful that it was just a false alarm, but then the Jeep changed lanes again without a blinker. Right in front of them.

"I don't like the looks of this," Michael whispered.

The yellow Jeep pushed forward, then, without any warning, slammed on its brakes. Adam had just enough time to hit the brakes himself.

"Jesus! What the fuck are they doing?" Michael bellowed. Adam just tightened his grip on the steering wheel and got ready. He checked his mirrors, keeping all options open.

"They're trying to make us stop," he said. "Whatever way they can."

"Just don't let them hit us," Michael ordered.

"I'll try my best."

He wasn't going to shake them on the highway like this. Chances were, all they were going to do was cause a ten-car pile-up when the Jeeps turned them into a pancake.

They whizzed past a sign on the side of the highway and Adam had to take a chance.

"Hold on, guys," he said. They rounded a tight bend and the green exit sign was suddenly right there. Before he could overthink anything, he turned the wheel with a sharp pull and swerved off the highway. The tires squealed and the whole SUV try to list to the side, but he got a handle on it and the tires caught traction again.

It wasn't enough to trick the yellow Jeep, however. It also banked right and peeled off with the exit, managing to fall right behind them. The white Jeep wasn't as quick and when it tried to follow them, it nearly crashed into another car it hadn't seen in the way. Adam caught sight of it in the rearview mirror, now a couple cars back but still on their tail. As they turned off the highway, he saw Jones and Miller pass by, unbothered and zooming down the highway. They probably had no clue what to do, but hopefully they would just stick to the plan. He was going to do everything he could to shake these assholes.

The off-ramp merged onto Route 46 eastbound. This stretch of highway was going to be tough, though. There were only two lanes and traffic moved much slower. Both sides of the highway were lined with various gas stations, restaurants, shopping plazas and hotels. Slow cars were turning off and on everywhere, but the late hour worked to their advantage. He just prayed everyone would stay clear out of their way.

"Where the hell are we going?" Billy yelled.

"A little detour."

Michael nodded. "Okay, but we've still got to shake these pricks somehow."

"Oh," Billy said, "I'll shake them for us."

He reached back and pulled out his Skorpion. Michael spun around in his seat and yelled as Billy rolled down the back window.

"What the fuck are you doing?"

Billy didn't look over, though. He got the window all the way down and took the safety off.

"I'm going to scare them off."

"Like hell you are!"

Billy tightened his grip on the gun and leaned a bit out the window. Michael yelled even louder.

"Billy, I swear to fucking Christ, don't you — "

The sound of the Skorpion going off in the car was deafening. Just as the yellow Jeep swung out into the left lane to try to get ahead of them again, Billy pressed the trigger. Billy had never fired one before and the moment he put enough pressure on the trigger, the semi had already blasted through sixteen rounds in a burst of noise and smoke that almost popped Adam's eardrums in an instant. The whole world went silent before a high-pitched siren faded in while his ears rang.

Two of the bullets hit the Jeep. One hit the windshield at a funny angle and ricocheted with barely a scratch to the glass. The other hit the driver's side mirror and sent the whole thing smashing off. The Jeep swerved but they had been too close to the cement barrier dividing the highway. The front bumper hit the cement, scraping and jostling them back to the right, and the Jeep lost control as it drove. It overcorrected and Adam caught the way it slammed back into the cement. The front headlight smashed out in a wink and the force of the second collision was bad enough that the Jeep instantly came to a stop in the fast lane, falling behind them, while they sped away.

"Fuck yeah! Did you see that?" Billy screamed. His voice was still a little wobbly-sounding as Adam's hearing phased back in. "That fucking did the trick!"

Michael reached back and pulled the gun clear out of Billy's hand. Billy immediately went to argue, but the look on Michael's face was almost enough to put Billy in the ground right then and there.

"What the *fuck* did I say? You're going to get us all killed or fucking locked up!"

Adam didn't have time to focus on the two of them shouting. The highway up ahead had a sharp turn coming up fast. While almost all the traffic behind them stopped in confusion from the wrecked yellow Jeep, the white one hadn't given up. It was behind them a ways, but he could tell it was them for sure when they floored it closer. Worse though, two cars were driving side-by-side up ahead, blocking the whole highway. His only hope was to take the tight inner breakdown lane and pull ahead.

He whipped them around the corner and the back tire hit the curb for a second, making the car bounce before it straightened back out. Billy went sliding across the backseat and thumped to the floor, cursing a blue streak.

"For Christ's sake, Billy," Adam yelled. "Get your seatbelt on!"

"Oh, *shut up*," he groaned.

"Do you have to fucking fight me over everything?"

The car behind them made the turn easy and followed.

"Just put it on, Bill!" Michael shouted. "Before you go flying out the goddamn window!"

"Fine, fine!"

Adam drove up too fast to a blue minivan driving in the lane in front of them, but he managed to skirt around it. The Perezes were almost on top of them again. He thought for a second that the Jeep was going to smash right into the back bumper of the van, but they moved directly behind him and skated by with an inch to spare. Once he was past the van, he swung back to the more open right lane.

The white Jeep kept to the left, however, but it wasn't trying to pass them anymore. Their passenger side window was open, and Adam caught the glint of a gun barrel at the last second.

Four gunshots blasted out in the night air. Adam's driver-side window exploded inward with a crack of broken glass. Shards of glass hit the side of his face and rained down into his lap, but he barely felt it in comparison to the bright flash of sharp pain that screamed from his left biceps. He didn't have time to look, but it felt like a huge piece of glass must have cut through the material of his jacket and into the flesh of his arm. Almost as quick as it came, though, the pain disappeared.

Billy, on the other hand, started screaming. The piercing shrieks sounded like an animal in surprised pain and agony. Adam glanced back — he was holding his right hand with his left, looking at it and screaming like he had stuck it in a hidden wasp's nest and was now paying the price.

"Jesus Christ! What the fuck?" Michael screamed over him.

"It's my goddamn *hand*!"

Adam had to think fast. Signs for the George Washington Bridge were passing overhead. They were going to have to go through the tolls, and tolls always meant police cruisers hanging around waiting. They would be screwed if he didn't lose the Jeep soon.

He had a couple seconds to brake and he swung them into the huge entrance of an empty gas station along the road. He pressed the gas pedal all the way down to the floor as he whipped them by the pumps and back out through the other exit, merging them back onto the highway and around a sedan with hardly a foot between them.

The bang of metal smashing into metal was loud enough that he jumped in his seat. He looked in the mirror and there was the Jeep, passenger side of the front crumpled in and practically fused with one of the bottom posts of the metal sign for the gas station. The towering sign was bolted into the ground by the exit and had stopped, and completely totaled, the car. There was no way that Jeep was moving another inch.

"WOOOOO!" Michael bellowed out. It was deafening in the tiny space, even with the blasted window open, and Adam's ears ached.

He finally took his foot off the gas. The adrenaline flooded in his system made the world lurch back into regular motion, like a spaceship leaving hyper-speed, as the SUV crept back down to a more reasonable pace.

"WOO!" Michael yelled again. "That was goddamn amazing!"

"Amazing? You call *this* amazing?" Billy hollered, holding out his bleeding hand and shaking it in Michael's face. Rivulets of blood were pouring off, dripping and splashing into the armrest, the seats and the carpet on the floor. The iron scent of it was powerful, even with air whipping in from the broken window. Adam risked a glance over and winced at the mangled flesh in the center of Billy's hand, like he'd run it through a meat grinder yet somehow kept his fingers intact.

"Just wrap the damn thing up in something!" Michael said. He sounded annoyed, like it couldn't matter less that Billy had been goddamn shot. "Take your jacket off and wrap it up tight."

"Then what? Huh? It's *destroyed*! They're gonna have to cut the whole fucking thing off!"

"Oh, come on," Michael argued. "Quit being such a pussy. It's not that bad." Billy scoffed out an incredulous laugh. "It's not! We'll get back and get you all patched up. Just quit bitching."

"Let's shoot you in the hand and see how much you bitch!"

"Just shut your fucking mouth! We've got another goddamn toll to go through. Wrap your hand up and tuck it out of sight. Adam, roll the window down all the way so we're not driving around with a blasted window."

There was no way they were going through a toll booth where a person could see the bullet holes and the shot man in the backseat. Thankfully, he only had to drop them down to an easy speed and they passed through the automated lane, the GO sign turning green as it picked up the transponder on the car and let them by.

A set of police cruisers were parked off to the side just like Adam had guessed. Both were idled and their occupants talking to each other through their open windows. Neither of them turned their heads when they drove by.

Michael turned to him and beamed a smile.

"Take us fucking home."

Chapter Thirty

Adam pulled the SUV back onto Elm Hill Avenue and swung it right in front of their warehouse. The street was still empty and quiet, but he spied Jones and Miller's SUV parked off to the side of the building, tucked into the shadows.

Billy groaned. It was long and pitiful, like a whining child. He had wrapped his hand up in his denim jacket. The bunched material was stained with huge patches of blood and it had to hurt like a son of a bitch.

"*Sssshit!*" he hissed between gritted teeth. "If I ever see Arlo Perez again, I'm gonna fucking end him."

Billy cursed like a sailor as Michael all but dragged him out of the seat. Adam rolled his eyes. It wasn't like he had gotten shot in the leg, after all. He could still friggin' walk.

"Miiiiiiike," Billy whined. "You've gotta take me to the hospital."

"Well, thanks to your little stunt, we can't. What, you think we can just walk into the E.R. and explain how you were shot in the hand? While there are probably reports out of a shoot-out on fucking I-95 on every cop's radio in a twenty-mile radius of here by now?"

"Oh, come on," Billy cried. Adam had to help Michael keep him upright as they walked, and they each took an arm and shuffled him to the entrance.

"Don't worry," Michael reassured him. "We're gonna do the next best thing. But first, we've gotta get you inside, buddy."

They reached the door, but Jones and Miller must have locked it behind them. They had to wait for Michael to fish out the keys from his jeans. Billy whimpered and shuffled over to the concrete wall where he propped himself up with a huff.

"Hey, Adam," Michael said, getting the key out.

"Yeah?"

"I can get Billy inside. You go grab the case from the trunk."

"Okay, sure."

He turned back to the car and hit the button on the key fob. The trunk popped open and there was the plain black briefcase just lying there. It had slid during the drive, but the latches had held fast, and it was intact.

Half of all the money from the trade was inside it. Two of the four million dollars. It was heavier than he'd thought.

He slammed the trunk closed and headed back to the front door. It was propped open with a broken cinder block on the front steps, so he kicked it to the side and stepped in. Jones and Miller were standing in the main room, crowded around Billy who Michael had gotten safely into a folding chair.

"What the fuck *happened*?" Miller asked, gesturing to Billy. "What happened to you guys?"

"What the fuck happened?" Billy sassed. "I almost got my hand shot clean off!"

Jones looked to Michael, desperate for answers.

"Was it the Perezes?"

"I think so."

"In the Jeeps?"

He nodded. "One of you, go grab some oxy from the back room for me. Billy's gonna need a couple."

Billy groaned again from his seat, his legs sprawled out as he tossed himself from side to side. His forehead was beaded with sweat and strands of his long hair stuck to his face.

"Okay, hold on," Jones said. He and Miller were still flabbergasted. "But how in the hell did you guys get away? Do you have the money still?"

"Right here," Adam said. He lifted the case and Michael reached out to take it from him.

"Yeah. Adam here did some quick thinking and we lost them on 46 before the bridge."

"Holy crap," Miller gasped. His eyes were bulging out of his chubby face. "No one else followed you here, did they?"

Adam shook his head. "I don't think so."

"Are we fucking done here?" Billy shouted. He looked like he was two seconds from foaming at the mouth in anger. "If you ladies are done clucking like some goddamn hens, I would *love* to get some fucking medical attention."

"Hold on, Bill. Jones is getting you a little something for the pain. I'm gonna call Miles and see if he's still around."

"What the hell is Miles going to do?"

"He's got medical experience."

"He worked in a goddamn morgue for two years!"

"And so he knows how to stitch up a wound," Michael said. It wasn't the best plan, but it was probably the best they were going to get. Miles knew the game so there would be no awkward lying, and hopefully his stitching was good enough.

Billy let out a frustrated groan, dragging it out with his whole breath. Jones came flying through the double doors from the back, handed Billy two pills and popped open a can of beer for him to chase them down. Adam took the second to nudge Michael's arm.

"Hey, uh, can I just talk to you for a minute?" he asked. Michael turned to him with a quizzical look, but then gave an easy nod.

"Sure. Come 'ere. Jones? Get Bill a new towel to wrap his hand up in and start getting him into your car. I'll be right there."

"Okay, Mike."

Jones and Miller scrambled to cater to Billy while he moaned, but Adam followed behind Michael, who headed for the back hall, briefcase in hand. They walked all the way back to the clubhouse. Michael flicked the lights on, stepped over to the fire-proof safe and spun the dial. The other case of money was sitting on the floor right beside the safe and Michael grabbed it to put both inside. The money would stay there overnight until he hand-delivered it tomorrow to their father.

"What did you want to talk about?"

"Here, this is yours." Adam pulled the snub-nose revolver from his back and held it out for Michael, who stared at it as though he'd never seen it before. After a moment, he reached out and took it. He turned it over a couple times as if admiring the polished steel as it glinted in the low light from the old standing lamp nearby.

"Look, Adam," Michael sighed. "I don't want there to be bad blood between us. You're my brother. Nothing is ever going to change that, whatever's happened in the past."

Adam couldn't tell if he meant Justin or their mother. Probably both, if Adam had to take a guess. Michael continued.

"I'm just trying to say thank you. For tonight. Shit could have gone a lot different if you hadn't gotten us outta there."

"It's all right, Michael. I just did the best I could."

"And I appreciate that," he said, slapping a hand on his shoulder like he loved to do. "I'm proud of you. You have a lot of potential here."

Adam's throat felt dry and his lungs felt empty. "Thanks."

"No problem. Are you sure you don't want to keep the gun? For just a little longer?"

It was obvious that Michael was extending an olive branch, but Adam couldn't take it.

"Thanks, really, but it's yours."

"If you're sure." He tucked the beloved revolver into the back of his jeans. "Why don't you get outta here. I can take care of Billy."

"Okay..." Now that it was finally happening, Adam had a hard time making himself leave. His feet felt heavy. If what he had planned next worked out, this would be the last time he ever saw Michael.

"Miles will get him all patched up. Don't worry," Michael said. "I'll give you a call in a couple of days."

"Sounds good," he lied.

"Come on. Let's get back out there. I'm sure Billy's ready to go." Michael slapped Adam's arm again, but this time Adam winced in pain. Michael pulled his hand back and frowned. "Holy shit, you're bleeding."

Adam looked down at his arm. He had completely forgotten about it from earlier. "Oh yeah, I think some glass from my window must have got me."

"Bullshit." Michael shook his head. He grabbed for Adam's arm and inspected the ripped material of his leather jacket and T-shirt sleeve underneath. "The car's safety glass. It doesn't shatter into shards — it's made to crumble."

"Really?"

Michael pulled the torn fabric apart and uncovered a long, weeping slash across the outside of Adam's arm. Bits of brown, caking blood clotted the edges, but the wound was still leaking.

"Damn, Adam. A bullet grazed you."

"Wait, really? I barely felt it."

"Yeah." Michael wiped his hands on his dark-wash jeans. "Do you want to come with us to Miles'?"

"No, no." Adam shook his head. "I'll just clean it up at home."

"You sure?" Michael didn't seem too concerned with it, though.

"Absolutely. You go take care of Billy. He definitely needs it more."

"That's for sure. I can't stand all the bitching," Michael said with a chuckle.

The two of them stepped out into the hall and Billy was audible way before they got to the swinging doors. He was bent over in his seat, clutching his wrapped hand to his stomach, but he seemed just as lively still.

"Let's go, everyone!" Michael shouted.

"Thank fuck," Billy said, sighing with relief. "It's about freaking time."

"Yeah, yeah, come on."

Jones and Miller scooped Billy under his armpits and shuffled him out the door. Michael followed close behind them, saying something to Billy that Adam couldn't quite make out. No one paid him a lick of attention as they left. He waited until they were out to the car before he grabbed the key to the garbage pit from the tiny hook on the wall by the front door. It would be returned to its place before any of them even came back to the warehouse.

* * * *

Adam wanted the night to be over. He wanted it all to be done with. There was still one hurdle left though, and arguably the one he had been dreading the most. Justin was waiting for him and Adam almost sent a text, but he was so close — just a little bit farther — and everything would be over. Surely Justin would understand once he explained.

Their father's penthouse was on the thirtieth floor of a skyscraper that overlooked a small park in Hunt's Point. The neighborhood was surrounded by banks, industrial companies from sheet metal to tubing and the whole block was probably filled with more millionaires than he cared to know about.

His backpack was heavy and he carried it on one shoulder. His duffel bag he carried with his left hand, but the slight weight was enough to make his arm burn, the biceps sizzling in pain from the bullet. Warm rivulets of blood oozed down his arm toward his wrist from time to time, making his skin sticky as it dried, but it was going to have to wait. At least it was dark, and it was nearly impossible to see the tear in his black jacket.

The building's lobby was dead empty at this hour of the night, the small cafe tucked into the back-left corner barren. In a couple more hours the early birds would be getting up and starting the busy day, but not yet.

The light above the elevator blinked off and the doors slid open for Adam to step in. It was dead silent as it took him up to the thirtieth floor except for the quiet hum of the cables and machinery.

There were just a handful of moments before he was at his father's floor. He hadn't technically *seen* his father since he had moved down to the Lower East Side, but it felt like just last week. He didn't have to be living under Shawn Creed's roof to still be living under Shawn Creed. He had tried to escape by moving out, but it didn't work like that. He knew that now, and no amount of nervous anticipation was going to change his mind.

He was doing this for Justin *and* himself. He had to.

When the elevator doors opened, he didn't hesitate to step out into their private foyer. He went right for the hallway door, walked inside and punched the code into the security panel on the wall to prevent the alarm from going off. The code was still the same. Some things never changed.

The penthouse felt more like a luxurious, private suite in a pricey hotel, not like someone's home. He didn't know how his brothers could stand to live here. He bet the pampered lifestyle was more tempting than anything else. When Shawn Creed was the kind of man who bought whatever he liked and only the best, who would blame them?

He headed straight back toward his father's office. He knocked twice on the door like he used to and walked right in.

Shawn Creed was at his desk across the room, turned to the side to watch a basketball game on his high-definition, flat-screen TV on the wall, mounted into its own custom entertainment center.

The office didn't look like it had changed a bit, but he couldn't say the same about his father. Shawn was sixty-two and still wearing one of his professionally tailored Italian suits that he took great pride in. The black dress suit was accented by pops of blue at his tie and pocket square, and when he finally turned his head away from the television, Adam saw that they perfectly matched the exact shade of his pale-blue eyes.

"Shouldn't you be at home, lying low after tonight?" Shawn asked, already turning back to the game. He spoke slow and lazy-like but his voice was deep and had a hard edge to it, as if he was just on the brink of anger seeping in.

"I wanted to come see you."

"To talk, I presume." He reached for the remote and muted the television. He turned and looked at him like he was sick of already wasting the two minutes they'd been talking. Everything that wasn't making Shawn Creed money only wasted his time.

"Yeah, to talk," Adam started, dropping his bags at his feet. He took a step closer. "I wanted you to know that I helped Michael and Billy like I was ordered to, and we almost got fucking killed while setting up this new connection that you apparently need."

If his father was shocked by any of this news, it didn't show on his face, so Adam continued.

"But I'm never doing it again."

That seemed to have piqued his father's interest, just a bit. He leaned back in his leather chair and rested his elbows on the arms, tenting his fingers in front of his chest.

"And what exactly does that mean?"

"It means," Adam said, "that I'm never doing any of this shit again. No more drug trades, no more going around stealing from these people every month. I'm not doing it. I won't be a part of any of this anymore."

His father's face was stone solid. The hard clench of muscles in his jaw flexed.

"You mean you won't be a part of this family? Because it's one and the same."

"If that's honestly the only way."

"Is this your latest way of disobeying me?" Shawn asked. "First moving to the East Village to get a job in that pathetic market? Then skipping out on your duties for the past three months? And now this?"

"This isn't something new. Don't try to twist it like that."

"It isn't? Are you sure?" he asked, raising an eyebrow. Something in the tone of his voice made Adam's skin crawl. "Are you positive that it couldn't have anything to do with Justin Turner?"

Adam's heart skidded to a stop and the air punched out of his lungs. He tried to keep his face neutral. "I don't know who you're talking about."

"Oh, let's see…" Shawn broke his stoic pose, reached over to the top drawer of his desk and pulled out a slim, unlabeled manila folder right off the top. He read out loud.

"Justin Turner. Age twenty-one. Son of Violet Turner and Matthew Barnes, both deceased." He scoffed and shook his head. "It says here that they both died of a meth overdose in some shit-hole in Queens. How pathetic."

Adam's blood felt as though it was pounding in his ears and he clenched his hands into fists by his sides.

"Resides now with Julia Turner at Three-Thirty-Four West Seventeenth Street, right between Ninth and Tenth Ave. Apartment four-oh-two. You know, I think I know the place. Villacourt Houses, right? I heard that place was a real dump. All sorts of things could go wrong with a building like that. The carbon monoxide detectors could be broken, or maybe even the wiring is shoddy and tends to spark. Really tragic things happen to buildings like that all the time."

"You son of a bitch," Adam growled.

"But you also know what? I think you knew these things about Mr. Turner already, because it *also* says here that you met with him on the eighth, fifteenth and twenty-second at Stephen Morita's little sex den in the Garment District. Oh, and also last night in Times Square, and that dive bar you frequent in the Village. And today as well at St. Anthony Hospital! Now, those are some strange places to be meeting your whore."

Adam was seeing red. That blaring anger screamed in his head, just like it had with Billy the other night. "He doesn't have anything to do with this."

"Either way, I think you and I are on the same page, Adam. You're right that tonight was the last time you helped us. Now that the deal is done, you are going to remove yourself completely from the picture."

"Excuse me?"

"You think I'm just going to let you saunter around the city like you're above the rest of us? After all this shame you've brought us?"

Adam had seen that same face before — to waiters in restaurants, to doormen at skyscraper entrances, to the lackeys that had come and gone in and out of their business. It didn't matter if Adam was his son, not now. He would recognize that disdain and disgust on his face any day.

"I want you to never again associate yourself, in anyway, with this family," Shawn ordered. "You are never to speak to either of your brothers, none of our associates, and I don't even want you using the name Creed. Change it to whatever the fuck you like — it doesn't matter two shits to me — but I don't ever want to lay eyes on you again. And if I do? I'll make damn well sure that you'll regret it."

That punched the wind right out of Adam's sails. He could, and at the same time couldn't, believe what he was hearing. His father was not only threatening Justin's and his grandmother's lives, but at the same time disowning *him*.

"You couldn't just let me go, could you?" Adam said.

"No, I can't." Shawn pushed his chair back and stood. "I have a reputation to uphold. My name has *weight* in this city. Fuck, the whole state even. After all the selfish things I've watched you do over the past few years and especially the past month, I can't trust you, Adam."

"You can't trust me? After everything I *have* done for this family?"

"Exactly," Shawn said. He didn't even blink. "Now get the fuck out of here before I call security."

Adam scoffed out a laugh in disbelief, but it turned into a real chuckle with his next breath. Then another. His father just glared at him with his dead-set eyes.

"Okay," Adam said, sounding like it was no skin off his back. "You don't have to tell me twice. I'm gone."

He bent down to scoop his bags off the floor. His father didn't say a single word as he gathered them, but Adam could feel him staring at him. A thousand different things he could say were flying through his mind, but none of them felt right in the moment. The angry, unsettled silence in the air stole his breath away. He let it linger, spinning on his heel and slinging his bag over his shoulder. The truth was, there was nothing left to say.

He reached the door and didn't close it quietly behind him.

Chapter Thirty-One

It was one-eighteen a.m. Jewels was already asleep in her chair. The movie had ended, and Justin had gotten himself ready for bed, but he knew there was no way he was going to sleep again. He had work tomorrow, but even the dread of an eight-hour shift with zero rest ahead of him wasn't enough to convince him to lie down. Instead, he crawled on top of the comforter and sat cross-legged with his phone in his hands.

He sighed. Staring at the clock was never going to help, but he couldn't stop.

He's not going to call.

The thought was terrible, but the sneaky voice in the back of his head wasn't done torturing him yet.

He's not going to call because he's not coming back. He's probably long gone by now like he originally planned.

His heart dropped to his stomach. He couldn't let himself think like that. Adam said he would find a way to stay. Why would he have asked him to be his boyfriend if he was secretly planning on leaving all along?

He looked over to his nightstand. Right beside his lamp was the book Adam had given him, *Scary Stories to Tell in the Dark*. He reached out and snagged it, dropping his phone to the bed. He turned the thin book over and over in his hands.

Maybe he changed his mind.

But that didn't seem like Adam, not after he had bought him this present, after he had taken him out on a real date, after the way they had slept together at Adam's place. Adam's heart was much bigger than Justin had ever anticipated, and he was devoted in a way that made him sure that he was going to find a way to stay.

His cell phone on the bed began to vibrate. The quiet ringtone started but had barely played a couple notes before Justin grabbed it off the bed and answered it.

"Adam?"

"Hey, Justin."

Justin sighed in relief and the muscles in his body relaxed. "I'm so glad you called. I was starting to get worried."

"I'm sorry," Adam said softly. "It's done, though."

"Are you okay?" There was a long pause from Adam's side of the line and Justin immediately tensed back up. "Adam?"

"Uh, well, mostly," he said with a surprising chuckled.

"Mostly?"

"I'm, um, actually down on the sidewalk outside your apartment building."

"What? You are? How did you — wait, never mind. Hold on, I'm gonna let you inside. Come on up, apartment four-oh-two."

He ran to the bedroom door, careful to open it without being too loud. He rushed past the living room where Jewels was snoring and reached the buzzer by the front door. He pressed the button and held it, counting to three in his head.

He let out a shaky breath and stepped back from the door. Holy shit, Adam was actually *here*. He unlocked the chain on the door, twisted the bolt-lock and stepped out into the hallway in his socks.

At the very end of the hall was the elevator. Justin closed his apartment door with a soft click and watched the numbers on the screen above the elevator doors as they ticked up to four. He wrung his hands together.

The elevator reached his floor and the bell chimed. When the doors slid open, there was Adam standing in front of him, still in his clothes from earlier at the hospital, and carrying two bags.

"Hey, sweetheart," he let out with a tired breath, dropping his bags to the floor. He looked exhausted and yet still more handsome than Justin remembered. Seeing him took his breath away. The smile Adam gave him was sweet and earnest and beautiful to see.

"Hey." Justin took a step forward, then two. Now that he was moving, he couldn't stop. Adam pulled him in tight when he finally reached him.

"I'm sorry for not calling," Adam whispered, squeezing him. Justin burrowed his face into Adam's neck and squeezed him back, twice as hard.

"It's okay. I'm just glad you're here."

Adam pulled back enough to cup the sides of Justin's face with both warm hands.

"I was going to call," he explained, "but when it was all said and done, I... I just had to come see you."

"What happened? Is everything all right?" Justin held his hands over Adam's. His whole body wanted to sway into the warmth of him being so very close, but he held himself back. Adam just stroked his hands down his neck, touching him reverently.

"Everything almost went to shit in the end, but we made it out. Billy got hurt, but he'll live."

The image of Billy flashed into Justin's head from the other night. It was mean-spirited, but he didn't feel that bad about that jerk, not after what he had said to the both of them.

"But what about you?"

"Well, uh..." Adam turned his head down to his left arm and Justin took a closer look. After a second, he saw the rip across the sleeve of his jacket, clean through the leather. Adam let him reach up and pull the fabric aside, but Justin gasped at the sight.

An angry-red gash ran sideways across the muscle of Adam's biceps. It had to be at least three inches long, but it was deep enough to expose the layers of skin and fatty tissue. Thick brown and black blood was caked at the edges, and he could see the rest of his skin was stained with it. Seeping rivulets were still dripping down.

"Holy crap," Justin whispered. "Adam, this looks bad."

Adam just shrugged. "It doesn't feel too bad now. Sort of quieted back down."

"Yeah, but it'll never heal up like this. It's too deep. Come on," he said. Without waiting, Justin picked up one of Adam's bags for him.

"What, inside?"

"Yeah, of course."

He opened the door and the two of them stepped inside his apartment.

"You know, I'm sure it's gonna be fine," Adam said. "The bleeding slowed down a lot already."

"Yeah, but a wound like that needs to be stitched up. Otherwise it'll get infected."

"But I don't want to be a pain in the ass."

"Don't worry about it."

"Justin?" Jewels called out from the living room. She was awake. "Are you talking to someone out there?"

"Yeah, Jewels," he called back. "It's Adam."

"Adam?" she said, sounding pleasantly surprised even though it was one in the morning and a stranger was in her house. She stepped out into the hall and gave them a huge smile, her hair in plastic curlers and her pink housecoat over her nightgown.

"Why hello there, Adam. I was just asking Justin when I was going to get to meet you," she said. She reached out a hand which Adam intercepted for a handshake.

"It's very nice to meet you, Mrs. Turner. I'm sorry to barge in like this in the middle of the night."

"Please, call me Jewels."

"Jewels. Thank you."

"We need your help," Justin said.

"Oh?"

"Adam's arm is hurt. He needs stitches."

"What?" she gasped. "Where? How bad is it? What happened?"

"Really, it's not that bad," he said, but it was hopeless. Jewels was already taking hold of his arm and ushering him into the kitchen.

"Nonsense," she stated. "You came to the house of Manhattan's best nurse for forty-seven years. At least, that's what they used to tell me on the floor just to butter me up. Either way, we're gonna take a look and get you all patched up."

Adam let out a laugh as she pushed him into one of their two chairs at the unused dining table.

"Well, how can I say no to that?"

"Exactly." She turned to Justin while she pulled up the other chair close to Adam's. "Justin, honey? Would you please go grab the first aid kit?"

"Sure." He gave a quick smile to Adam, who looked a bit sheepish sitting in his new boyfriend's place, talking to his grandmother and bleeding profusely. He wanted to tell him not to worry. Jewels had lived through just about everything the world could throw at her and she was a hard woman to offend.

He scurried off down the hall toward the bathroom and grabbed the kit from the cabinet under the sink. Adam was shrugging out of his jacket as Justin stepped back in. He pulled the whole thing off and Jewels made a sympathetic hiss of pain when his arm was free.

"Oh, that is definitely going to need some work," she said.

The sleeve of Adam's T-shirt had been slashed and was drenched in a spreading splotch of dark blood. The whole sleeve was almost stained through, but most of it looked like it had run down his arm. It was almost as if he had reached all the way down into a vat of blood. Justin stepped right up next to both of them and smelled the metallic tang of the blood.

"Here, Jewels," he offered.

"Thank you, honey. Look at this. I'm going to have to roll the sleeve all the way up."

"Okay," Adam whispered. His eyes were trained on Jewels when she put the kit aside and reached for his arm, and he held his breath when she touched him. The fabric peeled away, wet and sticky, and she rolled it up all the way to his shoulder.

"Oh…" she said.

Adam's shoulder cap wasn't so blood caked, but that only made the patchwork of heavy scars that much more visible. Adam was dead silent while Jewels took in the sight. Her face was drained of her light cheeriness while she looked over the scars.

"These are very old," she finally said.

"Yeah," he agreed. It was filled with a sad sort of humor. "Too old."

Her look of shock disappeared, and she was back to business. "Well, let's get started then, huh?"

She popped the top off the first aid kit and began pulling out her tools—a travel-sized bottle of rubbing alcohol, a stack of gauzes cut into small squares and a compact suturing kit. When she opened it, it was lined with a set of curved needles and a pack of sterilized suture threads.

"Justin? Please hand me a glass from the cabinet."

"Of course."

He fetched her a short tumbler and handed it to her. She unscrewed the cap off the rubbing alcohol and poured a good-sized glug and picked out one of the curved needles, which she dropped into the glass of alcohol. She grabbed a pair of rubber gloves from the kit and put them on while giving Adam a grave look.

"I'm going to warn you, this might be more painful than normal. I'm going to have to suture through some scar tissue and it's going to be a bit sensitive."

"That's all right," Adam said, his voice strong. "I'm sure you'll be as gentle as you can."

Jewels laughed. "Naturally. Don't worry, honey. You're in good hands. Isn't that right, Justin?" she asked as she picked up a few squares of gauze and dipped them into the alcohol.

He looked over at Adam's face and their eyes locked. It still made his stomach do a somersault when Adam looked at him like that, as though they were the only two people in a crowded room.

"That's right," he said.

A smile broke across Adam's face, but he tried to tuck it away, like he was saving it for later. The corner of his mouth was still turned up, though, just a bit. He reached over with his right hand and took Justin's in his. It was his turn to try to keep the smile off. Jewel's didn't pay them any attention.

"I wish I had something to numb you out, but I don't. This is going to be the worst of it," she said, and she shifted closer toward Adam, getting ready to work.

"That's okay. Just do it."

Jewels didn't hesitate or draw it out. She reached forward with the alcohol-soaked gauze and went right to swiping it over the entire length of the gash.

Adam instantly flinched when the alcohol burned deep into his flesh, but he schooled himself still with a low groan. His jaw was clenched tight, the muscles of his neck flexed, but he let her keep going and she swiped at the wound, making sure to thoroughly disinfect the cut.

Justin gave his hand a strong squeeze to try to help distract him. Adam let out a tense breath and squeezed his hand right back.

Jewels finished cleaning and leaned back, giving Adam a moment of reprieve. She went to work fishing out the needle and dried it so she could thread it. Adam slumped back into the chair with a huff.

"You really weren't kidding, huh?"

Jewels broke out a good laugh, her eyes sparkling. "And we're not done yet, tough guy, c'mon."

"All right, all right," he conceded. "You don't sugarcoat it, do ya?"

"No, I don't." She looked over at Justin. "I like him already."

Justin let out an embarrassed laugh.

"That's good," Adam said. "I just wish we had met under different circumstances."

"You've got that right. Now, I need you to hold still. I'm going to start stitching."

Adam steeled himself with a deep breath. "Okay, let's go."

Jewels used a pair of needle clamps to guide the curved needle. Adam sat like a statue as the needle plunged into his skin about a quarter of an inch from the end of the gash. She twisted the needle up with a fluid motion and it popped back out on the other side. She pulled the thread to nearly the end and, with practiced ease, threw a knot three times until it was perfectly tightened without puckering the skin. She plucked a tiny pair of scissors off the table and snipped the thread, getting ready for another one.

"And how did you say this happened again?" she asked.

"Oh, um, at my family's warehouse. I was just helping my brothers when a pane of glass fell. I guess it grazed me, but I barely felt it."

"Oh, my goodness," she gasped. It sounded earnest but distracted while she worked.

Justin knew that Adam wasn't telling the whole truth. Sure, he believed that Adam *had* been with his brothers, and Billy probably *had* gotten hurt, but Adam was playing it close to his chest. Probably best for Jewels anyway. If she thought any part of Adam's story was fishy, she didn't say. She was very focused on her work as she started the last stitch.

"Aaaaaand... Ta-da! All done."

Adam lifted his arm to peek at the neat line of sutures pinching the skin back together again through the edges of scars.

"Thank you so much. It was very kind of you," he said. "There was no way I could have done this myself in a motel bathroom."

"A motel?" she asked, completely shocked. "You aren't staying in a motel, are you?"

"Oh, just for a bit. I had to move out of my place today. It was...unsafe."

"Nonsense," Jewels said, shaking her head. "It's too late in the night to be out in the streets. You can stay here tonight, right, Justin?"

"Oh, yeah, absolutely."

"I don't want to be an even bigger pain in the ass after everything already," he replied.

"Stop, don't even. You're staying and that's final." She snapped the gloves off and stood up to dump all the bagged-up trash into the can. "Justin? Why don't you help Adam to the bathroom so he can clean up?"

"Sure, Jewels."

"Just make sure to bandage that up for me when it's all washed off, okay? There's plenty of gauze and tape in the kit."

"Of course, no problem."

"Thank you, sweetie. I'm going to head off to bed. Goodnight, Adam."

"Goodnight, Jewels. Thanks again."

"I'd say anytime, but I think we'd all rather not."

Adam huffed out a laugh. "Very true."

"Night, boys." She turned around and shuffled out back to her chair. Once she was out of earshot, Adam turned in his chair toward him.

"Okay, now I'm *definitely* going to have to order a butt-ton of flowers for her after all this."

Justin chuckled. "She would love you forever if you did. C'mon, the bathroom is down the hall."

Adam got up and followed him. Once they got to the bathroom and shut the door, it was finally safe to talk again without disturbing Jewels. God knew that the woman needed her sleep now. It had been a long, *long* day.

"Here, let me get you a towel," he offered. He turned to open the small linen hutch behind the door while Adam stepped up to the sink and started the tap to wash his arm. The pink-stained water was bright in the white porcelain sink and there was just *so much of it*. Adam didn't seem fazed in the least. Justin wondered how many times he had cleaned himself up like this in his life.

"So," he said, leaning back on the hutch door while Adam kept washing. "A pane of glass?"

Adam glanced back at him through the mirror for a second before he dropped his gaze.

"Not quite."

"And Billy?"

"He got what he deserved. It was his fault to begin with."

"How?"

Adam turned the sink off and turned around. Justin held out a towel for him and he gave a soft thanks. He scrubbed the bottom of his arm dry, but the stitches were still messy with blood.

"Here," Justin said. "Sit down. I'll take care of this." He gestured for Adam to sit on the toilet lid and took the towel from him. He placed the first aid kit on the sink and started pulling out supplies.

Adam cleared his throat. "Look, I…"

"It's all right," he interrupted. Adam raised an eyebrow.

"Oh really?"

"Yes." He took the bottle of rubbing alcohol out and ripped a paper towel off from the roll mounted to the wall. He inched closer to Adam, stepping between his spread knees.

"I don't want you to feel like I'm keeping secrets from you," Adam said, "but it's not safe."

"I know. That's why it's all right. But it's scary to think that you could have gotten a lot more hurt than you did."

"You're right, but I didn't. And it's over now," Adam said.

Justin dampened the paper towel in alcohol, filling the enclosed space with the powerful antiseptic scent.

"Hold on," he whispered. He dabbed the sealed line of stitches with the towel. Adam hissed in a breath as the alcohol touched the wound, but he held still for Justin to carefully clean off the blood.

"I want to believe you," Justin continued, "but how is it over? What if they call again and want you to do something else for them?"

Adam kept his eyes trained on Justin's face. "They won't be calling. I spoke with my father."

He paused and met Adam's gaze. "And what did he say?"

Adam shook his head and Justin's heart sank, but Adam gave another one of those sad laughs. "He disowned me."

"Adam, I'm so sorry."

"Don't be. At first, I was so *angry*. After I thought about it, though, I realized that it was perfect."

"Perfect?"

"Yeah. I've gotten what I wanted, just maybe not the way I had originally planned." He seemed to be lost in thought for a second, his forehead furrowed. "But either way, I'm finally free from all of it. It was worth it, if you'll still have me."

Justin hadn't been expecting that. Adam had gotten himself disowned to be able to stay with him. He never imagined that Adam would go to such lengths, just for him. It left him speechless.

"So," Adam continued, "I was thinking about getting a new place. Somewhere a little bit further from the Bronx. A small change of scenery."

"Oh?" he asked. He remembered he was supposed to be doing something and finished up cleaning the last of the blood. He tossed the paper towel in the metal trash can and picked up a paper-wrapped piece of gauze and medical tape.

"Yeah. Maybe somewhere in Brooklyn. Something nice, with two baths and two bedrooms, you know…so Jewels can have her own room."

Justin froze, halfway through taping the piece of gauze to Adam's biceps. "Wait, you mean, like for all of us?"

"Yeah," Adam, finally smiling again. "What do you think?"

Justin placed the last piece of tape on and put the roll aside. Adam took his hands when he finished, and they were large and warm when they enclosed around his. It was nice, but after all that had happened tonight, it wasn't enough.

He pulled his hands from Adam's and wrapped his arms around his neck, dropping to his knees to be on his level. The second he was, he surged forward and pressed his lips to Adam's.

Adam met the kiss with hungry passion. He wrapped his arms around Justin's back to pull him as close as possible, deepening their kiss and opening his mouth to let him taste.

The blood seared through Justin's veins, stoked by the eager way Adam took his kiss and returned it. He wanted to press his whole body against Adam's and stay wrapped up in his arms forever. He almost whimpered when Adam pulled back, but he whispered something against Justin's lips that he hadn't been expecting.

"Justin," he said, "I love you."

His stomach swooped in the best way possible. "I love you, too."

"So, will you think about moving in with me?" Adam finally asked. Justin grinned and let out a laugh.

"Yes, absolutely."

"Perfect. And you don't mind me staying in your bed tonight?"

"No, although it might be a bit small."

"That's fine, as long as the springs don't squeak too loud."

Justin let out a peal of laughter he had to smoosh down or risk waking Jewels up again. He leaned in for another quick kiss, feeling elated. When he had sent his application to Eros what felt like a lifetime ago, there was no way he could have guessed things could have turned out like this. The past month had to have been one of the most strange, exciting, terrifying and rewarding months he had ever lived through, and maybe Adam would say the same.

He figured it showed that there was no telling what a single decision might end up leading to, that sometimes doing what seemed difficult could be most rewarding, and that putting in the effort to get to know someone was worth it to find that beauty beneath.

Want to see more from this author?
Here's a taster for you to enjoy!

Starling's Again
Aver Rigsly

Excerpt

It wasn't until ten o'clock rolled around that Peter Corcoran began to get impatient enough to think about grabbing his jacket off the back of his chair and making his way home. There was only so long that he could pretend to enjoy people-watching.

The Starling Club in Bowery was as busy as it was every Friday night. The dance floor was crowded enough that couples had only their two-foot square to dance in, and the bar counter on the left wall had people trying to squeeze in to any space they could to shout out their orders. The hall was a fair enough size, but it always felt smaller than it was when people were packed like sardines, which was every time he came. They stood in packs in floating groups around the few wooden columns that held the wood beam-laced ceiling up. The wax-polished cherry wood dance floor glowed in the glimpses between dress shoes and heels, but it would certainly need to be buffed again tomorrow after a night of wear and tear. As for the bar, he could hardly catch sight of the bartenders as they worked to sling whiskeys, southsides and gin rickeys as fast as humanly possible.

It was busy, but Peter had still managed to get his usual seat at the corner-most table in the back, where about two dozen tables were placed so people could sit when they needed to smoke a cigarette or rest their feet for a song. It was his usual seat for a reason. Sitting all the way in the back meant that no one looking for some drunk small-talk, or perhaps to bum a cigarette, would drift close enough to bother him. So instead, he was able to watch the crowd in peace by himself.

There were plenty of the neighborhood faces he recognized tonight, but his gaze landed on a group of women standing by the edge of the dance floor. The four gals had to be the most gorgeous flock of dames who played together and broke hearts just for fun in their spare time. He had no silly daydreams about even being close to their league, but why would he care? *Leave that to all the thick-headed men who like to drink all night then parade over to try to woo them like strutting peacocks during mating season.*

Especially the blonde. Peter could acknowledge when a woman was a bombshell beauty. Her platinum-blonde hair was always perfectly in place all night long, as if she had her own private stylist, like a movie star. Her skin was crystal clear of any blemishes and her garnet-red lipstick was the best match for her fair ivory complexion. Not to mention her wide eyes, which were baby blue, expressive like a doe's, and always framed by lashes so long that any guy would be drawn to them. Of course, any man here would kill to have her eyes on him, but she had her gaze fixed across the hall. He traced her eyeline with ease and wasn't surprised to find her attention set on a handsome man leaning an arm on the bar to settle with the tender.

The man looked a bit flushed, but it didn't hurt his natural attractiveness—quite the opposite, really. He could easily be an actor, with a face like that, or maybe a model for one of those department stores on Fifth Ave. He wore a nice set of navy-blue trousers with an impeccably pressed white dress shirt tucked in. They certainly weren't his finest set of clothes, like a formal suit for big affairs, but they were close. His sleeves were rolled up to the elbow, showing off his well-muscled forearms, and the button near his throat was undone from the warmth, but that only piled on the natural magnetism that radiated from him.

Peter looked back at the ladies and the whole band of them were watching the man at the bar now. They patted the pleats of their skirts smooth and tucked loose curls of hair behind their ears, each one hoping that he was about to stroll over and ask her for a dance. He had danced with each of them over the past few hours, but they all wanted at least one more. He could see it in their eyes as they ogled him and whispered to each other with their cherry lips.

He could also understand their disappointment all too well when the man at the bar didn't turn back to the dance floor when he pushed off from the counter. Peter dropped his eyes to his glass. The man walked straight through the smattering of rickety tables and wooden folding chairs nearby, but the glass in his hand was empty and a poor excuse for his attention. He only glanced up again when the guy got right to his table and rested his hands on the back of the chair next to him.

"Hey, you think you're about ready to head out?" the man asked.

Peter shrugged, pretending that wasn't what he had been contemplating for the past hour now.

"Sure, Dan. If you think you've had enough."

PUBLISHING

Sign up for our newsletter and find out about all our
romance book releases, eBook sales and promotions,
sneak peeks and FREE romance books!

About the Author

Aver Rigsly was born and raised in the Boston, Massachusetts area and spends her days working at a travel agency in Quincy. Some of her favourite places to visit are Washington D.C., Bangor, Maine, and most of all New York City. When she isn't working a trip or writing LGBTQA+ romance obsessively, she spends her free time relaxing with knitting, needlepoint, video games, or marathoning horror movies with the family.

Aver loves to hear from readers. You can find her contact information, website details and author profile page at https://www.pride-publishing.com